The Book of Memories

Holly Jacobs

The Book of Memories
Copyright © 2025 Holly Fuhrmann

ILEX Books

Dedication: For Papa John, Marge and Jean...I'm proud to call you friends and family.

Two roads diverged in a wood, and I—
I took the one less traveled by,
And that has made all the difference.
~Robert Frost

The Book of Memories
Holly Jacobs

They say that history is written by the victors.

No one can accurately pinpoint who really coined the phrase, which is probably why people attribute it most often to some unnamed *they*.

Well, my idea of history—of memories, which are a form of personal history—can be definitively attributed to someone specific. Someone who will never be a name lost in time.

The originator was a woman named Ida Hunter Hall.

She was my mentor.

She was my friend.

She was my family.

She wrote the first *Book of Memories*.

Then she showed me how to write my own as well.

She taught me that all memories are subjective. They are arranged, rearranged, and shaped by time and perspective.

More importantly, Miss Ida taught me how to use my memories to navigate...well, life.

Prologue
Sapling

Chapter One

"But Mom, I don't want—"

"Sadie Mae Hanson, when you whine like that you sound like a toddler, not a teenager. And as a teenager, you are old enough to realize that in this family we help our neighbors. Miss Ida is alone and she's getting on in years. You *will* go over on Saturday mornings and help her."

"But Mooooommmm," I drew out that one syllable word to be at least four syllables worth of word.

"There is no *but* in the world that will get you out of this job. And may I remind you that polite young ladies do not say the word *but* to their mothers. They say *yes ma'am*. Besides, think how nice it will be to have some spending money of your own."

My mother, Bette Lee De Butes Hanson was a gentile southern lady who'd been transported to the north by my father, Big Henry Hanson. They called my father Big Henry to differentiate between him and my grandfather, Old Henry Hanson.

We lived on the east side of Erie, Pennsylvania in a small cape cod house in a middle class neighborhood. The house was white with green shutters. There was a big red maple in our front yard and an even bigger silver maple in our side yard, along with a mulberry tree and a chestnut tree.

I'd been on my back under that maple staring through the branches and watching the clouds blow by when my mother had called me inside to inform me about my new job.

Our house was small, but the perfect size for the three of us.

Mom and Dad's room was on the first floor.

My room was on the second floor, though it wasn't much of a second floor. The sloped roofline of the cape meant it was more like a one-and-a-half floor.

The back half of that second floor was our attic.

I had the small front room with a large window on my only outside straight wall. That window looked out on that giant silver maple that grew beside the driveway.

On the other side of the tree was Miss Ida's house. I could barely make it out in the summer because of all the leaves, but in the winter, her house was clearly visible.

Yes, I called her Miss Ida. She'd been a fixture next door for as long as I could remember. I waved at her when I saw her outside, but that was the extent of our interaction.

None of my other almost-sixteen year old friends referred to non-parental adults as *Miss This* or *Mister That*. Although my father might have relocated my mother to a northern state, he couldn't take the south out of her soul, her voice, or out of her childrearing techniques. And according to my mother's southern rules for parenting, anyone her age or older was *always* referred to by Miss or Mister by my mother's children...namely me.

I'd always regretted that I was an only child because I was the focus of all my mother's considerable parenting energies.

And my mother decreed that Miss Ida was Miss Ida.

Thus, Miss Ida was Miss Ida. Not Mrs. Hall, though that was how any of my polite friends might have referred to her. I knew that once there had to have been a Mr. Hall, but I had no memory of anyone at the house next door other than Miss Ida.

"Saturday mornings, Sadie Mae," my mother said one last time.

There was no fighting my mother when she used that particular tone, though to an outsider, there would be nothing remarkable or overly intimidating in her voice.

But there was a warning in that soft, southern drawl. My mother ran our home with a voice laced with the accents of her youth. Only those who knew her best knew that magnolia and julep voice hid a core of iron.

"Yes, ma'am," I said, acquiescing to the inevitable.

Which is why that Saturday at precisely nine a.m. I found myself at Miss Ida's front door, knocking politely.

"Come in dear," she called.

The floor creaked as I let myself directly into the living room.

There was no foyer or even a true entryway in the tiny house. But there was a medicinal smell. Like rubbing alcohol or some other old time remedy for some sort of old person's ailment.

Miss Ida was sitting in a large flower-patterned wing chair, wearing a grey cable-knit sweater, a plain black shirt and jeans. Not trendy jeans to be sure. These were too light and high-waisted to be cool, but still they were jeans. Her hair was coiled into a bun of inordinate size that couldn't seem to make up its mind as to what color it was. Dark brown and white hair seemed to be at war.

It appeared that the white hair was winning.

From my point of view there were three types of people. Kids. Adults. And old people. Miss Ida was a *really* old person.

"Sadie Mae, dear, thank you so much for offering to assist me." Miss Ida's voice, despite her age, wasn't nearly as soft as my mother's. It was firm and steady. It sounded like a younger person's voice.

I didn't mention that *offer* wasn't quite the way I would describe how I'd come to be here, but I'll confess,

12

looking at Miss Ida, it was impossible to feel bitter about my mother-enforced job. "It's my pleasure, ma'am. Where would you like me to start?"

"Growing old is not for the faint of heart. My grandmother was old by the time she was forty, so I'm pleased that I was able to hold my decrepitude off until my seventies. But as hard as I tried to run from it, it finally caught me because of my knees. They just won't work the way they did when I was your age."

It was hard to believe Miss Ida had ever been my age, bless her heart. But I didn't say so to her. Not that she would have let me have much of a chance to say anything. Bette Lee always said Miss Ida could have an entire conversation all on her own.

She sucked in a quick breath and continued, "It's my darn knees that have made it difficult for me to scrub the floors. I'm embarrassed by the state of them. Would you mind starting with that?"

And so, my first working week, I scrubbed Miss Ida's floors. Her house was even smaller than ours. It was a one story, two-bedroom home with hardwood floors throughout. The master bedroom had a huge bed that looked as if it would swallow Miss Ida whole. The smaller bedroom across the hall had a twin, canopied bed and a huge dollhouse on a chest of drawers. But it was the painting that caught my eye. Two walls and part of a third filled with random pictures. A town. Some woods. People. Cars.

I recognized Miss Ida's image in some of the pictures. There was one of her, sitting in a rocker, with what had to be a baby wrapped in a pink blanket.

In one she was standing under a movie marquee holding a man's hand.

This must be Miss Ida's husband, though I had no recollection of him. And from the look of the room, I realized she might have had a daughter, though no daughter ever came to her house to visit that I could remember.

I didn't ask her about either.

Bette Lee Hanson had very firm opinions about *being cheeky*.

Asking Miss Ida about her husband and daughter would definitely be counted as such, so I didn't ask, though I was curious. I wished I had time to stay in the room and study the pictures.

Instead, I continued with the floors.

It was more than an hour later when I finished. The house smelled of Murphy's Oil Soap now. It was definitely an improvement over its previous antiseptic smell.

"What next, ma'am?" I asked after I'd emptied the bucket for the last time.

"Why don't you make us a cup of tea and come visit for a moment before you run off."

Visiting with a woman who had to be close to one hundred was not my idea of a good time, and yet, I did as Bette Lee Hanson would have insisted...I accepted Miss Ida's offer.

I put the pot on the stove and popped back out to ask where the tea bags were.

Miss Ida laughed, as if my question was standup-comic worthy. She set down a large leather-bound book that I hadn't noticed before and creaked her way to her feet with an audible grunt. Then she beckoned me into the kitchen.

She pulled out a small brown teapot and then got a metal tin and spooned loose tea into the pot. "It's a four cup teapot, so it's four heaped scoops," she instructed.

She pulled the teakettle off the flame before it whistled. "You want to get it before it comes to a full boil. Just a pre-boil. Pour the water into the teapot and put the lid on it. Now we wait about five minutes. When you pour the tea into the cups, you use this." She held out a small strainer. "It will catch any of the leaves that are floating."

14

She went back to her chair and I followed her to wait for the required five minutes.

"What were you reading?" I asked.

I spent a great quantity of my life to date in books. Bette Lee said I started reading cereal boxes when I was a baby and had continued reading ever since.

"Oh, I wasn't reading," Miss Ida said with a kindly smile.

She reminded me of Mrs. Santa Claus.

"I was writing down a memory," she added as if that explained everything.

"A memory?" I knew what memory was, but I'd never heard of someone writing one down.

"Every day, I add at least one memory to my book. My Book of Memories." She said *Book of Memories* in such a way that I knew the words started in caps.

She smiled and opened the book. It was a large book and she opened it to the last quarter of the pages. "Sadie Mae Hanson has come to help whip the old homestead into shape. She's a tiny dynamo. She..."

She stopped reading and looked up at me. "I don't know how to thank you. I was truly mortified by the state of my floors. You were a great help."

I smiled at the compliment. "Thank you. I'm more than happy to get a few more jobs done."

She shook her head. "No, that's enough for one day. I'm old, but I can still manage most of it myself. If you would be so kind as to pour us both a cup of tea, I'd love the company before you leave."

I nodded and got up.

"There are cookies in the cookie jar," she called.

The cookie jar was shaped like an English house, with a thatched roof and yellow flowers climbing up a trellis that surrounded the door. I lifted the thatched roof off and found a box of store-bought cookies.

My mother wouldn't approve—Bette Lee Hanson baked her cookies from scratch—but I didn't mind store-bought cookies.

I placed a half dozen of the chocolate circles on a plate and carried it out to Miss Ida and then went back for the tea.

"I wasn't sure if you had a tray," I said as I carried out the two delicate teacups and saucers. Her kitchen was in disarray. There didn't seem to be any order to her dishes or her pantry.

Bette Lee believed in a well-ordered world. There were rules about everything.

Pantries were organized by food types.

Daughters called elders Miss or Mister.

Big Henry put his dirty clothes in the hamper.

"I'm sure I have a tray," Miss Ida mused. "Reorganizing the kitchen is on our list for some future Saturday...that is if you're interested in making the job a permanent one?"

And suddenly, I found I was.

I'm not sure if it was the store-bought cookies, the tea, or the prospect of bringing order to her chaotic kitchen.

I suspected it wasn't any of those. No, I suspected it was Miss Ida herself.

"Yes, Ma'am, I would."

"Then let's have a civilized cup of tea together and I will see you next Saturday."

"You write down a memory every day?" I asked, steering the conversation back to her book.

Miss Ida nodded. "Every day with very few exceptions—" She looked sad for a moment, as if those days that were exceptions weren't happy ones. "—for more than sixty years now."

"Why?" I asked.

Miss Ida smiled and for a moment, seemed so very much younger.

Although, when you were as old as Miss Ida was, even *very-much-younger* was still unbelievably old. She had so many lines on her face that I couldn't help comparing it to how our pond at camp rippled when I tossed a stone in it.

Miss Ida had so many wrinkles that I'd have had to toss a boulder in the pond to get a similar effect.

"How did it start?" she mused more to herself than me.

"It was the week before my eleventh birthday. Junie Malks was the most popular girl in my class. I had plain mousy brown hair, though these days it's getting harder to tell as the grey is overtaking the brown."

"It's more white than grey," I said, then wondered   if   that   was   sassy.

Miss Ida grinned and said, "Why thank you, dear."

I guessed it was okay.

She continued, "Now, that Junie Malks, she had beautiful blonde hair that hung in ringlets. She didn't have to curl it or anything—it was just naturally curly. There was some cartoon character that used to brag about naturally curly hair, wasn't there?"

I didn't have a clue, so I shrugged.

"Well, Junie was proud of her hair and she was popular, though not because of the hair. She was popular because if you crossed her, she'd torment you, so no one crossed her. Where was I?"

"Telling me about your book," I prompted.

"Oh, yes. So one day, Junie said something mean to me at school. And this is important," Miss Ida said, with emphasis. "Though I remember it was Junie Malks, I can't for the life of me remember what she said or did. I do remember that I came home in tears. And I remember that my father found me crying on the back glider. I was trying to get myself under control before I went into the house, but my father always could sense when someone was hurting. It was like some sixth

17

sense. He wasn't a demonstrative man by nature. Not like your father, but he loved me and without saying much could make me feel better no matter what. So that day, he asked me what was wrong and I told him that I was never going to forgive that Junie Malks for being so mean."

She laughed. "Junie ended up marrying a minister named Hiram Bucks the Fourth. I can't imagine why anyone would ever think that there should be more than one generation of Hiram Bucks, but that family certainly did like that name. I guess there is no accounting for taste. Do you think Junie had a son and named him Hiram Bucks the Fifth? If so, poor boy. Names can make or break you when you're young. I often wished my mother had named me something other than Ida Mary. But Ida was a family name. And before her, there were Edas. More than one. My mother was keen on her family tree. They came from New England—Providence by way of Boston. They were related to the Browns University Browns. A man named Chad Brown. Someone down the pike in our tree married a German Eda, and Eda became Ida. And that's where my mother got my name. But back to Hiram Bucks number four, he was a nice man, and maybe his niceness was contagious. The last time I met up with Junie, she was very sweet to me."

"What did your father say that day when he found you crying?" I asked, trying to steer her back to her original story.

I knew that if Big Henry found me crying on a back glider he would have smacked my back and told me to *buck up*. Big Henry thought most of the world's problems would be solved by people *bucking up*.

Miss Ida pointed to a portrait on her wall. It was a man wearing a suit, with dark hair and a serious expression. "The only time I saw my father not smiling was in his portrait and the day my mother died. He was a quiet man, but he was a glass-half-full sort of man as well. That day he told me that we have over a thousand minutes every day and every one of those minutes was a potential memory. *You can't take all of those memories with you, Ida,* he said in that very deep voice of his. His voice, it was so deep it sort of reverberated through your whole being."

She was smiling, remembering her father and his very deep voice. "He said we'd buckle under the weight of all our memories. Why just think of it, Sadie Mae. All those memories you make every day. Who you saw, conversations you had, what you ate, what you dreamed. So many memories, one on top of the next. Why yesterday I talked to a neighbor and she told me about her garden. She itemized everything she planted and offered to bring me zucchinis. She said of all the things she grows, she grows those best. I wrote in my book that I was looking forward to frying the zucchini she brings me this summer. That act of kindness I'll remember, but by next week, I doubt I'll remember the rest of the conversation and I certainly won't remember her itemized list of what she's planting in her garden."

"Oh, I see what you mean. I went to one of Big Henry's family reunions and met a bunch of Old Henry's cousins. I've forgotten most of them, except for one named August. He belched after he ate his picnic lunch. I mean, really let it rip. He said in some countries it's a compliment to the cook and there were a lot of cooks, so he had to make it long and loud. My mother assured me later that no southern gentleman would ever dream of complimenting a cook like that. She was aghast."

Oh yes, my mother's sense of propriety had been shocked that day. It had amused me almost as much as August had. "I'll remember him, but I've already forgotten most of the rest of the people I met."

If I had a book like Miss Ida's, I'd have written about August and smiled every time I was reminded of that day, that very loud belch and my mother's insulted sense of propriety.

Miss Ida nodded, as if she understood. "You're so young, Sadie Mae. Why you've hardly started adding to your own Book of Memories, but someone as old as me? Can you imagine if I'd kept every one of my life's memories? I wouldn't be able to wade through them. So my father that day, he said, *since you can't take them all with you, you can pick the best of them to save.*"

"Just the best of them?" I repeated.

Miss Ida nodded. "That day, he went out after dinner and came back with this." She laid a loving hand on the large leather book.

Now that I was closer, I could see that the leather was cracked with age and use. And spots she handled were worn to a much lighter color. "I don't know where my father got the book, but it was full of hundreds and hundreds of blank pages. So almost every day since, I've added a memory. A *good memory*," she clarified. "Sometimes it's just a sentence, sometimes it's more."

She gently closed the page with my entry and moved to the front of the book. Its binding gave a small moan, as if moving back that far in time took some effort.

The noise sounded similar to the sound Miss Ida had made when she stood up.

I smiled at the thought. The book that Miss Ida had written in for sixty years had aged right along with her.

"Here," she said. "*Daddy gave me a book for my memories* is my first memory in my book."

"Only the good ones," I murmured again.

She nodded. "He was right. I couldn't see the sense in saving the bad ones, so I didn't write down whatever it was that Junie said or did to make me cry that day and honestly, I don't have a clue any more. There's something to be said for losing the bad memories and holding on to the good ones."

She looked sad again for a moment.

20

"Miss Ida?" I asked.

She gave her head a small shake, sending one of her brown sections of hair tumbling out of her bun.

"I'm fine dear. It's just that some memories won't fade regardless of whether we write them down or not."

I cleaned up our teacups and the cookie plate then walked across the lawn to my house.

"Now that wasn't so bad, was it, Sadie Mae?" my mother asked.

I shook my head. "No, it wasn't so bad at all."

The next week, I was surprised to find I was looking forward to going to Miss Ida's.

My mother gave me a look of approval when I said, "I'm heading next door now."

But my mother's approval wasn't the reason why I'd been anticipating going back all week. And the idea of doing housework wasn't either.

It was Miss Ida.

She intrigued me.

She seemed optimistic. I liked that.

So I went back across the yard and Miss Ida asked me to wash her windows.

After I finished, we had tea and cookies. This time, I made the tea with no assistance. I let the water almost boil before I added it to the teapot. Then I waited five minutes before I poured our cups.

Miss Ida had strawberry wafer cookies in the English cottage cookie jar. I put six on a plate.

When I sat down, she handed me a large box and said, "It's for you."

I opened it.

Inside, wrapped in tissue paper was a large, leather-bound book. And I knew before I opened it that all the pages were blank.

"For you," she said. "I hope you fill it with a lifetime of happy memories."

I went home that night and wrote, *Miss Ida gave me a book for my memories.*

I promised myself I'd only write the nicest of my memories in it.

At least one memory every day.

Miss Ida's Book of Memories

Sadie Mae Hanson has come to help whip the old homestead into shape. She's a tiny dynamo. She reminds me of Barbara at that age.

Part One
Back to the Woods

Chapter Two

Ten years later
"I'm heading home..."

I'm not sure if it's truly possible to be bored to death, but I would readily testify in a court of law that it was possible to be bored into a state of catatonia. A place where the edges of reality soften and blur. A place where even the most annoying conversation becomes the faintest buzz of an insect.

"...of course, white linen is so very classic. Maybe with a colorful centerpiece, or black accents..." Charles' mother, Francesca Lewiston droned on and on about linens and tables.

In my head, I called her Frannie, because she was the least Frannie-like person I'd ever met. And she would be the first one to agree with that fact.

My mother might have rules for proper etiquette, but hers were considered subpar by *Frannie*.

They hadn't met yet, but I suspected that Frannie's queen-of-the-castle airs would not mesh well with my mother Southern-debutante ones.

Sometimes I tried to imagine the mash-up.

Frannie coming out of one corner, dropping names as if they were bars of soap while my mother sweetly blessed-her-heart and began to lay out my family lineage like a colorful quilt on a winter's bed.

Bette Lee would of course work in the picture of our relative, a certain Martin Gambill who had a Paul Revere-esque ride down south, but alas, no one ever wrote an epic poem about his ride, so he was largely ignored by historians, despite a massive portrait in

Asheville, North Carolina, the hub of civilization according to my mother.

I'm not sure Frannie would be impressed as she lobbed the names of Michigan's society elite at poor Martin.

I'd told Bette Lee how much I was dreading today's wedding conference and she'd said, "Someone who's trying that hard has something to prove or something to hide, bless her heart."

I might have grown up a decided northerner—much to my mother's chagrin—but my mother made sure that my southern heritage was at my core.

And just as I knew that adults my mother's age or older were Miss or Mister, I also knew that *bless-her-hearting* someone was a sweet way to insult them.

I'd once come downstairs in jeans and a t-shirt for dinner with my parents. My mother had smiled as she looked at me and said, "Did you need help choosing an outfit?"

"No, I thought I'd wear this," I'd said.

"Bless your heart, you certainly could if we were visiting my great-grandfather's stables."

I changed my clothes without any further prompting.

Frannie didn't seem to notice my meandering thoughts. To be honest, she rarely needed any help carrying on a conversation.

Miss Ida could talk the ear off a brass monkey—I had no idea what that meant, but Bette Lee used to say it. Suddenly I couldn't wait for Miss Ida to meet Frannie. I wondered who would emerge with their ears talked off like that brass monkey's?

Frannie was still droning.

I'd once gone through an entire meal with Charles' family without saying as much as *pass the butter* and no one seemed any the wiser.

"Dee," Frannie said sharply.

I'd started going by that nickname in college and was accustomed to it by now. Sadie or Sadie Mae sounded simply too old fashioned.

To the world I was Dee. I tried to live up to the shorter, more fashionable name. But in my heart, I suspected I'd always be my mother's Sadie Mae who thought biscuits from a refrigerator tube were as wrong as iced tea with no *sweet* in front of it, or in it.

"Dee," Frannie said again, as if she had finally realized I was drifting away. "And we have to talk about the centerpieces…"

I looked her straight in the eye and nodded, which is all she needed in order to start talking centerpieces without my ever saying a word.

I didn't care about tablecloths or centerpieces.

I didn't care about what color was used for what part of the table settings.

I'd wanted a small wedding. Something intimate.

Charles did not.

I'd always imagined that I'd spend my late twenties traveling the world. I'd never imagined I'd be in Michigan planning my gala wedding.

I was not one of those little girls who spent her childhood dreaming of her wedding. When Charles asked me to marry him, I immediately envisioned the two of us with our families in a small chapel saying I-do.

My wedding was not going to be that at all.

We had guest list that included hundreds of people. I'll confess, having guests that numbered in the triple digits wasn't my idea of a good time, but Charles came from a *well-respected family of judges and statesmen,* a fact that Frannie reminded me of on a regular basis.

By statesmen, she meant politicians.

Charles' cousin, Max, was in the state congress.

Charles had higher ambitions than state government.

The fact that he did was not a good thing in my estimation.

I refrained from telling Frannie that my mother's family had come to Virginia pre-Revolution and had statesmen and doctors here in the US, and a titled family back in England.

My mother was a member of the DAR and proud of the fact.

I didn't tell Frannie because I wanted to witness what happened when she started her high-and-mightying in front of my mother.

Watching Bette Lee slap Frannie down to size, in the most genteel way imaginable would be a sight to behold.

I tried to wiggle out of the large wedding by pointing out I couldn't afford that kind of money, and I wouldn't let Big Henry and Bette Lee pay for that kind of useless extravagance, especially because that's not the way our family did weddings.

Rather than considering a wedding like my parent's, Charles had immediately offered to cover the expense and before I could agree or disagree he was inviting *Frannie* to help me pull it all together.

Charles was always very clear on what he wanted. That decisiveness had been something that had attracted me to him. But...

I pushed the *but* away and turned my attention back to Frannie.

"Did I tell you that Carol called me?" Frannie went on.

I could have told her I didn't have a clue who Carol was, but I couldn't really muster up the energy.

At that moment, Charles walked into his mother's office. He glanced at the large whiteboard that had wedding pictures and notes tacked all over it. He rolled his eyes and grinned at me.

I managed to shoot him a small smile in return.

For a moment, I forgot my annoyance about planning a society wedding I didn't want. His smiled reminded me of the day I'd met him. Charles had walked into my poli-sci class. He'd been there for a meeting and stopped into see Professor Ralph and then later...

I pushed the thought away, but tried to hold onto the sweetness of that first meeting though annoyance over the wedding plans made it hard. I couldn't help but think that it was easy for Charles to waltz in and find my torture amusing. I tried to tell myself that I understood the wedding was important to his family. I tried not to mind that this wasn't the type of wedding that I wanted.

Bette Lee had a hurried wedding with Big Henry when she was twenty-one. My grandmother had done the same with Old Henry when she was only sixteen. Both had told me the stories of loving someone so much they couldn't wait to plan a wedding. They'd just hauled the people who mattered with them to the chapel and said their I-dos.

That's what I had wanted with Charles.

I looked at him smiling at me as indulgently as Frannie had and felt—

My phone rang, giving me a reprieve from naming exactly how I felt about this whole big-wedding business. My mother had said she could try to come help plan, but after one single conversation with Frannie, Bette Lee had said it sounded as if we had it handled.

I looked at Frannie's pictures of *my* wedding and knew I didn't have anything to do with the *handling*.

"I've got to get this," I said, acting as if the unknown number with the recognizable area code must mean something. "Francesca, why don't you ask Charles' opinion on the table linen. You always say he has impeccable taste."

She always said it in such a way that his impeccable taste somehow only emphasized my lack thereof.

Charles shot me a look of horror that salved my annoyance. I smiled and winked at him to let him know I'd done it on purpose.

He smiled that long, slow smile that had been one of the first things I'd liked about him.

I felt lighter as I answered, "Hello?" and walked out of the room.

"Hello.   Is this Sadie Mae Hanson?" an unfamiliar voice asked using the name that no one but my family ever used anymore.

"It is."   I glanced back at Frannie thrusting tablecloths into Charles' hands and smiled again.

"I'm calling on behalf of Ida Hall..."

The stranger explained she was with social services at the hospital. She talked about HIPAA and Miss Ida's limited permission in such a way that I knew there was more she'd like to say but couldn't.

What she could say was Miss Ida had been in the hospital for three days and was ready to be released. The doctor and the social worker both felt she would be best served in a nursing home, but Miss Ida had refused.

"What's wrong with her?" I asked.

The woman hesitated a bit too long before she finally said, "You'll have to ask her about that. I have permission to tell you she's here and right now she's fine. But she really can't go home by herself and though she wants to go back to her house a nursing home is a better option..."

As I listened to this stranger tell me all the reasons I needed to agree to convince Miss Ida to go into   a   home,   I   kept   thinking   about   *paffles*.

After a few months of Saturdays, Miss Ida proclaimed she was going to make me breakfast the next week. She asked me if I liked pancakes or waffles. I jokingly said, "Both."

The following Saturday morning when I came over, she called me into the kitchen and set a plate in front of me, wearing a look of triumph.

"What is it?" I asked.

"A paffle." Miss Ida laughed as if she'd just told a joke. "You wouldn't tell me which you liked, so I made both and used cinnamon butter as a paste to stick them together. Try it."

I used a fork and realized that the concoction in front of me was indeed a waffle sandwiched between two pancakes.

I doused it with maple syrup and as the first bite melted in my mouth, I realized I had a new favorite food.

I didn't have to look through my book to remember that day's entry. *Paffles*, it simply read.

Paffles became a regular tradition for us.

I could almost taste the syrupy sweetness as I asked the nurse, "When will you release her?"

"I'm not sure you understand. I found a bed for her at a nursing home—"

I cut her off. "Does she want to go into a nursing home?"

"No," the woman admitted. "She's adamant about that. That's why I called. I'm hoping you can convince her—"

Even if I were inclined to try to convince her, Miss Ida wasn't someone you could convince any more than you could convince Bette Lee of something. They had different styles, but both styles included stubbornness.

"Please tell her that I'll be there tomorrow to take her home. I'll figure out what to do after I've talked to her."

The social worker sighed as if I was every bit as trying as Miss Ida.

I decided to take it as a compliment and felt she was lucky she'd called me not Bette Lee.

31

The woman gave me details and promised she'd have things lined up for me in the morning.

I wasn't sure how I was going to make it all work, but I'd figure it out.

"It's okay if I come tomorrow?" I asked, double-checking. "She doesn't need me sooner?"

"Tomorrow will be fine," the social worker assured me.

"Then tell Miss Ida, I'll be there around lunch," I said.

"I will," the woman promised me.

I stood for a moment looking out at Frannie's beautiful manicured lawn. There was a white gazebo at the edge of the property. I'd escaped and sat there a few times, but otherwise I'd never seen anyone else use it.

Actually, the only time I'd seen anyone in the backyard was during Frannie's parties. The yard was just for show.

I thought about Miss Ida's small yard that was mainly eaten up by her flower garden. All the neighbors were used to finding random bouquets on their porch when they needed some pick-me-up. Miss Ida had an uncanny ability to know something was wrong even if the person in question hadn't said a word about their problem.

I realized that I missed home.

I wondered if Detroit would start to feel like home after Charles and I were married?

I couldn't answer that question, but I could start to organize things so I could leave for Erie in the morning.

I didn't need to call the Brain to know he'd let me go. Heck, he'd help me pack. We'd been talking about me looking for a new job. By *we*, I meant *Brian* had been talking.

He said I was wasted working for him, though he'd happily pay my salary forever to keep me. But he said he was friend enough to know I needed more challenges.

He'd handed me articles on virtual assistants. With the Internet, I could still keep him on track from wherever I landed he assured me.

I knew he'd call this a test run.

I mentally started arranging things in my head as I walked back into the office and found Frannie going over her schpeel with Charles.

I was pretty sure he wasn't having any more fun than I'd been having. Under any other circumstances, I'd have laughed, but I was too caught up in my plans to focus on the wedding I didn't want.

"Charles, could I talk to you please?" I asked.

"What's wrong?" Frannie asked.

Normally, I wouldn't risk offending Charles' touchy mother, but right now I needed to talk to him.

Just him.

I needed him to hold me and tell me he understood why I needed to go.

His care and understanding could be my memory for today.

Charles nodded and followed me out onto the terrace. "What's wrong?"

"It's Miss Ida. She's been in the hospital. They wouldn't tell me what's wrong, but they did say she couldn't go home by herself. They wanted to put her in a nursing home, but she doesn't want that, and I can't say that I blame her. So I said that I'd head home and help her figure out what to do next. So I'm leaving—"

He looked confused. "The elderly neighbor you used to work for?" he asked, obviously not having processed more than my first sentence.

I knew that he knew who Miss Ida was. He was asking why I was going to take care of her.

Technically *neighbor* was an accurate description for our relationship, but Miss Ida was more

33

than that. I'd tried to explain it to Charles in the past, but he'd never really seemed to understand.

He'd come home with me once to meet her, but he'd been stiff and monosyllabic in her company.

I was furious on the way home, but he told me *old people* made him nervous. He'd sent her roses the next day, as if his gift could make up for his behavior.

I remembered my first day of work thinking she was *really* old, but in retrospect, she'd been a very young soul in her seventies. She'd be the first to tell you she had old knees, but the rest of her was eternally young in spirit.

As that memory rose up, so did my fury. I tamped it down and reminded myself that though he could sometimes be insensitive, he could also be caring. When he was in college, he'd volunteered at a local literacy center. He had a notebook of letters his students had written him in his office.

That memory took away some of my red-hot anger.

"She's so much more than just a neighbor to me," I said softly. "I'm leaving in the morning to go to Erie."

He hugged me, just as I'd hoped. "That's one of the things I love about you. You have a generous heart. Will you be home in time for our show on Saturday?"

His question took away some of the sweetness from the memory I'd planned to write down.

I shook my head. "I'll be in Erie indefinitely. The woman from the hospital wouldn't tell me much because of all the patient confidentiality rules. But from what she *didn't* say and the way she *didn't* say it, I think this is serious. I'll know more after I talk to Miss Ida..."

"Wait. You're thinking that you're staying with some elderly childhood neighbor in Pennsylvania indefinitely?"

I realized that his hug was not going to be today's memory because his question had just taken all the sweetness from it.

"More than thinking about it, Charles. It's what I'm doing," I said.

His frown deepened. "What about work?"

"I'll tell the Brain I'm going to work virtually for a while."

To be honest, I'd never intended to be a personal assistant. I'd fallen into the job.

Brian Thompson, aka the Brain, worked at the university. At first glance, no one would consider him a professor other than he had the look of a younger Neil deGrasse Tyson, only with dreads, holey jeans and far less charisma.

I'd taken his basic science class. He was that absurd kind of smart that seemed to function on a different level than most of humanity. One day as he tried to explain *Schrodinger's Cat* to me and I realized that unlike Dr. Tyson, Dr. Thompson had no ability to relate with lesser beings.

Then Brian had told me about wanting to write science books that would make kids like science.

He'd showed me his idea.

The Brain might know science, and he could even teach it to non-genius college students like me as long as they were equipped with a good thesaurus and a friend who was on the geeky side of things, but I wasn't sure he knew kids.

Frankly, I wasn't sure he'd ever been a child.

I tried to tell him he didn't need to talk down to kids, but he couldn't speak *scientist* to them either. He didn't quite get it, so I took his idea and showed him what I meant.

He'd hired me to clean up that book months later. That worked for me since I was graduating with an English degree and no specific job aspirations.

Gradually, I took on more duties and my part-time job turned into a fulltime job.

My title was *personal assistant*. What that meant was I helped the Brain with office stuff as well as life stuff. I found a certain satisfaction in organizing his life.

I'd wondered about how a college professor could afford a fulltime personal assistant, but when I took over his accounts, I found out the Brain was rich. Looking at his ledgers was the only way anyone would ever know it though. He lived in an apartment building that was predominantly student housing and his apartment looked more like a student's room than a wealthy adult's.

The Brain used the term Spartan as his decorating guide.

Charles occasionally made noises about me finding a job more worthy of my talents, but I suddenly wondered if he liked that my job organizing Brian's life left me time to organize his.

I realized I hadn't done a good enough job at tamping down my anger.

"How long?" Charles asked, interrupting my thoughts.

I was pretty sure I knew what he was asking, but I wanted to be wrong. "Pardon?" I asked, giving him a chance to clarify.

"How long will you be gone? There are so many plans for the wedding..." Whether Charles heard what he was saying, or saw my look of disappointment, I wasn't sure. But he gave himself a little shake. "No, you're right. I'm sure Mother would be willing to pull it all together. She—"

And suddenly I knew that Miss Ida had inadvertently given me a temporary way out of this massive wedding I didn't want.

I felt an overwhelming surge of relief.

I interrupted Charles, blurting out words I'd hardly even thought, "I think we'll have to put off planning the wedding until I have a better idea what's going on."

"I'm sure your Miss Ida wouldn't expect you to throw your life into turmoil for her. My life runs so much smoother when you're here."

Ouch.

I wanted more than to be the oil that kept Charles' life moving smoothly.

"I'm glad things are better when I'm here," I said, hoping that's what he'd meant. "And you're right, Miss Ida wouldn't expect me to throw my life in turmoil. That's just one of the reasons she's as amazing as she is. And that's just one of the reasons I plan on doing just that. I'll throw my whole life into turmoil to be there for her."

"I don't understand you and this woman's relationship." He looked truly mystified.

"Miss Ida is…"

There were so many ways I could describe Miss Ida. My mentor. My friend. A keeper of memories. After I went to work for her, her memories intersected with my memories frequently.

If I were writing a dictionary that's how I'd define family because it's not DNA. It's a lifetime of tangled memories.

Charles wouldn't understand any of those explanations. But they all could be boiled down to something simple he should be able to comprehend. "She's family."

"It's not like you aren't close with your parents," he said. His tone indicating that my being close to my parents was not a boon in his eyes either.

We'd gone to stay with them twice in Virginia in four years we'd been together, and they'd come to see me here. Charles had never suggested we get our parents together, but to be fair, neither had I. More than that, I'd noticed when they visited Detroit, Charles got very busy at work.

"You're right. We are close. I love them and they love me. But Bette Lee and Big Henry are complete in and of themselves. They love me, but they don't *need* me. Even when I was young, I recognized that. Miss Ida needed me in a way they never would. And to be honest, I needed her."

"What is it with you and old ladies? You and your neighbor now are thick as thieves," he muttered.

"First, I'm going to do you a favor and not tell Miss Carol that you called her old. She'd tell you that she's upwardly mobile. And to answer your question, she's a friend, too."

He snorted, as if my being friends with either lady was incomprehensible.

"You collect old ladies like old ladies collect cats," he muttered.

He continued his one-sided argument and when we went back into the house, he enlisted Frannie's help and she argued as well.

I didn't need to take part in the debate. They did just fine without my input. But as I listened to them both, my initial feeling of relief seemed to grow and blossom.

I was relieved to have a legitimate reason to postpone planning my wedding to Charles.

And that struck me as all together wrong.

I thought about my mother and Big Henry, and my grandparents. They'd been in a hurry to join their lives together.

I realized that I didn't feel that sense of urgency.

I loved Charles. Of course, I loved him.

I loved how he laughed. When we'd first started dating we'd gone out for ice cream one night. I'd been torn between the pralines and cream and the strawberry cheesecake. I'd been still debating when he'd ordered me both.

I'd said something like I really shouldn't.

I remembered exactly what he'd said. I'd written it in my book. "Life's short. Always get a double scoop." He'd laughed. I couldn't capture the sound of his laughter in my book, but remembering the moment I could hear it all over again.

I realized I hadn't heard enough of it lately.

Today hadn't been his shining moment of love and support. Well, actually the wedding plans hadn't been either. But there were other moments. Better moments.

The day he surprised me with tickets to Hamilton. The tickets had been hot for a long time. I wasn't sure what strings he pulled to get them, but I'll confess, I melted a bit when he gave them to me. I went on and on about how excited I was that he was going to take me and give theater a try.

The memory wasn't quite as sweet after Frannie casually asked how I'd enjoyed the show and then asked what friend I'd taken. That's when I realized Charles hadn't intended on going with me.

I wasn't sure why I had suddenly remembered another moment that felt as if Charles had let me down.

There were so many other times he'd done lovely things. Flowers for no reason. Walks in the evening holding hands and talking about our day and our plans.

But this wedding...this wedding wasn't something I was going to love. I'd tried to dial it back but Frannie had steamrolled ahead and Charles seemed happy to let her have her way. I couldn't blame her takeover on him. I hadn't fought for what I wanted. I'd expressed my concerns, but hadn't insisted they pay attention to them.

After my trip home to Erie to help Miss Ida, I'd come back and put my foot down. I'd insist that we find some compromise. I didn't want to start my married life off resentful that my desires had been completely ignored.

But for now, I pushed aside worries about the upcoming wedding and concentrated on what needed to be done in order to get to Miss Ida.

I kissed Charles' cheek before I left. "I'll keep you posted."

He gave me a stiff nod and stalked back into the house.

Normally I'd be disturbed that he was annoyed, but since I was annoyed myself, I didn't feel disturbed at all.

I thought I was heading home to pack, but instead I went to Brian's office because he had office hours today. The door was closed when I arrived and I had my suspicions why, so I knocked.

"Come in," he called out. Even though I couldn't hear him sigh through the closed door, I knew there'd been one. I opened the door and found him alone in the office, just as I suspected.

"*Brain*," I said with a heavy emphasis on his nickname, "you're supposed to leave the door open so students know you're here and available to help."

He sighed again. "If they really want or need my help, they'll knock. Like you did."

I took a seat on the couch, knowing that the chair he kept in front of his desk was not only uncomfortable by design, but had uneven legs. It always felt as if at any moment you could fall over.

Which was his intent.

He thought that chair made students get to their point more quickly.

I patted the cushion next to me. "I need to talk to you about work."

"You found a new job?" He sounded pleased about the prospect as he took the seat next to me.

I mock-slugged is arm. Brain wasn't someone comfortable with physical contact. He'd be apoplectic if I hugged him, but he could handle an occasional slug or pat. "No. But I need to go to Erie. I don't know for how long, so I thought we might try out your idea of my managing things long-distance."

He grinned. "That's fantastic. When are you going?"

This time I sighed, though I couldn't hide my underlying grin. "You could pretend to be distraught that I'm leaving you."

He gave me that quintessential snarky look that he made so well.

"You'll miss me," I warned.

"Yes," he admitted. "You are one of the few human beings who don't make me want to pluck out my eyeballs. But we've had this discussion. You need to do more than just manage my life. To be clear: I'm not letting you off the hook. You still have to manage me, but you're too comfortable here."

"How about you?" I challenged.

"What?" he asked.

"When's the last time you stepped out of your comfort zone?" I said.

The Brain once said that we made such a good team because we each filled in what the other one was missing. I didn't argue, but secretly I thought there was a chance we worked well together because we were so much alike. I don't think many people—including Brian—would notice, but the truth was, we were two people who liked status quo. We liked knowing what to expect. We were very good in our comfort zones, but not-so-much in the rest of the world.

"We're not talking about me," Brian said.

"*I am* talking about you. Let's make a deal, I'll try managing you long distance and you ask a girl out...on a date."

Brian frowned. "You already told me you were going to manage me long distance."

"That's what makes me such a good bargainer. I hid a clause in our contractual bargain. Say yes, *Brain*."

He gave me that odd little look he always gave me when I called him by his sister's nickname for him. I thought he might fight some more, but finally he nodded. "Fine. I'll go out on a date." He added another classic Brian sigh.

The sigh was too much. "That was too easy. With who?"

He shook his head. "Hey, I said I'd go. I didn't say I'd give you all the gory details."

There was definitely more going on here. If I had time, I'd stick around and worm it out of him.

"You will eventually."

He laughed uneasily which made me laugh.

"Oh you're so going to tell me," I assured him as I patted his shoulder. He looked uncomfortable. I wasn't sure if it was the thought of my worming his mystery date out of him, or my patting his cheek. "I'm leaving first thing in the morning."

"I'll miss you," he said as I let myself out of his office.

"I know," I agreed.

Visiting with the Brain had given me a moment's respite in my worry over Miss Ida. But as I walked out of his building, I was back in full worry mode.

I went to see Miss Carol before I went in my house. She readily agreed to water my plants and collect my mail.

I couldn't help but think about Charles' comment when Carol's cat, Marmalade, curled around my ankle.

That night, I couldn't write about Charles' support in my Book of Memories, so I simply wrote: *I'm heading home.*

I flipped back to that day my sophomore year of college. And found the entry I'd made the day I'd met Charles.

I fell over a man today. He was smart, sophisticated and oh-so sure of himself. We went for coffee and are going to dinner tomorrow.

I remembered every moment of that first day, and just looking at that short entry took me back in time...

I was making myself sick, trying to put together next semester's schedule. I felt even worse as I tried to decide on what to declare for a major.

I'd thought I'd drop in on Professor Ralph, but as I approached his office, I saw he was talking to someone already in the hall by his door. I'd come back later and see if my advisor had any wise, sage words of advice.

They stood on opposite sides of the hall, and there was no way to get by without crossing between them. "Excuse me," I said and promptly tripped over the other man's foot.

I fell with a hard thud on my knee. My book bag and purse added a secondary audible thud.

"Are you all right?" Mr. Handsome asked.

Professor Ralph might have said something too, but I only had eyes and obviously ears for Mr. Good-Looking.

"I'm fine."

"I'll talk to you later, Professor. Right now, I'm going to walk this damsel in distress wherever she was going."

"That's not necessary," I assured him.

He smiled at me then and any arguments about what was necessary evaporated along with all thought.

"What's a pretty girl like you doing in a class with him," he asked loudly enough for the professor to hear him as he picked up my bags for me.

"You don't have to carry those," I said. "I'm fine."

"What would my mother say if I didn't try to rescue the princess?"

I snorted. "Princess? More like court jester with that fall."

Before I knew it, we were walking across the campus chatting. He introduced himself as Charles and I introduced myself as Dee.

He told me he was a lawyer and alum, then he asked about my major. I'd confessed I hadn't declared one, but knew I needed to.

"I knew I was going to be a lawyer from the first," he'd said. "I was going to follow in the family footsteps. Never any doubt about that."

I wondered what it would be like to always know exactly who you were and where you were going.

"Would you like to get coffee?" he asked as we approached one of the school's coffee shops.

"Yes," I said, realizing I really did want to.

We grabbed a couple coffees and settled at a table and as I set my bag down, next term's schedule fell out.

Charles picked it up. "Classes?"

I sighed. "I don't have any clue on a major and have taken all the core classes. It's time to figure out what I want to do so I can know what I need to take. That's the problem with the schedule. My English comp teacher said that my schedule has been English heavy and it makes sense, but seriously, what do you do with an English degree? If you're a scientist you know you're going to be doing science stuff. If you are an engineer you'll be doing..." I hesitated.

"Engines?" Charles asked with a grin.

"Yes. I just don't know what kind of job opportunities an English degree will present. I know I don't want to teach, so that's out."

"Do you like English?" he asked as he took a sip of coffee and studied me.

I thought about it and nodded.

"Then get the degree. Life's too short to do something you hate."

"But that's the point, what will I do with an English degree?"

"Anything you want." He pulled out his phone, tapped on it a few times, then read off, "Copy editing, human resource, technical writer, English as a second language, archivist..." He left the word hanging, then looked up and grinned. "The world's your oyster. And I would think if you're going into any graduate program, that would make a great degree to build off of."

I laughed because something in me settled. He had vocalized what I hadn't been able to say to myself. My parents had said the same sort of things. "Thanks."

"You're welcome," he said. We chatted amiably as we finished our coffees. As I got up, my knee felt tight, but I worked not to limp at all because I didn't want him to feel bad because of my klutziness.

But he obviously noted because when we reached my car he said, "My mother would be appalled that I maimed a beautiful woman. She'd say I needed to make it up to you. How about dinner tomorrow night?"

I'd replied, "I'd like that."

I ran my fingers over the words on the page and just those three sentences were enough to take me back. For a moment I was that younger girl who'd loved that Charles was so sure of himself...sure of every decision.

Was that what had attracted me to him? I was young and confused and he was the opposite.

Opposites attract they said. A small voice inside of me added, *not always*.

I flipped back to today's entry. As I looked at the words on the page, I realized how much I missed Erie and Miss Ida.

I couldn't wait to get on the road.

Sadie Mae's Book of Memories

My mother is a force of nature.

She is a hurricane, blowing everything in her path out of her way.

Most people don't realize her power because she covers it with bless-her-hearts and sweet smiles.

I don't feel like a force of nature. I'm a leaf in the wind, being blown from one thing to the next with very little say on my direction. I literally fell over Charles. I fell into my job with Brian.

I've never chosen.

I have never been a force in my own life like my Bette Lee.

I am heading home.

I have chosen this direction.

> Maybe I'm becoming more of my mother's daughter...finally.

Chapter Three

"Today, I saw a double rainbow over the lake..."

I left Detroit at four the next morning.

I hadn't slept well. I wasn't sure if I was excited to *get away from* or I was excited to be *going to* my home.

I threw my suitcase in the backseat of my car and left my small house by the university before the sun came up.

I drove past the campus on my way to the highway and realized that I'd lived my entire life near a university. It struck me as ironic, since I'd never felt an overwhelming need for a degree.

I'd gone to college because my parents expected me to. Big Henry might have been persuaded that life experience was a better path for me. Maybe I would have discovered something I was passionate about and gone to school with a plan instead of drifting through my four college years and having a nice, but not overly useful degree in English.

But putting off college hadn't been an option for me. Bette Lee wasn't someone who could be persuaded about life experience holding more value than a piece of paper. Sometimes I wondered if she wanted me to go to college for a degree, or if she wanted me to go so that she could start the next chapter of her life with Big Henry.

Yes, I was absolutely sure that my parents loved me but they'd never experienced the slightest twinge of empty nest-itis. They seemed to revel in their childless state.

After I went to school, Big Henry indulged my mother's homesickness. They'd picked up stakes, bought a small place in Virginia and used it as their home base between trips. Their phone calls were always filled with stories of some new place they'd visited.

I'd never felt the urge to travel to that extent. Oh, an occasional trip out of town was nice, but by nature I was a homebody.

My small house in Detroit near the university was enough for me. I'd decorated it in *early book nerd* and had wonderful neighbors. I could walk to the Brain's.

But no matter how much I loved my place in Detroit, I knew that Erie would always be my real home.

I caught glimpses of the Great Lake to my left. Depending on how I-90 curved, it came in and out of view. Each time I caught sight of it, my excitement at going home grew.

I grew up within a few miles of that lake.

My childhood home was within walking distance of Mercyhurst University, where Big Henry had worked. The university sat on a ridge that towered over the city and the lake. When we walked home down Parade Boulevard from the campus, I could see the water in the distance.

I remember walking up the hill to meet my dad so I could walk home with him after work. The crackle of the leaves under our feet in the fall, the slip-sliding steps through the snow and ice in the winter. Mud in the spring when the bottom of the hill could get so boggy that you'd sink if you strayed off the sidewalk. And in summers, after most of the students went home, I'd walk through the relatively empty campus and revel in how quiet it was.

All those memories kept unfolding as I drove east on I-90 towards Erie. I knew if I thumbed through

48

my Book of Memories, many of them would include those moments with Big Henry.

When I saw the signs for Presque Isle, I knew I was home. I exited I-90 and took I-79 north towards the Bayfront Connector. But rather than go straight to the hospital, I took a detour. I drove down that last few blocks of State Street to the dock on the bay.

I parked my car and walked to the edge of the pier. I'd seen pictures of the earlier version of the dock from before my time. There had been a deck with a small spire at the back that had stood at the end a cement outcrop into the bay.

Now, we had a tall tower—The Bicentennial Tower—there. You could ride an elevator to the top and look out over the bay to the peninsula and beyond to the Great Lake itself. If the conditions were right, you could sometimes see Canada across the lake.

It was drizzling today. I could hear the water beating against the dock. Seagulls flew overhead, crying out plaintively. There were ducks east of the dock who quacked and grumbled to each other. I heard all those sounds and more, but they didn't stand out individually to me. They blended into a wonderful harmony that said, *you're home, Sadie Mae. You are home.*

I stood at the end of the dock listening to the lake's music and looking out over the water towards the peninsula.

Home.

I was home.

It had been two months since I'd been back to visit Miss Ida. I normally came down once a month, but I'd skipped last month.

I regretted that now.

I glanced at the clock on my phone. One minute to ten.

Almost on cue, my phone rang.

"Where are you?" Charles asked with no salutation.

"Almost at the hospital. I couldn't sleep, so I left a little early. I stopped at the dock first." I drew in a deep breath.

Some people might say the water smelled fish-ish. And I guess it did, but to me, there was more. If asked, I'd swear I could smell the poplar trees that grew on the peninsula across the bay. And there was a sweet undercurrent of spring flowers.

"Well, get to the hospital, figure things out for your *friend* and hurry home. I need you."

I need you.

Not that he missed me or was worried about me.

"I'm sure you'll survive on your own, Charles." The words came out a bit more snarkily than I intended.

Charles didn't seem to notice as he asked, "Do you know where my purple tie is?"

I hated that tie and didn't feel bad that it was hidden in the back of his closet. But I wouldn't be there to see him wear it, so I happily confessed, "I think it's back behind your grey suit."

"Thanks. You are so organized. Things don't run as smoothly if you're not around."

I wasn't sure that being missed because of my organizational skills qualified as love poetry. I didn't want to think about Charles' needs right now. "Listen, it's misty out here and I don't want to damage my phone. I'll talk to you tonight," I promised.

"Fine," he said, annoyance lacing the single syllable.

"I love you," I said, though he'd already hung up.

I stood another moment at the edge of the dock, staring across the bay and realized there was a faint rainbow over Presque Isle peninsula.

Not just a rainbow. A double rainbow.

It seemed like some optimistic sign.

I smiled and wondered if there was a pot of gold buried out there.

I wouldn't be surprised if there was.

May had always felt like a time of rebirth. Of rediscovery.

I hung onto the sight of the double rainbow as I got back in my car and drove the short distance to the hospital.

I walked through the revolving doors and realized no matter how homey they tried to make it look, it was still a hospital. It was a place filled with pain, illness and sadness. I had to think a nursing home would feel the same.

I didn't blame Miss Ida for wanting to go home instead.

I pushed the button and the elevator immediately appeared. I was anxious to see Miss Ida for myself. I thought again about our tangled memories and smiled.

I think I made a lady on the elevator nervous with that smile, and I tried to offer her a reassuring look, but she got off the moment the doors slid open. I stayed on as they slid shut again and the elevator moved upwards.

Miss Ida meant so much to me.

She'd always been my biggest cheerleader. In many ways, she was my best friend. She knew me in a way no one else did. Not my parents. Not Charles.

I felt bad at the thought. I needed to make more of an effort with him when I got home.

The elevator door opened and I got out this time and walked to the nurses' station.

The nurse went over Miss Ida's forms and promised to send a home healthcare nurse over later this afternoon. She'd be able to help with Miss Ida's care.

Miss Ida had been having dizzy spells and had fallen. The nurse emphasized it was important that Miss Ida use the walker for stability.

I asked about a wheelchair, but the nurse said to ask her home healthcare nurse.

Then I followed the woman down the hall to Miss Ida's room. I was nervous about seeing her. Afraid her hospital stay would have changed her.

She was in a wheelchair and she smiled when she saw me.

Something in my chest loosened, as I was reassured that she was still Miss Ida. She was the same woman who taught me to make tea and hold onto the memories that counted.

Oh, maybe she seemed smaller physically and her hair was pure white these days, but her smile showcased the depth of her spirit and that hadn't changed at all.

I remembered seeing her that first day, sitting in her flower-covered chair holding her Book of Memories. I remember thinking how very old she was that day.

She was eighty-one now. Yes, it was still old, but she didn't seem nearly as old now as she'd seemed on my first visit to her house.

Funny how time and perspective changed things.

"Miss Ida," I said, as I leaned down to hug her and realized how fragile she felt.

"I'm so sorry they called you, Sadie Mae. I told that doctor and his minions that I've been caring for myself for years and I'm capable continuing to do so even if I get a bit dizzy now and then."

I smiled as she said my name. It was just another sign that I was home.

Bette Lee had never adjusted to the idea of me being Dee. She said that Sadie Mae was a perfectly wonderful name. I had three grandmothers at various points called that. There were a lot of Bette Lees as well. My mother said that southerners valued their roots, which is why there were so many names that were repeated generation after generation.

"Miss Ida, I'm glad they called." And because she looked so worried, I added, "I'm inviting myself to stay at your house. Please don't tell Bette Lee. You know her southern soul would swoon at the idea of me being so forward. She'd blame Big Henry for his northern influence."

That made her laugh and the tight lines of worry relaxed. "I won't tell."

"Then let's go home."

An aide helped us to my car and I put Miss Ida in the front seat and her small bag of belongings in the back with mine. I folded up her walker and put it in the back as well.

"The nurse was vague on your diagnosis," I said as I drove the familiar streets. Perry Square looked as different as the dock had, with its new brick stage area and sitting wall that wrapped around the edge of the sidewalk. But as I moved onto Erie's side streets, things looked much more familiar. The sameness was comforting.

Miss Ida didn't answer me and I realized she'd fallen asleep.

That wasn't like her. It might not mean anything other than she'd been ill and was recovering.

Yet, as I glanced across the car, I was afraid it might mean more.

She woke as I pulled into her drive.

"Miss Ida, why do the doctors think you're getting dizzy and falling?" I asked again.

"Darling, I'm getting old. Old people fall and you know I've always been a bit dizzy. Albert used to say I was a whirling dervish. I wrote it in my book the first time he said it. *Whirling dervish.* Do you know that the term came from a religious group who literally whirled in circles?"

I smiled. "No, I didn't."

When I was little I loved to twirl in circles and then fall onto the ground under the silver maple. I loved to feel the world spin around me as I looked up at the branches and their leaves.

"Yes," Miss Ida continued. "It's an order that uses that whirling as a kind of prayer. I like the idea of praying with all that movement. It seems joyous to me. Maybe my dizzy spells are a sign that I should start whirling in earnest? I'll have to think about that."

"Miss Ida, I think that whirling in prayer is a bit different than whirling because you're dizzy."

She gave me a stubborn look I'd never seen her use before. "Well, if you just help get me settled, I'm sure I'll be fine."

As much as I wanted a clear diagnosis, it was obvious she wasn't in the mood to be pushed any further, so I shook my head. "We'll talk about that later. Right now, let's get you inside."

It looked like a long way from the car into the house. I wished they'd sent her home with more than a walker. I hated the thought of her getting dizzy on the cement stairs and falling.

I glanced at her. She seemed to be thinking the same thing.

I thought for a moment. "Miss Ida, you stay put for just a moment. I have an idea."

I had a key to her house on my key ring, so I took both of our bags and let myself in. I went back to her room and the small desk in the corner.

I got the chair—the big office chair with thick padded arms and wheels—and went back to the car. "They didn't give us a wheelchair, so we'll improvise."

Miss Ida's smile was contagious. "Oh, Sadie Mae, you are a wonder. I wasn't sure I could make it inside. They kept me in that hospital for too long. I'm not the type to vegetate in bed for days on end. I tried to tell the doctors I could go home sooner, but they wouldn't listen to reason."

"I should have insisted on a wheelchair at the hospital. But they're sending someone over later and we'll ask then. For now, your chariot awaits. " I turned the chair backwards and tilted it before attempting the stairs. I didn't want to tip her out. I got her on the level porch and, still going backward, underestimated how far it was to the lone step at the door and backed myself into it.

It was enough to send me off kilter and I fell backward onto the step.

"Sadie?" Miss Ida said.

I tried to answer, but I was laughing at myself.

She swiveled the chair and saw me sitting on the step and laughed along with me. "We're quite a pair," she said.

"Yes we are."

I got back up and opened the screen, ready to bump the chair up that last step when a man on the other side of the street called, "Do you need a hand?"

"No, but thanks," I called back, then asked Miss Ida, "Do you think he saw my stumble."

"If he did, he's gentleman enough not to mention it. He's my new neighbor," Miss Ida said as we bumped up that last step and into the living room. "He's the one that busted me. I fell getting the mail and he wouldn't just prop me up and take me inside. He called the ambulance instead. I think I may need to be fierce with him."

I laughed. "You are as fierce as a kitten."

I thought of Charles saying I collected old ladies like old ladies collected cats. If I told Miss Ida what he'd said, she just might be a bit fierce and I wouldn't blame her. "I thought the Nick house sold last year. It's sold again since?"

I might have moved out of the neighborhood a decade ago, but I still felt a sense of connection. Miss Ida kept me informed. These days I didn't know the people who went with the names she threw out, but I still heard their stories.

I'm sure some people would call her a gossip, but she only ever shared the nicest stories, so there was no harm.

"No," she said. "He's the one who bought it last year. A year is still *new* when you're practically a hundred."

"You're eighty-one," I said. "You're almost two decades away from a century."

Miss Ida's accident made me realize just how old she was. I guess there comes a point in everyone's life when they're closer to death than birth.

The thought of losing her someday hurt. I was determined to get her well and make sure that day didn't come for a very long time.

"It's all right, Sadie Mae. I know I'm old. I've always thought life was a grand adventure. I'm betting that what comes after is an even bigger one. I know there are a lot of people just waiting for me to come to the party."

Miss Ida had always painted pictures with her words. Whenever she shared a memory from her book, I could see it almost as if I'd been there. Right now, I could see people gathered together, waiting for her to come join the party. I'd seen pictures of her Albert. He was in the front of the group in my mind's eye.

"Well, I'm lobbying for a lot more time here partying with me," I said.

I'd do what I could to help. I'd be more attentive. Once she was better, I wouldn't miss a visit and I'd call more often.

"Sadie-my-darling—" She said as if it were one word, blurring the word *my* so that it almost sounded like Mae. "—everyone dies. I've kept my wits about me and I have been blessed with good friends and happy memories. Speaking of which, would you..."

She didn't have to finish asking. I got in her bag from the hospital and handed it to her with a pen.

I realized how much closer to the end of the book she'd gotten over the decade since I first saw it.

"*Today, Sadie Mae came home,*" she wrote, echoing my own thoughts.

"Miss Ida, we still need to talk about what caused you to fall," I said.

She smiled. "I'm old, Sadie Mae. I get dizzy now and sometimes I fall. But I don't have any complaints. I'm as sharp as I ever was. Now, some might claim that isn't all that sharp, but I haven't lost ground. I've got my house and my friends."

"Will you let me talk to the home health nurse about your actual diagnosis?" I asked.

"We'll see," she said cryptically.

I had a sinking feeling that Miss Ida's diagnosis was not a good one.

Was she sheltering me?

Or was she sheltering herself?

Maybe it wasn't real to her if she didn't have to name whatever the problem was. I decided I'd wait a little bit before forcing the issue.

Later that night, after settling Miss Ida in her bed and dealing with the very nice visiting nurse who ordered a hospital bed and wheelchair for us and promised to make arrangements for physical and occupational therapy, I went into the bedroom across the hall from Miss Ida's.

I looked at the beautiful mural and wondered about Miss Ida's daughter. I knew more about her now than I'd known that first day. Her name was Barbara and she was older than me. She used to love tea parties with Miss Ida. She loved to paint. When she was just a toddler, she'd gotten her hands on a pen and had tattooed herself with pictures on her arm, the day before she'd had an appointment with a photographer.

Miss Ida had taken Barbara for those pictures, despite the fact the marks were very visible.

Miss Ida displayed it with other Barbara pictures in her room.

I liked that tattoo picture best. Barbara had a devilish twinkle in her eyes.

Other than that, I knew very little about her.

I'd asked Bette Lee about her once and she'd just said, "She's gone and I don't think she's coming back."

I looked at the section of the painting closest to the head of the bed. I realized it was a glider and a man was sitting across from a young girl on it.

I'd heard the story of Miss Ida's book and how it had started. Barbara had captured Miss Ida's memory. The entire wall was her memories. Some I recognized, some I didn't.

A movie theater. A train. An old looking car.

So many of Miss Ida. A woman with a massive bun. Her hair wasn't white in the pictures, but then it hadn't been totally white back when I met her either.

I turned at the wall next to it. These were darker pictures and I didn't recognize any of them. There was a picture of a girl under an arch. A bridge maybe? She was sitting on cement and her eyes were half closed, as if she were dreaming.

The picture disturbed me, though I wasn't sure why, so I didn't study these any closer.

I turned back to Miss Ida's wall and after a while, I got out my own Book of Memories. *"Today, I saw a double rainbow over the lake and I brought Miss Ida home."*

It wasn't a long memory, but it was a good one.

I woke up at two and checked on Miss Ida. She was sleeping peacefully.

It wasn't until I tiptoed back across the hall that I realized Charles hadn't called to check on us. He *had* texted me about a missing suit. I reminded him he'd taken it to the dry cleaners. He hadn't bothered texting back as much as a thank you.

Before I could become annoyed, I realized, I hadn't thought to call or text him either.

Miss Ida's Book of Memories

I dreamed of Albert last night. Even after all these years, seeing him is such a comfort. He told me to relax, that Sadie Mae was going to take care of everything.

And sure as the sun rises in the east, Sadie Mae swept in and had everything organized just like Albert said. I have a wheelchair and a fancy bed to use.

Right before I woke up, Albert said he'd see me soon.

According to the doctors, he'll be right about that, too.

Chapter Four

"Today I laughed myself silly as I burned breakfast..."

"I think it's time we admit, that despite the fact I love watching cooking shows, I am not a cook," I told Miss Ida as we both laughed hysterically.

Oh, *Alton, Rachel* and *Giada* would be so disappointed in me. And let's not even start on how *The Pioneer Woman* would feel. My breakfast had been a comedy of errors. It was more worthy of a sitcom than *The Cooking Channel*.

I'd burned the toast, which made the smoke alarm start pinging. And it turned out the alarm was hardwired and there was no off button.

"I thought about trying paffles," I said.

Miss Ida laughed. "I think just trying toast was a good decision."

I opened the doors and windows, but the alarm beeped for at least five minutes. The neighbor next to Miss Ida's—not my old house, but the other side— finally yelled out his window to either call the fire department or turn off the beeping.

"Nor am I an electrician," I said to Miss Ida. "Let's hope I can do better at pretending to be a nurse."

"Despite what they said at the hospital, I don't need a nurse, but I'm happy to have a friend here, dear," she said.

I'd offered to make more toast, but we opted to eat our scrambled eggs without another toasting attempt on my part.

"I do make a very good pot of tea," I said. "I learned from the best."

She smiled.

"So here are my plans today. The home health nurse is coming back to make sure we have everything set up. After she comes, I'm going to call your current helper—"

"Julie," Miss Ida supplied.

"I'll call Julie and see if she'll come sit with you after school for an hour or so while I run to the store. And I'm going to spend my morning making a few calls to get the house organized."

"Sadie Mae, what about your job—" she started.

"The Brain can manage his own life for a while. He's been pushing me to figure out an actual career. Oh, he's blatantly informed me that he's not saying I don't have to work for him, but keeps pointing out that I could manage him from any computer. So, I'm trying out being his virtual assistant for a while. I promised him I'd call or text every day with reminders. And he owes me about a bajillion days of vacation anyway."

"This isn't a vacation for you," Miss Ida scolded.

"Are you kidding?" I asked. "You've saved me from a fate worse than death."

"What's that?" she asked.

"Wedding plans with Frannie. Oh, Miss Ida, it's torture." I grasped my heart with an exaggerated tortured expression.

"Tell her no," Miss Ida said as if it would be that simple.

"But Charles wants a big wedding, too," I pointed out.

"What do you want, dear?" she asked.

That was the five million dollar question.

I knew what I didn't want.

I didn't want that elaborate horse and pony show they were planning.

I shrugged. "When I look at people like the Brain and Charles...they've always known what they wanted and who they are."

"Maybe you're not exactly sure what you want to do with the rest of your life, but I know who you are," Miss Ida said. "You are a young woman with a huge heart and a knack for organizing things. You're a woman who loves reading and doesn't mind old ladies."

I almost added, and cats, thinking of Charles' comment about my collecting old ladies like they collect cats.

Too bad there wasn't a job in that.

I didn't say it. Instead I said, "I'm hoping that some time away gives me an opportunity to really think about what I want."

What I wanted to do about Charles and the wedding...what I wanted to do about a career?

She patted my hand. "Then, I won't feel guilty about you spending some time here."

Thinking about my wedding, I asked, "Would you tell me about your wedding?"

Despite our long friendship, there was so much I didn't know about Miss Ida.

"Go in the living room and bring my Book of Memories and the small black photo album on the top shelf."

I'd never looked in the photo album.

Miss Ida flipped to the first page. There was a picture of a young woman in a simple white dress and a man in a dark suit. "That's me and my Albert."

She ran a finger over the picture, tracing his face. "Albert Dulaney Hall. I always loved the sound of his name. If we'd had a boy, I would have used the Dulaney Hall part. Not the Albert part. I mean, I loved my Albert, but it was *despite* his first name, not because of it. Although with a name like Ida, I couldn't throw any stones. Still I do think there's something nice about the name Ida Hunter Hall. We got married at the church, then had a small reception at my mother's. Everyone I loved was there. My mother made this pink cake with coconut on the frosting. And tiny cucumber sandwiches with no crusts. We toasted with grape juice. Albert came from Baptists and none of them drank a lick. Not that my family were drinkers, mind you. But we weren't opposed to an occasional beer or glass of wine. Except my Uncle Carl. He would drink himself silly, but he was a funny drunk and never drove so no one minded. My Aunt Cheryl said half the time she didn't know who dropped him off at home after he'd been out. He complained about the alcohol free reception. But I didn't care whether or not we toasted my wedding with champagne or grape juice. I just wanted Albert."

"What was your memory for that day?" I asked.

She flipped through the pages and when she stopped, she ran her finger gently over the page. "*I never realized I only had half my heart, until I found the other part. Today both halves of my heart came together and I was finally whole.*"

She looked up and smiled at me. She had tears shining in her eyes. "It wouldn't have mattered if we got married at an affair as big as Princess Di's, or simply eloped to a judge's office. He was the other half of my heart and I just needed to be whole."

My eyes watered in a way that had nothing to do with the lingering smell of burned toast and everything to do with the image Miss Ida had just painted with her words.

"You must miss him fiercely," I said softly.

"I do, but I know he's still with me. He's never really left me. Sometimes, when I wish I could hear him again, I'll look through my book and find a memory to remind me. After he passed, I spent time going through my memories and realized that when he was here, most of my memories involved him. Like the day he shaved off his mustache. He'd always had one and then one

64

day, for whatever reason, he just up and shaved it off. Well, when he came out of the bathroom with his hairless face, I must have looked shocked. He asked if I liked it. I tried to say the word *yes*, but I just couldn't manage it. I nodded my head, but I don't think I was very convincing. He grew it right back and never shaved it again. Some men just naturally look better with a mustache, and my Albert was one of those. Not that I like the scruff so many men—"

Someone knocked on the front door. "I'll see who it is."

I opened the door and realized it was Miss Ida's neighbor from across the street. He had dark hair, a couple days worth of stubble covering his face. Given what she'd just been saying, I smiled when I noticed it. He had light green eyes that stood out given the darkness of his hair and complexion.

I realized that he looked familiar, but I couldn't place him. So I smiled and said, "Hi. Miss Ida says you're new to the neighborhood. The one who busted her to the doctors. Be careful. She's planning to be *fierce* with you. I'm her old neighbor. I actually grew up next door." I extended my hand to shake. "Dee Hanson."

"Reese," he said, taking my hand in his. "And you weren't always Dee, were you?"

"Pardon?" I asked.

"I remember a little girl who always had her nose in a book. She rescued dogs and classmates with the same degree of compassion. That girl went by the name of Sadie Mae."

I hadn't thought about the dogs, Poke or Prudence, in years. Bette Lee did not believe animals belonged in homes, but when I showed up with the two puppies I'd found in a bag in the woods behind the University, she'd been outraged. She said we'd keep them overnight and take them to the shelter the next day. Instead of the shelter, she'd taken them to the vets, then brought them home again. And they'd stayed. I had thought they'd be my dogs, but they were Bette Lee's through and through. They'd both passed away within days of each other and Bette Lee had been heartbroken.

She'd never even considered finding a new dog.

I looked at the man who knew my name and still couldn't place him, though he obviously knew me.

"You look so familiar, but..." I shrugged. "I'm so sorry." I dug through my memories, trying to find him in them. He looked to be around my age.

"Sorry," I said again, finally admitting defeat.

"Like you, I went by a different name back then. My given name is Mad—"

He didn't get any further. "Mad Dog Reese," I said. I remembered him.

I remembered a lot about him.

Mad Dog was the kid who skipped classes on a regular basis. He was known for playing imaginative pranks. My particular favorite was one that became known as Mad Dog's Cups. He'd lined the hall next to the teachers' lounge with small plastic cups of water. Wall-to-wall cups of water. No one could walk down the hall without kicking a cup.

The principal never could prove it was Mad Dog, but every student knew it was.

His smile dimmed as I mentioned his high school nickname. "I prefer Reese these days, if you don't mind. Though Maddox will do as well."

Given his reaction to Mad Dog, I was glad I hadn't remarked on his infamous prank.

"Sure," I said. "I'm sorry. Would you like to come in?"

He shook his head. "No. I just got a call from Mr. Gerald. He said Mrs. Hall was burning down her house. I thought I should probably check on her."

"It wasn't Miss Ida," I admitted with a sigh. "I've decided there's a chance the Cooking Channel will not be calling to offer me a show of my own."

"What did you burn?" he asked.

"Promise not to laugh?"

He looked serious as he made a cross over his heart.

I sighed and admitted. "Toast."

I'll give him credit. He didn't laugh. He did smile and snort, however. He got himself under control quickly and said, "So let's agree up front, if we ever do dinner, I'll cook."

"I'm engaged," I blurted out.

"You are engaging," he said with a smile that said he was just being kind and not asking me for a date.

I felt my face flush as I realized I'd been presumptuous.

"But speaking of dinners, I do have an invitation for a barbecue tomorrow. And yes, I'll be cooking. I meant to ask Mrs. Hall earlier this week, but there was her fall and we weren't sure she'd be back in time. You're invited, too. Not a date, I promise," he assured me, teasing.

Ouch.

Mad Dog had put me in my place in the sweetest way possible. He smiled so infectiously, there was no way to take offense.

"If you invite us to the barbecue, I'll bring a salad. Even I can't mess up some lettuce and veggies."

"Deal." He paused and asked softly, "Is she all right?"

"She's been having bouts of dizziness and took that fall, but she seems fine. Although, at her age, falls are very concerning."

"Sadie Mae Hanson," Miss Ida called. "I might be getting older, but I have ears like a bat. *At my age?* Indeed." She came to the door slowly, leaning heavily on her walker. "Reese, don't listen to this sassy girl."

"I came to invite you both over for a barbecue tomorrow," he said.

"We'd be delighted to accept," Miss Ida said, answering for both of us.

"Well, Sadie Mae already made sure I know she's engaged, so we're all on the up and up." He shot me a cat-that-ate-the-canary grin and I knew that if he'd been wearing that expression when I first opened the door, I'd have known exactly who he was from the get-go. With that smile firmly in place he was the boy with the water-filled glasses and so many other high school hijinks. "Dee warned me that you might be annoyed with me."

Miss Ida shook her head. "You are a good boy so I'm going to overlook your tendency to snitch on your elders."

"You just yelled at me for referring to your age," I teased.

"Well, now, I'm sure Bette Lee would tell you that you should never comment on a woman's age, but no one can stop me from commenting on my own age."

"You're probably right," I admitted.

Reese chuckled at our banter and then asked me, "How long are you here for?"

"Long enough to get Miss Ida back on her feet...literally," I said.

"Try not to burn the neighborhood down while you're here," he said. There it was, that smile again.

"You used to make Mr. Holcomb crazy when you shot him one of those smart ass smirks," I said.

"It's okay, he made me crazy too. He spoke in that soft, monotone voice that made half the class fall asleep and the other half *want* to fall asleep."

He nodded at us both, then turned and walked back towards his house. If he'd been wearing a hat, he'd have doffed it. I imagined Reese in a cowboy hat and smiled.

"He's been a good neighbor," Miss Ida said.

"What do you know about him?" I asked.

"Not much. He moved into the Nick's house a year ago February. We had that huge storm this winter. I was planning to call my plow service, but when I got up, everything was already shoveled. Reese did it."

"That was nice. He dropped out of school before our junior year. There were all kinds of rumors about why. I personally favored the joined-the-foreign-legion theory."

She laughed. "He's a cop now."

I shook my head. "That doesn't sound like Mad Dog to me."

I looked across the street at the Nick house. They had been a loud, raucous family. Four boys and their parents stuffed into a little cape cod house. I'd never asked where they made all the boys sleep.

The grass had always been haphazardly mowed, much to Bette Lee's annoyance. I never figured it mattered much, because it was hard to see the grass under all the toys and sporting equipment that littered the lawn.

Mad Dog Reese.

It was a small world.

The rest of the day was a whirlwind. A nurse who introduced herself as Doran made sure everything had arrived as promised and she did a walk through the house and made a few safety suggestions, like moving the throw rugs to avoid more falls.

She spent a half hour with Miss Ida, doing a check up.

When she came out, I asked, "So what exactly happened? She's dizzy. I helped her into the shower last night and I thought for sure she was going to fall again."

"She's getting on in years," she said vaguely. So vaguely that I was sure Miss Ida had sworn her to secrecy about whatever was wrong with her.

Doran made some calls and set up an appointment with Miss Ida's primary doctor for Monday.

The day flew by.

I tucked Miss Ida in that night.

"Miss Ida, what aren't you telling me?" I asked.

"I'm sure there are many things I'm not telling you," she said. "As much as I loved Albert, I'm sure there were things I didn't tell him as well. No one can share themselves completely with anyone else."

"You're being deliberately obtuse," I complained. "Are you sick?"

She made a cross over her flowered flannel nightgown. "I do not have any dread disease I'm not telling you about. I'm as healthy as a... I was going to say horse, but let's just say I'm as healthy as a woman in her eighties tends to be."

I sighed. "Miss Ida—"

"Do you know what my memory for the day was?" she asked, interrupting me. She patted her book on the nightstand.

"No," I said.

"*A handsome man asked me to a picnic.*" She laughed. "Of course, we'd just been talking about Albert's short-lived attempt at no facial hair. So when I saw Reese's scruff, I laughed to myself."

"I thought the same thing. You don't like scruffy facial hair?"

"Well, not on most men, but with Reese it doesn't seem to be for effect, but rather because he simply forgets to shave. So I don't mind. Or I like him and because of that I don't mind. Now there's something to think about. When we like someone it's easier to ignore things we don't like about them and maybe sometimes that's okay, but sometimes we probably should say something."

For a moment she seemed sad. As if she remembered a time she didn't tell someone something she should have.

"Well, being asked to a picnic is a lovely memory," I said, trying to pull her away from whatever made her feel so bad. Since my faux pas about Reese asking me to dinner, I didn't think I'd be using that same memory for the day. "I think my memory will be about burning not only the toast, but my hopes of entering a cooking competition. I might not have made a definite decision about what I'm going to do when I grow up, but chef is off the list."

"Maybe you'd have better luck with barbecue," Miss Ida said and with a pregnant paused added, "Given how smoky everything was this morning you might find that's just your style of cooking."

She started laughing at her own joke and I couldn't help but join in. I was relieved that whatever had made her sad had given way to a happier thought.

"I've missed you," I said. "I'm sorry I haven't been here more often."

"Sadie-my-darling, you call and visit more regularly than most women's granddaughters do. But I missed you, too."

I was still chuckling over Miss Ida's barbecue comment when Charles called. Her house was small, so I went out to the front porch so as not to bother her. Rather than sit on the bench, I moved onto the grassy hill that sloped from her house to the street.

"Hi, Charles," I said as I picked up.

"How are things?" he asked, getting straight to the point.

"Fine. I have the house all set up. I pulled all the throw rugs up so Miss Ida doesn't trip over them. And with the help of the home health nurse, I have a hospital bed in her room, a wheelchair and we've installed a seat in the shower and grab bars as well. Yes, that's right, I drilled into tile and screwed the handles on. You can call me Norm Abram."

"Who?" he asked.

"*This Old House?*" My parents watched PBS more than any other station. I'd grown up with the Norm, Kevin, Rich and the rest of the guys on the show.

"Oh," Charles said, not pursuing the subject of the show. "I just wanted to say that I miss you."

That was sweet and warmed my heart. Charles was not a man prone to flowery prose. Most of the time that was fine, but an occasional *I-missed-you* was welcomed.

"I miss you, too. Maybe you want to drive down this weekend? I'm sure Miss Ida wouldn't mind if you crashed here. The guestroom only has a small bed, so we'd have to snuggle." I tried to sounds as suggestive as I could. But I wasn't sure it came across as such. I was more girl-next-door than seductress.

"Sorry," he said. "I have plans with my parents, remember?"

I didn't, before I could confess as much, he added, "Mother said she can get the ballroom at the club for the second Saturday in November, if that works for you. Six months is the bare minimum for getting everything in order."

"Charles, I think we should put off our plans until I get Miss Ida on her feet again. I think there's more going on with her than she's saying." I didn't just think it, I knew it in my heart of hearts.

"Don't tell me that you think you'll still be there in November?" he asked.

"No, I'll be back by then I'm sure, but I'm not sure if I'll be around to plan things. And I know that Francesca," *Frannie*, I added mentally, "thrives on that sort of thing, but I want to be involved in planning our wedding. I realized that I have some very specific ideas on what I want and I don't think I've been clear enough about it. I thought a lot about it on the drive here. Our wedding should be about us. About both of us. I need to compromise, but so do you. I—"

He interrupted. "I think we should talk about this when you get home."

"Fine. But start to adjust your reality, Charles. This wedding won't be exactly what either of us wants. It will be collaboration...a mix of our tastes. The compromises will set the tone for our marriage. I—"

He interrupted. "What about your job?"

Charles was many things and focused was definitely a big part of who he was. Sometimes one-track-mind was even closer to the appropriate description. I tried to remember the day I met him. I'd found his certainty comforting then.

"The Brain and I worked it out. I'm using some of the vacation days he owed me. I've told you that he was pushing me to do more than build a career around being his babysitter—though goodness knows that's a fulltime job. For now, I'm working as his virtual assistant, so I'm still drawing a check." I might feel bad about that, but even on a virtual level, keeping the Brain on track was hard work.

"Dee, I don't know what to say. You'd quit a job you loved?"

"It's not something I ever planned on doing. I do I love parts of it. And I love Brian. I'm very good at organizing his life but the job wasn't, and isn't, my calling or anything. I've never felt I truly found where I was supposed to be."

That familiar sense of being lost swept over me. It seemed that by the time someone was closer to thirty than twenty they should have an idea what they wanted to do when they grew up.

I never had and still didn't.

"Somewhere out there my dream job is waiting. I just have to find it. Brian's been encouraging me to find it." And suddenly I realized that the Brain kept pushing me to find what I really wanted, but Charles never had. He wanted me to want what he wanted and to be content with that.

Shouldn't someone you love push you to be the best possible version of yourself and not encourage you to be content standing in their shadow?

I tried to push the question away, but I could feel it itching in the background like a mosquito bite.

As if on cue, Charles said, "So what should I tell Mother about the wedding?" He was back on the wedding? I was telling him that I felt lost and he was worried about how it would impact him.

"No," I said firmly. "Tell her no. Tell her things are on hold for now."

"Fine. I'm working on a speech for Dad's club. If I send it to you, would you take a look?"

Ask me if I want more out of life than finding your suits and cleaning up your speeches. Ask me what you can do to help me find myself. Ask me...

But Charles didn't ask me any of those things. He simply waited for me to reply about the speech. "Yes."

"It's easier when you're here," he said not for the first time. "We'll talk about this again tomorrow."

He hung up without saying goodbye.

I saw Reese across the street pulling out his trashcan. It must be garbage night. I walked around the side of the house to get Miss Ida's can.

When I got back to the front, Reese was waiting on my side of the street.

"Did I say come over about three tomorrow?" he asked.

I shook my head. "No. You didn't give a specific time. I figured when we saw neighbors heading your way, we'd head over, too. We'll see you then."

I started to turn, but he took my hand, lightly holding me in place. "And Sadie Mae—Dee—it's good to see you again. Welcome home."

He dropped my hand as if just realizing he was holding it.

"You, too, Reese." I used his last name as he'd asked, but in my head, I thought *Mad Dog*. I smiled as I walked back into the house.

I thought again that it was a very small world.

I locked the door and in the dim light, I really looked at the very small painting next to the door. It was an outdoor scene. There was a field in the forefront, and a copse of trees behind it.

I'd seen it before, but now I really studied it.

The copse was more than a few trees. It was the edge of a forest, I realized.

There were two broad and distinct paths weaving their way into the woods. One went towards the right of the frame, one towards the left.

At the very bottom was the artist's name.

I turned my phone's flashlight on and looked closely.

It was the letter B.

I was growing to recognize Barbara's art. It was as distinct as a fingerprint. Miss Ida's part of the mural made me smile at her memories. The other side left me feeling disquieted.

This painting made me feel...

I realized that it made me feel as if Barbara understood me, though I couldn't remember ever meeting her.

I wasn't sure why, but I felt a kinship to Miss Ida's daughter. This painting told me she knew what it was like to feel lost and to search for where you belong.

I suddenly wanted to know more about her.

Maybe while I was here, Miss Ida would share some Barbara stories.

And I wondered, not for the first time, why she had never shared stories of her before and what had happened to Barbara.

Miss Ida's Book of Memories

Barbara is still at that toddler stage where she tastes everything. Except crayons. I gave her a box and a tablet of construction paper and she sat for more than an hour, drawing. She pointed to a blob of green and said, *Mama*. Then she pointed to a blob of blue and said, *Bea*. And as I looked closely, there was a line of green and a line of blue touching, as if we were holding hands.

I like to think that she knows I'll always be there for her. I'll always hold on tight.

Chapter Five

*"I'm done stumbling through the woods.
It's time to turn on my GPS and figure out
what direction I need to go in."*

The next day, I wheeled Miss Ida across the street to Reese's house with a large tossed salad balanced on her lap.

As I pushed her up the driveway apron onto the sidewalk, I practically ran over John Henry Gardner.

The world was definitely small.

Way too small at the moment.

Or maybe it was just Erie that was too small. After all, I never had problems like this in Detroit.

Of course, I had an entirely different set of problems there. And thinking of my life in Detroit as a problem gave me pause. On its heels, another small thought crept in—maybe I couldn't blame my problems on a place. Wherever I was, I brought my problems with me.

That was profound, but I didn't have time to concentrate on it because John Henry was shooting me a genuine smile as he said my name. "Sadie Mae."

Finding a happy memory for my book on the day John Gardner broke up with me was probably the most difficult entry I'd ever had to come up with.

I remembered exactly what I'd eventually written. *"Ice cream and a friend can help anything heal."*

It wasn't exactly a happy memory, but as I looked down at Miss Ida, then back at John, I realized that there was a truth to it.

Mom and Dad had been...

Wow.

I suddenly realized that I didn't remember where my parents were that day. I just remembered they weren't home.

That first day, Miss Ida had told me that memories would fade and she was right. I'd completely lost the memory of where my parents were the night John broke up with me. All I remembered was that they hadn't been home on the day he'd called and *Dear Sadie Mae'd* me. I did remember that I'd walked across the yard to Miss Ida's house and cried my eyes out on her shoulder.

I also remembered that she'd gone to the kitchen. I thought maybe she was going to make tea, but instead, she came back with two pints of Hagen Daz.

"You pick," she'd said.

I even remembered the flavors. I'd picked some chocolate brownie thing. She'd eaten chocolate chip.

And as we ate our ice cream right out of the small cartons with spoons, Miss Ida regaled me with inventive tortures that she would happily inflict on John Henry Gardner.

The memory helped me smile as I looked at the boy I used to love. He was all grown up now. "John. It's nice to see you," I lied. "You remember Miss Ida? Miss Ida, you remember my old friend, John Henry Gardner?"

I could see by the way she subtly straightened her shoulders that she did. "I would never have guessed you were my Sadie Mae's age, bless your heart," she said in an attempt to Bette-Lee him and call him old.

It wasn't the smooth sort of cut my mother would have managed, but I really appreciated the effort. I smiled as I said, "Nice to see you."

I wheeled Mrs. Ida away as quickly as I could and I managed to hold back the laughter until we were in Reese's backyard. "Oh, Miss Ida."

"We are going to call Bette Lee tonight and tell her that I *blessed his heart*," she said as she laughed as well.

"Oh we certainly will," I promised.

I felt a stab of guilt that I hadn't called my parents sooner. I didn't have a landline, so if they called, they'd get me on my cell no matter where I was, but still not keeping Bette Lee apprised of my whereabouts might land me in the doghouse. And she'd be sure to let me know she was annoyed. My mother was so much better at subtle torture than Miss Ida was.

I decided to avoid John as much as possible. But I couldn't help but wonder what he was doing now. Why he was back in Erie? He had been so eager to move out of town. We'd talked about seeing the world together.

We'd talked about a lot of things.

I sighed and tried to shake off thoughts of my ex as I wove Miss Ida's wheelchair through the people to the table Reese had set up for dishes.

He was standing at a huge stainless steel grill, flipping burgers like a pro.

"You made it," he said with a smile.

"I did. And I made salad."

"I think the neighbors will appreciate that." He had a devilish look in his eyes that told me he was teasing.

"You're right they will," I agreed.

"Go mingle," he said.

So I mingled. There were very few people left from when I was a kid. Miss Ida and Mr. Gerald were about it.

A single mom and her eight-year-old daughter lived in my old house now. Heidi and Lulu. They'd moved in before Reese had bought the Nick's house, but not much before. I'd seen them a few times when I'd visited Miss Ida, but this was the first time I met them proper.

"Do you like your room?" I asked Lulu.

She nodded shyly.

"I lived in your house when I was little and that was my room. I had my bed right by the window. I liked to sit there at night and look out at the neighborhood. I always thought it looked so friendly at night when everyone had their houses lit up. Sometimes, the moon was so bright, it was like a nightlight."

Talking about the moon was all it took to set Lulu in motion. She told me she was going to be an astronaut, but she didn't want to visit the moon, she wanted to go to Mars.

She used terms that sounded a lot older than her years.

I listened and felt a bit jealous. Here was an eight-year-old who had a surer idea of what she wanted to do when she grew up than I did.

"She likes you," her mom said when Lulu ran off to see a friend.

"She seems like a very nice kid," I said.

"Thanks for telling her how much you liked the room. She wasn't excited about moving here. She still misses the old house a year and a half later."

"I'm sorry. I can understand that. I haven't lived in Erie since college, but I still miss it. I still feel like Erie is home."

"I hated making her move, but it is what it is." From her expression, I could see that Heidi hadn't wanted to move any more than Lulu had. She gave herself a little shake and added, "You'll have to come over sometime and see your old place. Of course, be prepared to talk about all things space. Lulu's idea of fun is watching launches on YouTube."

"So now I feel like a slacker because cute animal videos are about all I ever watch."

Heidi nodded. "And baby videos. Laughing baby videos."

I genuinely liked Heidi. Maybe it was that she clarified she liked *laughing* baby videos. Anyone who preferred their babies laughing was someone I could like. Heidi and Lulu made me feel good about the old house. I guess it felt as if we'd passed it on to people who would love it as much as Bette Lee, Big Henry and I had.

When Heidi got called away, I moved to a back corner of the yard and looked at all the people mingling with ease.

I had never been an easy mingler. I was horrible at small talk.

But Miss Ida was in her element. She held court. Neighbors came over to say hi and chat with her. She was a fixture in the neighborhood. People came and went, but Miss Ida was constant.

There was a comfort in that.

"It was a very good salad," Reese said as he approached a while later.

"I do cook non-cooked food best," I said.

John came towards us. "John, do you know—" Reese started.

I nodded. "We were all in school together, remember?"

Reese laughed. "That's right. Didn't you guys date once upon a time?"

"We did," I admitted. "But that was a long time ago."

I didn't add that it hadn't ended well. It was the truth, but no one other than John Henry and I needed to know that.

For a moment, I could remember the passion of my first love. I'll confess, I'd never felt that same heady rush with Charles, but that made sense. I was older now. I knew that love was more than the flash. It was a long, steady glow.

But oh, how I'd had that flash with John Henry. I'd been mad about him.

I had loved that his middle name was Henry. No one else used it but me. I'd written about it in my Book. I remember thinking it was a good omen.

Old Henry, Big Henry and a John Henry. They all fit.

And I liked it when things fit.

For the first time I wondered if his middle name was one of the reasons I'd dated him. He fit my weird need for order.

"John works at the high school now," Reese said. "He's teaching Phys Ed and coaches."

"That's how Reese and I met again," John said. "He visited the school and spoke about drugs to the health class."

I must have looked confused, because Reese said, "I'm a cop."

Miss Ida had been right. But Mad Dog Reese as a cop didn't seem to fit at all.

"After you dropped out of school, I always pictured you in the Foreign Legion," I blurted out. Smooth. No one could say I wasn't smooth. I sighed. "Sorry."

Reese looked amused. "I might have joined if I'd given it any thought. I just knew that for me, high school was a waste of time. I dropped out, took my GED and started college in what would have been our junior year of high school. I joined ROTC in college and then afterwards the Marines. Now, the police force. I know, it's not quite the Foreign Legion, but I like it."

My impression of Reese the bad boy tilted.

I didn't have time to try and adjust my view of him because I caught a glimpse of Miss Ida. She was starting to wilt.

"I'd love to hear more about that, Reese," I said. Then turned to John, "It was nice to bump into you. I've got to run. I think Miss Ida's had enough."

"Could we get coffee sometime and catch up?" John asked.

"I can't imagine why you'd want to. I'm in town to help out Miss Ida. I don't think I'd be able to go out. And I can't imagine your wife would appreciate us catching up any more than my fiancé would."

"I'm divorced," he said as I hurried to Miss Ida.

I remembered how hurt I'd been when he'd *Dear Sadie Mae*'d me. And a year later, when I heard that he'd married, the pain had struck again.

I shook my head. Then turned to Reese, "Thanks again for the invitation." I hurried to Miss Ida and said, "Let's go home."

"Sorry to be a spoilsport," Miss Ida said.

"You're not a bit of it," I assured her as I wheeled her toward the street. "I'm ready to go back myself. I promised the Brain I'd set up his calendar online today."

"How is he?" she asked as I rolled her through the yard.

"The man is brilliant. I mean, a genius sort of brilliant, but he'd forget to eat if someone didn't remind him."

"That's why you call him the Brain?" she asked as I eased her chair over the curb. "I never asked before."

We were friends, but obviously both had questions we'd never asked. I thought about Barbara. I had questions too, but they'd keep.

"I didn't start that nickname," I told her. "His little sister couldn't say Brian when she was little and called him Brain...and it stuck. After I started working for him, she told me she still called him that to keep him humble."

"How does reminding him he's smart keep him humble?" Miss Ida asked with laughter.

"I don't know the whole story. He made her swear not to tell me, but I did notice that he listened better if I call him Brain. After a while, it became habit."

83

She laughed. "My Albert was a humble man by nature. He told me once, *Ida, I don't know what I did to deserve you, but I do know that I'm a lucky man.* I laughed and told him I didn't know what he'd done either and then I assured him that regardless he was indeed lucky. But truth be told, I was the lucky one."

I thought she'd start one of her longwinded stories. Maybe some people would have found them annoying. Miss Ida did tend to hop from point A to point Z and then back again to Point C. She moved around stories like an Energizer Bunny, skipping from one point to another, then back again.

But she was quiet after we got home. She was in bed by six that night. The outing had exhausted her.

As I helped her into bed, I realized how frail she was beginning to look. Her skin was soft and paper-thin except for the vivid blue bruise on her forearm from her fall. Her hair had thinned. It was still long, so the thinness wasn't terribly noticeable until she took it out of her bun.

"Do you know what I wrote today?" she asked drowsily as I started for the bedroom door.

I stopped and walked back to her bedside. "No."

"*I'm so glad that Sadie Mae's here. I can't help but think that our Barbara might have been like Sadie if things were different.*" That was all she said and I realized her breath had evened out and she was asleep.

I tiptoed out of the room, shutting her door gently behind me.

I looked in the bedroom I was using. I'd speculated about her daughter often enough. All that was left of Barbara was the mural on the wall, the picture by the front door and some assorted furniture in the room.

Miss Ida, who would talk in depth about anything, never talked about her daughter.

Maybe some pain was so vast you couldn't let it out without risking collapsing under its weight. I wish I could do something to help her.

It was too early for me to go to bed, but I didn't want to disturb Miss Ida so I went out to the front lawn.

"Miss Dee," Lulu called from my old bedroom window. "Wanna come see my room? Your room?" she corrected quickly.

"Is it all right with your mom?" Surprise visitors weren't high on everyone's list.

Lulu disappeared from the screen and a few minutes later, was at the side door. "Mom says anytime. And anytime means now," she added in case I hadn't understood.

I laughed as I walked across the lawn.

Lulu opened the door and I walked into the house.

The kitchen was a small long galley to the right. Heidi was washing the dishes.

The kitchen had the same maple cupboards I remembered, but the appliances were shiny stainless, and the walls were painted a soft tan instead of my mother's sunny yellow.

Bette Lee used to say Erie wasn't sunny enough and I always thought her bright paint choices were her way of compensating.

"I hear you're *dying* to see your old room," Heidi said with a smile and an eye roll in Lulu's direction.

"You're sure it's okay?" I asked.

"I always mean what I say. It must be interesting to come back to your childhood home and see everything from an adult's perspective. Make yourself at home."

The kitchen was a nice mix of the familiar and new. I wondered what the rest of the house held.

"Come on, Miss Dee," Lulu said, obviously not patient enough for me to have a trip down memory lane.

Miss Dee.

I felt old and then realized that to Lulu I must seem old.

Perspective was everything.

Lulu pulled me hurriedly through the living room. The walls were a rich red now instead of Bette Lee's white and blue wallpaper. We zipped past the master bedroom. The door was closed, so I couldn't see how that had changed. I wouldn't have had time anyway. We were climbing up the oak stairs to the slanted walled bedroom.

"When you turn off the lights at night, the stars glow," Lulu said, pointing to the star decals on the grey-blue walls.

"How cool," I said.

"I would have put them up in constellations, but Mom doesn't know much about stars or constellations and she did it as a surprise, so I don't mind too much. That's what I think of when I look at them. *Mom did it.* She knows that I'm going to be an astronaut."

I laughed. "That is a great memory. Miss Ida taught me to write down my good memories so I'd never forget the good ones."

"Write down your memories?" Lulu asked.

I realized I liked the thought of writing down the good memories spreading beyond Miss Ida and me.

I nodded. "Miss Ida says as you get older, you forget things." Like where your parents were when your first love broke up with you, I thought, but didn't say. "So every day she picks out the nicest parts of her day and writes it down, so they're the memories she remembers."

"And mom putting up the stars wrong is a good memory," Lulu said.

"Your mother knows you love the stars and space and tried to do something special for you. I think that's the best kind of memory."

Lulu looked up at her sloped ceiling and nodded. "Me, too."

I sat in my old room, next to Lulu looking out the window. The trees were bigger, but otherwise, it was the view of my childhood.

Lulu talked about space, hopping from one subject to another with the nimbleness of Miss Ida. The Space Station, Mars missions, landing on comets...

After I said goodnight to Lulu, I had a glass of ice tea with Heidi.

"She's a great kid," I said.

"She is. Sometimes I wonder if I'm doing enough for her."

I thought of the stars on Lulu's ceiling and said, "You love her. That will offset a multitude of things."

Heidi smiled, but I wasn't sure she believed me. "I thought when her father left, it was for the best. And if he'd just left me, it would have been. But he left her, too. I'm not sure I'm enough to make up the difference."

Before I could try to think of some wise response, Heidi said, "Sorry. He just sent the child support check with no note or mention of seeing her."

I reached over and patted Heidi's hand. I realized there was nothing to say. I might not have children, but I knew that watching your kids suffer had to be the worst sort of pain. "She knows you love her. That's enough."

I hoped I was right for both their sakes.

When we finished, I tiptoed back into the house to check on Miss Ida. She was still sleeping and I wasn't ready for bed. So I took my Book of Memories out onto the front lawn.

Some days I wrote paragraphs. Occasionally I wrote an entire page. Most days I wrote simply a sentence or two.

What would I want to remember from today? Seeing John after so many years? He'd broken my heart when he Dear-Sadie-Maed me. But my heart had healed and I hadn't thought about John Henry in a long time.

How much things had changed in just a decade.

87

Maybe I should write about Reese? Bad boy turned cop. Marine then cop no less.

I could write about Lulu and Heidi.

Maybe all of it?

I tried to pinpoint the happiest memory of the day.

My phone rang, interrupting my what-should-I-write musing. It was Charles. "Hi, Charles. How was your day?"

He droned about the people he'd seen at the club, name-dropping as if it mattered to me. If he told me he'd seen a friend, or even some family member, I might have cared, but belonging to the correct social circle meant very little to me.

My mother would have done better with Charles and his circle. But she'd have done equally well at a party like Reese's.

Bette Lee Hanson didn't see class or status. She saw people. And she treated them all with impeccable southern manners.

Even when they annoyed her and she blessed-their-hearts she was never malicious.

At that moment I missed my mom with a physical ache. I wished I could walk back across the lawn to our house and go inside. Heidi had served unsweetened iced tea. I was northern enough to drink it. But if Bette Lee was next door right now, she would give me some sweet tea, despite the fact I had never fully fallen in love with it. She always insisted if I kept trying it I'd learn to. After we had our tea and I poured out my heart to her, she'd hug me.

My mother always smelled of sweet peas. A light, barely-there fragrance.

As Charles told me about a judge who knew someone in a local congressional office, I texted my mom. "Thinking of you. Miss you."

Finally Charles asked, "How was your day?"

"We went to a neighborhood picnic. I met the little girl who lives in my old house. She wants to be an astronaut and—"

"I'm glad you had a nice time, but I really wish you were home with me. I really have to go," Charles said. "We're having cocktails with the Valancias. You were invited too. It was a couples thing. I'm going to have to go solo."

The last name made me think of oranges. It wasn't really funny, but it was the most interesting thing he'd said all night.

"Sorry, but I'm sure you'll be fine," I said.

"I'll look like a man who can't get a date," he muttered.

"You'll look like a man whose fiancée was busy."

He sighed, just so I wouldn't miss how annoyed he was. "Gotta go."

And he hung up. Mentally I counted up my words. *We'd* talked for twenty minutes and I'd said less than fifty words.

I suddenly wondered if that was part of my appeal for him. I not only could and did organize his life, I had time to do so. I didn't have some high pressured, crazily demanding jobs some women did. Sometimes I thought one of those high-octane women would suit him better. But maybe the fact I wasn't that was part of why he chose me.

It wasn't a pleasant thought.

My phone rang again. I didn't need to look at caller I.D. to know it was my mom.

"What's wrong?" Bette Lee asked by way of salutation.

And I told her. My words tumbling one after another as if I was Miss Ida telling a convoluted story.

I told Bette Lee that I was in Erie, about Miss Ida and how worried I was. I told her about visiting our old house and my sense of nostalgia. I told her about

89

slowing down the wedding plans, about seeing John Henry and about Reese's picnic.

"Do you want a hug, a kick in the butt or advice?" she asked in her sweet, lilting voice. I'd noticed that since they'd move down to Virginia, her accent had become more pronounced.

Big Henry even said ya'll to me once. I about lost it laughing at him. He'd joined in and pretty soon all three of us had laughed.

Hug? Butt kick? Advice? "Any or all of the aforementioned," I said.

"Then here's a hug over the phone, which isn't very satisfying. And a kick, which is even less so. As for advice, Sadie Mae, I think you and I both know what you want to do in your heart of hearts. And I think we both know what you don't want to do."

I didn't say anything, and Bette Lee sighed. "You don't want that wedding that Frannie and Charles are planning."

"I've already said as much to him. I want a wedding like you and Big Henry had. I told Charles that we're both going to have to compromise and find some middle ground."

"That's good, but honey," she paused a moment, then said, "I'm not sure you want Charles any more than that wedding he and his mama are planning."

"I love him," I said.

"I believe you do, but answer me honestly, have you missed him since you went to stay with Miss Ida?" She paused and clarified, "Missed him like I missed Big Henry the time he went and spent a week with Old Henry and Bea?"

Bea. My grandmother's name made me think about Miss Ida's Barbara, who'd signed her painting with just her first initial.

"I didn't think I'd make it through the week," Bette Lee continued.

90

I realized I hadn't been sure she would either. My mother had spent the entire week my father was gone as wilted and sad looking as last week's flowers.

"No, ma'am," I admitted. "I don't think anyone's ever missed anyone like that."

"I wouldn't marry a man unless I missed him like that when he was gone. And I'd want him to miss me like that, too. Big Henry lost ten pounds that week, bless his heart. Of course, I didn't lose a pound and that is just another reason life is unfair." She'd voiced that complaint before and I laughed on cue.

"Maybe it's different for ya'll," she added softly.

Maybe it was.

But maybe it shouldn't be.

"I'll talk to Big Henry and maybe we'll drive on up to see you and Miss Ida soon. We've been talking about going on another adventure. I've missed you, too, darlin'"

And while my parents were complete in and of themselves, I knew Bette Lee had missed me. I knew that if I said, *come right away*, she would.

But *soon* was soon enough. "That would be wonderful, Mom."

"I know you're really in a state when you start calling me, Mom."

"I'm fine, *Bette Lee*." I said her name with emphasis.

"Humph," she said, letting me know she wasn't buying it. "I'll call you tomorrow. I love you, *little miss*."

Little miss.

I looked at my memory book, still in my lap.

I moved to one of the first pages and found the one I was looking for.

Ways to know Bette Lee's pleased with me. When she calls me Little Miss, Sweet Pea, Honey, Darlin', Sugar...

I was in my teens the first time I called her Bette Lee. I'd thought the name often, but one day it just slipped out.

I remember feeling like a deer in a headlight, but Bette Lee just laughed and went on with whatever she was saying.

I realized that I didn't remember what she'd been saying, just that she didn't mind my calling her by her first name—names.

I looked back at yesterday's memory—*Today I laughed myself silly as I burned breakfast for Miss Ida and me. Not the entire breakfast, just the toast. Sometimes all you can do is laugh at your mistakes. Afterwards a handsome neighbor who turned out to be a schoolmate, tried to ride to the rescue. Mad Dog Reese. He invited us to a picnic.*

That was a memory I didn't mind taking with me into the future. Miss Ida laughing over my failed attempt at breakfast.

Reese. He'd dropped out of school, so I'd assumed he hadn't made much of himself. But he was a cop. He'd figured out what he wanted and didn't want and taken his own path.

I had to confess, I was impressed by the way he cared for Miss Ida. Shoveling for her, calling an ambulance for her and inviting her—us—to his picnic. Maybe the way to measure a man was to see how he cared for the vulnerable.

If that was the case, Reese more than measured up.

But Charles...

I felt guilty as I finished the thought. Charles did not measure up in that respect.

I tried to assure myself that he had many other fine attributes. A good head for business. Political ambitions. He cared for his parents.

I didn't feel better.

I flopped down on the grass and watched as the sun started to set below a group of roofs and trees.

I picked a dandelion gone fuzzy and held it up against the pinkening sky. I took out my phone and snapped a picture of it, all without even sitting up.

I wasn't the type who spent a lot of time snapping pictures. I didn't Tweet or Snapchat. I did use Facebook, but just on occasion.

But the dandelion against the pink sky spoke to me.

I blew the fuzz off the dandelion. Watching the tiny seeds take to the air seemed to illustrate how I was feeling. Blown about.

I flopped back, still watching the pink sky give away to deep purples and finally black.

I sat up and reopened my book. In the gloom I wrote, *I want a man who misses me like Big Henry missed Bette Lee. I want to miss him when he's not with me the same way. I'm done stumbling through the woods. It's time to turn on my GPS and figure out what direction to go in.*

As I closed the book, I realized that I'd written a-man, not Charles.

I felt guilt, relief and restless all at once.

I pushed aside my dandelion wish and before I called it a night, I ordered a large leather journal online and had it shipped to Lulu next door.

From Lulu's Book of Memories

"Miss Dee gave me this book for my memories and my Mom gave me the stars."

Chapter Six

"There is nothing more satisfying than looking at a well-organized pantry..."

"Miss Ida, do I still have organizing carte blanche?" I asked Sunday after breakfast as we finished reading the newspaper in her living room. She was in her chair, the flower patterned wing chair and I was its plaid counterpart. The small table between us held our coffees, the paper, a lamp and a glass dome display *cloche*. I'd had to look up the term for it years ago. There was a small metal hook under the glass where things could be displayed. There was nothing now but the empty hook.

I'd suggested moving it once, but Miss Ida had insisted it stay there and everything about her expression said the topic was not open for discussion, so I didn't ask why and the cloche remained all these years later in the same spot.

When I was young and spent my Saturdays with her, Miss Ida eventually stopped assigning jobs and just let me do my own thing. That's when I added organizing to my cleaning schedule.

Some people have very noticeable gifts. They're gifted in a sport, music or an academic subject.

If asked, I'd say my biggest gift was organizing. Not only was I good at it, I loved it. I was well aware of the fact that I couldn't organize my life. If I could have, I'd have found my true vocation by now. But I could organize the heck out of a pantry or linen closet.

And not just organize things in a way that made sense to me, but I could organize them in a way that made sense to someone else. It's what made what I did for the Brain work so well.

And all those years ago, it made working for Miss Ida a joy as well.

Some people drank when they were stressed. Some took a bubble bath.

I organized something.

I might not be able to control the world, or even my life, but I could control a pantry or closet.

"So what's wrong?" Miss Ida asked me.

"I just thought as long as I was here, I'd straighten things up."

"Do you remember your senior year when Bette Lee was insisting you choose a college, but you were unsure?" Miss Ida asked.

I nodded.

"Sweetheart, you reorganized my pantry every Saturday for the month of April. You were never satisfied with the results. And after that John-boy broke your heart, my linen closet was so beautifully put together that I hated taking sheets out of it. So I repeat, what's wrong?"

Miss Ida wore a look that brooked no evasion or argument.

"I feel as if I fell into my job...into my life. You know the small painting?" I pointed across the room at it. "It reminds me of that poem about two paths in the woods."

"I think that was the poem that inspired Barbara to paint it," she said, looking...

Wistful? Sad?

I couldn't read her emotion. I waited, thinking she was finally going to tell me about Barbara. This woman who could talk the chalk off a board remained silent on the subject. Maybe some things hurt too much to share.

So, I filled the void. "I was thinking about Barbara's painting and the poem last night. I don't think I've ever even found the paths to choose from. I've spent the last few years simply stumbling through the trees."

Miss Ida said, "Sometimes the best things in our lives happen when we're not looking for them. I didn't plan on marrying my husband. Did I ever tell you that?"

I shook my head.

Miss Ida reached for her book, flipped through the pages to the first quarter. She skimmed for a moment, then read, "*I met a true gentleman today while I was out with a cad.*"

"What happened?" I asked, ready for a Miss Ida story.

She ran a finger lightly over the line in her book, then looked at me with a smile that didn't involve just an upturn of her lips, but twinkled her eyes and put a shine on her cheeks. It was almost as if time rewound itself and Miss Ida was again a young girl with long dark hair and a lifetime of living and loving still in front of her.

"I was out with a boy...I can't remember his name. My father would be proud that I've forgotten it. I didn't write it down on purpose."

I remembered the first day I'd come to her house and she'd told me about her father's gift and I couldn't help but think he'd given me a gift that day as well and maybe I'd passed it on to Lulu. I liked the thought of that.

"I swear," Miss Ida said. "That boy I went out with was very pretty to look at. I'd taken a job as a secretary at a car dealership downtown. He came in to buy a car and kept coming around. After three visits, he asked me out on a date. We went to the theater. I don't remember what movie we saw. It was an early autumn evening and just a bit chilly. I remember I wore my red sweater."

Miss Ida was quiet for a moment. "My date put his arm around my shoulder. I thought it was a bit forward, but I didn't protest. Then he grabbed my..."

she paused and stage-whispered, "my bosom. Well, I let him have it."

"You slapped him?" I asked.

Miss Ida gave me an *are-you-crazy* look and shook her head. "No. Of course not. I slugged him. Right in the nose. He swore—I mean said a bunch of words that would have made my father punch him, too. His nose started to bleed. I mean, it spurted blood everywhere. And he sat there looking so unbelievably shocked. Well, I just climbed over everyone in our row and stomped out to the lobby. When I got into the light, I could see that I had some of his blood on my shirt. That made me even madder. I liked that blouse. It had tiny red flowers on it and looked so nice with that sweater."

Remembering her bloody blouse seemed to make her even madder, all these years later.

"Miss Ida, I don't ever think I've seen you angry," I said.

"Sweetheart, I'm as human as the next person. I get mad...and sometimes my heart breaks," she added softly and then looked surprised that she'd said it.

I couldn't help but wonder who had broken her heart.

"I guess as I've gotten older, I've realized that anger doesn't get you anywhere. Action does. But in retrospect, I guess I did take action that day, too."

She chuckled a rather pleased-with-herself sort of laugh.

"Remind me never to annoy you," I said, laughing as well.

She nodded. And her laughter faded as her smile grew broader and her voice grew quieter. "The boy who was taking tickets at the theater ran over to me. Later he told me because I was a bloody, angry mess he'd thought I was hurt.

"'*Are you okay?*' he asked.

"I nodded and told him the blood was the other guy's. I explained that my date was too forward and asked if I could phone my father for a ride home. He told me his shift was over in a half hour and he'd be happy to drive me home. He had the manager come over and assure me that Albert was a gentleman. When my date came out of the bathroom, Albert tossed him out of the theater."

Miss Ida sighed and her eyes got a faraway look as she lost herself in the memory.

"I met Albert in September and we were married in December. I didn't set out looking for him. You could say I was just wandering in the woods with no particular path in mind, but I found myself exactly where I belonged. He's been gone so long now but there's not a day I don't miss him. I miss the way he called me *dear*. I miss the way he brought me a cup of coffee every morning. I miss the way he hummed all the time. You could never really make out the song he was trying to hum. Poor Albert was tone deaf, so it all came out like the whine of the emergency siren on television. But oh how I miss the sound."

She reached across the table and patted my hand. "Sometimes you do have to choose a path. Life puts options in front of you and you can weigh them and pick the one that makes sense to you. But sometimes you don't even know you're choosing until you're partway down one path or another. If you're lucky, you end up exactly where you belong without even trying."

"Well, I'm certainly not choosing anything," I groused.

Miss Ida found my statement amusing. The only reason I laughed was because she started it.

That didn't seem to bother her. "Well, just know you have my permission to organize the house to your heart's content," she said, circling back to where this conversation had started.

I got up and kissed her weathered cheek.

"Can I get you anything?" I asked.

"No. I'm fine." As she leaned back in her chair, her eyes looked heavy. As if her visit to the past had left her wanting more.

I glanced back at her from the kitchen doorway. Her eyes were closed and a light smile played across her lips. I was pretty sure she had indeed returned to that movie theater so many years ago.

I walked into the kitchen and felt an almost giddy glee as I looked at the pantry. That's where I'd start.

I took everything out of the pantry. I washed it out with Miss Ida's favorite cleaning agent, Murphy's Oil Soap, and then started putting things back in a more organized fashion. I put all the cans in long, perfectly straight rows. Vegetables, soups, tuna... I arranged all the boxes, spines out so it was easy to see what was what.

I checked all the expiration dates as I loaded the items back in. I didn't need to toss too many things.

I could almost feel the tension ease.

When as I searched for the expiration date on the cinnamon, I realized that I was humming *Wild Mountain Thyme*. I don't know why, but it made me thing of Miss Ida's Albert's tuneless humming and I felt even better.

I refused to think about paths in the woods or why I wasn't happy and content.

My discontent had become an itch that was always there, reminding me to figure out things. But organizing the pantry was working like calamine. Temporarily easing the feeling.

I put spices on the lazy Susan, hummed and enjoyed the feeling that this pantry I could control.

I gave the lazy Susan a soft twirl and smiled as the herbs and spices whirled by. Cinnamon, oregano, basil...

The doorbell rang.

100

"I'll get it, Miss Ida," I called.

"I think it's for you," she said as I came into the living room. John was standing at the screen door. When he spotted me he held two cups aloft so I could see them through the screen.

"Since you couldn't come out for coffee, I brought coffee to you," he said.

"I won't be long," I said to Miss Ida. "We'll be on the porch. You holler if you need anything."

"I will, dear."

I'll confess Miss Ida did seem to be getting along pretty well. It helped that her house was small and everything was contained on one floor. I wasn't sure *she* needed me here, but I was beginning to suspect *I* needed to be here.

However, I didn't need John bringing me coffee.

My not quite happy-to-see-you attitude must have been apparent because he frowned as I walked out on the porch and took the coffees he extended. "I wasn't sure how you took your coffee."

Of course he didn't know how I took it. He'd left before I drank coffee.

I'd been so young. And I realized he'd been very young, too.

Suddenly my annoyance faded and I smiled as I said, "Thank you."

I nodded at Miss Ida's bench and he joined me.

"So you're back in Erie and teaching," I said.

"And you're still taking care of Miss Ida," he said.

He'd picked up my name for her all those years ago in high school. She'd never been Mrs. Hall to him. I smiled as he used it again. "She's having a few health issues, so I'm here for a bit."

"And when you're not taking care of your old neighbor?" he asked.

"My friend," I corrected. "And when I'm not here, I'm working as an executive assistant in Detroit.

Which is a fancy title my boss gave me. In reality I'm part babysitter, part organizer and part translator."

Translating his science-speak into every day English was a skill that had grown over the last couple years. I was intimidated at first, but I started to look at it like organizing a pantry. I just had to take all his scientific bits and reorganize them in a way that made sense to everyone else. Spices in one column, canned vegetables in another...

"And you?" I asked, more because it seemed polite than because I wanted to know more about my ex. Even as I had the thought, I saw through my own lie. I very much wanted to know what John was up to.

"We both left town and both ended up right back here," he said. "After the divorce, I couldn't see staying in Harrisburg."

I couldn't think of anything more to say so I took a long sip of my coffee. It was bitter and strong. I wished he'd brought me a cup of tea instead. Something light and smooth. Green tea, I decided.

He took a long sip, slurping slightly to cool it as he drank.

I forgot how often he did that, but the sound brought it back to me. Back then he'd slurped soup or hot chocolate after a cold Erie winter's day. I could see him the day we went sled riding behind Behrend College. His cheeks had chapped and his lip had cracked. I'd offered him my chapstick, but he was too manly for that.

I'd laughed. We went down the hill again. I could almost feel the wind biting at my own cheeks as we raced down that huge hill, snow kicking back in our faces.

And I could remember the moment we tipped and were buried in a snowdrift, practically nose-to-nose, and John had kissed me so tenderly. For a split second, I was that young girl who was head over heels in love with a boy.

This boy.

"Listen," John said. "I wanted to see you in order to apologize for all those years ago."

Maybe I'd been angry over his *Dear-Sadie-Mae*, but suddenly I realized how very young that girl and that boy had been. I felt a sense of nostalgia instead of anger now. "John, people break up. Especially people as young as we were. Long distance romances rarely work out, regardless of age."

I wondered if my being in Erie again for a time would be too much distance between Charles and me? The thought didn't make me want to hurry back to Detroit.

That was telling and I was pretty sure I knew what it was telling me.

"I know," John said. "You, very rationally tried to break up before I left for college. I was the one who argued we could make it work. And then, two months later, I called and broke up with you. I've always felt bad about it. I was young and..." He shrugged.

"I think the fact we were young is a good enough excuse. So you can stop there," I said.

I took another sip of my coffee and realized it didn't taste as bitter to me now.

John grinned.

Oh, how I remembered that expression. Half devil, half hunk.

"Then, can I see you again while you're here? Maybe a movie, or a cruise down State Street like we used to. Dinner? Whatever you want."

"I'm engaged," I felt obliged to point out. I wasn't sure if I was informing John, or reminding myself.

"Nothing romantic," he assured me. "Just two old high school friends catching up. We could ask Reese to join us, just to keep things on the up and up with your fiancé."

"How about we catch up here on the porch for now," I offered.

He hesitated a moment and then nodded.

I didn't feel as if I were cheating on Charles if I simply sat on the front porch.

"Tell me how you ended up teaching. Last I heard, you planned on the NBA and..." I left the sentence hanging.

John picked it up. "I realized somewhere about my sophomore year, when I spent more time warming the bench than playing, that the NBA was a pipe dream. But I loved the game and knew I didn't want to give it up, so I started watching the coaches. Let's face it, there's not a lot to do on the bench. My junior year, I pitched in and helped with the freshman. That's when I realized if I wanted to coach, teaching would be the logical career. I switched majors my senior year. I had to stay a fifth year to get the necessary classes in, but my coaches let me help with the team, so when I graduated finally, I had a year of coaching assistance under my belt. I worked at a high school in Harrisburg, and moved back home last year."

He went on telling me about his classes and his team. He was animated and his excitement was palpable.

I remembered back in high school thinking I would love him forever. I'd pictured the house we'd live in and the family we had.

John Henry Gardner was a path I thought I'd stay on, but had veered off. I wondered what our lives would look like now if we'd stayed together. He hadn't talked about his ex and I hadn't talked about my fiancé.

"Sadie Mae, I hate to bother you," Miss Ida called from inside an hour later.

"Coming." I stood up. "Thanks for the coffee and catching up."

"You never got your turn," John said.

"Not much to tell. Fell into a job and I'm engaged."

"Maybe I could bring coffee again next Sunday and you can do a better job of it."

Sitting on Miss Ida's front porch was absolutely not a date I assured myself. I nodded. "Make it tea. Green tea for me."

John smiled as he stood up. For a moment, he leaned toward me, as if he was going to hug me, but I stepped back, keeping distance between us.

He nodded, as if acknowledging that he understood. "I'll see you next week."

I went inside and Miss Ida smiled. "I don't want to keep you from your friend, but I wondered if you'd get me something to drink?"

"He had to go anyway, Miss Ida. And I have a kitchen to finish organizing. After I get you a drink."

I took her out iced tea and asked, "Are you okay?"

She nodded. "As okay as a woman who's older than Croesus was rich can be."

That night, when I went into the bedroom, I looked at Barbara's mural. The images were so small, but I easily recognized a movie marquee.

I was right. This wall represented Miss Ida's stories.

Barbara had turned the bedroom wall into another version of Miss Ida's Book of Memories.

I wrote in my book. *There is nothing more satisfying than looking in a well-organized pantry. Too bad it isn't as easy to organize a life.*

Miss Ida's Book of Memories

The wind chimes in the pear tree are really tinkling tonight. Albert gave them to me years ago. As the threads age, the chimes fall off. I pick up the pieces and restring them. I've done that four or five times now. I think of him whenever there's a breeze and I can hear them.

And I wish that a heart could be restrung just as easily.

Chapter Seven

"Maybe if you look back, it will give you a clue how to move forward."

Miss Ida had a doctor's appointment Monday morning at ten. I asked to talk to the doctor with her, but she said no. It wasn't just suspicion now. I knew something was going on.

She hadn't fallen since we got home, but I was pretty sure that was more because the walker gave her support than because she didn't feel dizzy.

"What did the doctor say?" I asked before I started the car.

"I'm fine and dandy," she said with a smile.

Her answer disappointed me. "I wish you'd trust me enough to tell me the truth."

"Sadie Mae, you already feel responsible enough. You don't have to take on my healthcare, too." She snapped her seatbelt in place and looked out the window, rather than at me.

"Miss Ida, I do feel responsible, but not in a bad way," I said softly. "I feel responsible because I love you. Love means we get tangled up in each other's lives. And all those tangles are strings that tie us to each other. So yes, I'm worrying. And I'm worrying more because you're not filling me in than I'd worry if you did. I can deal with almost anything if I know what it is."

She didn't say anything as I started the car. We picked up subs and soup at Tickle's Deli on the way home.

As much as I enjoyed Detroit, there were so many things I missed about Erie. Our local restaurants and diners. The lake. The peninsula. The people.

Speaking of people, Reese was just finishing mowing Miss Ida's front lawn as we pulled into her driveway.

"That boy," she said. "He started mowing my lawn whenever he did his, right after he moved in. He won't take anything for it, but I'm tricky."

"How are you tricky?" I asked with a smile.

"I bought a gas card. If he's mowing for me, the least I can do is buy the gas."

I laughed. "That is very tricky. Should we ask him for lunch? There's certainly enough."

"What a lovely idea, dear," she said.

I got out of the car as Reese turned off the lawnmower. "Would you like to join us for lunch?" I called.

"You don't have to ask me twice," he said. He left the lawnmower where it was and beat me to the passenger side of the car. "Miss Ida, would you like me to get your wheelchair?"

"I think I can make it with the walker, though I wouldn't mind a handsome young man walking with me."

He kept a hand lightly on Miss Ida's back, ready to catch her if he needed to.

I followed them carrying the lunch bag.

"Shall we eat in the kitchen, or would you rather put your leg up in your chair?" I asked Miss Ida.

"I think I can manage the table."

Reese helped her get settled while I cut up the foot-long sub and dished up three bowls of soup.

"Reese, what would you like to drink?" I asked. "We have iced tea, water or milk."

"Iced tea is fine," he said.

I poured three glasses and brought the sugar bowl and sliced lemons, then took my seat.

"No work today?" I asked as I squeezed a lemon into my tea. Miss Ida reached for the sugar first.

"I'm on second shift today," he said. "I change shifts monthly."

I laughed. "I have a fluid schedule, too. The Brain teaches a couple classes for the university, though most of his job involves research."

"The Brain? And you do what?" Reese asked.

"I do everything," I said honestly. "As for his nickname, that's how I think of him and I forget to use his real name when I'm talking to people. His name is Brian, but his sister called him the Brain, like in Marc Brown's Arthur books, though I'm not sure that's where she got the idea. She couldn't say Brian when she was little, and Brain just stuck. I picked up the habit."

He looked blank. "Marc Brown?"

"He's a children's book author from Erie," I said.

Still nothing.

I laughed. "I'll confess, since I left home, I look for anything Erie related, even children's authors. I don't think I realized how homesick I was until I got back here last week."

"Sweetheart, you always have a place with me," Miss Ida said.

"I know that. And I appreciate it. Even though Mom and Dad moved, I still feel like I've got a home base here."

Reese told us anecdotes from police department. Nothing dark or dangerous. Funny stories. Reese was much more socially aware than my poor, awkward boss.

I glanced at the clock. I'd promised to check in with the Brain at one.

"I don't want to be rude, but speaking of work, I need to check in. Would you both excuse me a minute?"

I texted:

Brain??

I wasn't shocked when he didn't respond.

So I called. It rang so long I thought it was going to voicemail, but finally the Brain picked up. "Yeah?"

"*Hello, Dee. How are you today?*" I said in my mock-Brian voice.

I could almost hear his small, rueful smile. "Hello, Dee. How are you and how's Miss Ida?"

"Much better," I said. "And we're both fine, thank you for asking. I texted but you didn't respond. How are you?"

"Good.   I worked all night and I think I'm almost..." he faded off, which meant he was still working as he tried to talk to me.

Talking to him was tough on the best days. I'd tried to explain conversations were like ping-pong. You had to hit each conversational volley back to the other person.   Most of the time, he forgot to pick up the paddle, much less hit anything.

"Did you stop for breakfast?" I asked loudly.

"Huh?" he said.

"Food, Bri. Have you eaten any food?" I asked.

"Yeah, I ate yesterday sometime."

"It's one. You need to stop, get something to eat, take a shower and be at your class by two."

I knew what was coming before he said the words, "But I—"

I interrupted. "We agreed that you were going to try to keep yourself on task. Eat, shower, class...then back to the lab if you want. Or maybe, shower, eat, class. I'll leave the order up to you as long as you're in class by two."

"You're bossy." It was his normal complaint.

I just laughed. "I know. Next time pick up my text. I don't think my bossiness is quite as apparent in texts. And check your inbox. I sent you those pages back with a few notes."

"How was it?" he asked.

"Better. I sometimes worry that I've hung out with you for far too long and have lost my every-man

110

view. I mean, I know who Schrodinger is and I even understand about his cat being alive and dead at the same time. Once you explained it was a hypothetical cat, I didn't even mind the concept. And I understand why Scott Kelly is younger than his identical twin after his year in space."

I would never be a scientist, but I knew more than the average Joe. "I think you've warped me. But I also think you've learned to speak regular-people."

The line was silent.

"Put it down, Brain. Go get your stuff done, then come back to it."

"Bossy," he muttered. "I will never marry because I don't need a real wife as long as I have you as my work wife. Even long distance, you're a good work wife."

"And a good friend. But about work. Miss Ida still isn't saying precisely what's wrong." I'd decided I'd wait a bit longer for her to tell me. Maybe she had to adjust her own reality to the problem before sharing it. "I don't know when I'll be home," I added.

"Dee, you can nag me better long distance than anyone else could manage up close and personal. It's fine. I'm fine," he said.

"And?" I prompted.

He sighed and I heard something thump. "And I put it down. I'm on my way to shower, eat and get to class."

"Good," I said. "I'm sure your students will appreciate that you showered."

He hung up without saying goodbye. But I wasn't about to complain. He'd not only conversed with me, but actually followed instructions.

I turned and Reese was standing in the doorway. "Miss Ida said something about cookies?"

I smiled as I went back inside.

I reached for the thatched roof cottage cookie jar.

111

Things moved at a different pace here.

And I was discovering I liked it.

We shared cookies and tea with Miss Ida, then she went to take a nap and I walked Reese to the front door.

"Thanks for mowing the lawn," I said. "Can I ask you something?"

"Sure. I'm an open book."

"Why a cop?"

"I like to feel I'm a part of something bigger than myself." He chuckled. "Okay, that sounds full of myself. I know people think that the police spend all their time locking up criminals, and that's a part of our job. But the other part is making a difference. I was at one of the local schools last week at dismissal. Having a patrol car present makes drivers slow down and drive with more care. So if I'm not on a call, I try to show up at one school or another. But rather than sit in my car, I get out and said hi to the kids who walked past. A week ago, one of them started to tell me a test he had coming up. I told him to study. I saw him again this week, and he ran up to me to tell me he aced the test. I gave him a sticker and he ran off to show his friends. I know that's not anything big, but it's something. Kids need to know adults care and take an interest and..." he shrugged.

I looked at him. I didn't see Mad Dog Reese anymore, I realized. I saw Reese. A man I truly admired. "I'd say it's definitely something. You made a difference."

Now, he seemed embarrassed. "It was just a sticker."

"It was more than that." I thought about Barbara's painting. "Maybe life is like a Choose-Your-Own-Adventure book."

He chuckled. "I really want to see where you're going to take this."

I grinned and tried to articulate the thought. "Choose-Your-Own-Adventure books let you pick the next chapter. And chapter after chapter you do that. You choose which direction you want to go in. You chose the military, then police work. And you chose to sit outside a school and take an interest in a child. You can't see where each choice will lead, but it will lead somewhere. Just think, someday that boy could be president. And maybe that dream all started when one cop asked about a test and took an interest."

"I like how you think," Reese said.

I felt myself blush. "Thanks."

"And in case no one else has said it, you chose to be here, to help a friend. That's a choice that I admire. It's a choice not everyone would make."

I didn't know what to say about that. So I deferred to Bette Lee's training and just said, "Thank you."

"See you later," Reese said.

I watched him walk across the street to his house.

I realized that I no longer thought of it as the Nick house. It was Reese's house. And I liked that he was just across the street.

I sat up in bed late that night and listened. The house was completely and utterly quiet.

Silent.

Too silent.

I crept out of bed and saw that Miss Ida's bedroom door was open. Her small nightlight was enough to let me know that her bed was empty and her walker was missing.

I turned and saw that the front door was open, leaving the screen door as the only barrier separating the inside from the outside.

I padded across the hardwood floors and peeked out the screen door.

There was Miss Ida, a blanket wrapped over her bathrobe-covered shoulders as she sat on the bench. She barely filled her corner.

"Miss Ida, is something wrong?" I asked softly as I opened the screen door.

"I'm sorry if I woke you. I tried to be quiet," she said.

Bette Lee told me when I was little, I'd creep into her room and stand silently next to her bed waiting for her to wake up and notice me. She always woke up quickly because she said my silence was louder than most people's screams.

Miss Ida's were as well.

"You were too quiet," I assured Miss Ida. "What's wrong?"

"Nothing, dear. Really, nothing. Sometimes I like to sit out here and watch the world at night. I think most people miss so much of the beauty because they sleep through it. Even if they're awake, it never occurs to them to come outside. Maybe that's a gift of old age. You don't sleep well anymore, so you get to enjoy nights like tonight."

I sat down next to her. The sky was clear, so the stars were visible. Looking at stars made me think of Lulu. I glanced at her bedroom window, but the light was off.

"Do you see that house down the hill?" Miss Ida asked, pointing to a house way down the hill on the other side of the street.

"Yes."

"The light in that back window is always on when I come out at night. I wonder if the people who live there have children and leave the light on so when they get up at night they can find their parent's room."

"Or the bathroom," I quipped.

She chuckled. "Or that."

We were both quiet a moment, then she said, "I think I saw the space station whizz by the other night."

"They have an app that lets you know when it's coming by your part of the world," I said.

She laughed. "They don't make apps for my landline."

"We could get you a smart phone," I offered.

"I'm just as happy not walking through life tied to one. I'll confess, I see groups of children walking by, all of them tapping away on their phones, not talking to each other. I'd rather interact with real live people, not just letters on a screen."

There was no condemnation in her voice—it was just an observation.

She went on and said, "Even without the app, I'm pretty sure it was the space station. Or a UFO."

I laughed.

She smiled. "You believe in UFOs?"

"It would be hubris to believe that humans were the only intelligent species," I hedged.

She let the question of UFOs go and patted her book on the small table next to her chair. "I was writing about you being here. And as I wrote, I realized more than a quarter of the pages in my book are empty. I've always written very sparingly. I never wanted to have to buy a second book, so I saved pages for something big. I should have filled those pages and bought another book...or two even. What a waste of all those memories. I could have saved them for nights like tonight. Or maybe I should have made more memories. Done more."

I snorted. "I understand that. I don't think I've filled my life with enough worthwhile things. I don't think I'm filling my book up very fast either."

"What do you think you should have done?" she asked.

"I don't know. I don't know what I want. But I think, since I've been here this week with you, I'm beginning to know what I *don't* want. Maybe that's something."

"That's definitely something, dear." She paused and then added. "Sometimes when I feel a bit lost, I go back through my book and reread my memories. I went through a very hard time years ago. I don't think of myself as a lightless soul so I didn't know how to function with the dark pressing down on me from every direction. I went back in my memories to happier times. I opened my book up to a random spot every night before bed and relived a happier memory. When I went to sleep, I dreamed of those happier times. And slowly, the darkness receded. Maybe if you look back, it will give you a clue how to move forward."

"Maybe," I said slowly. I'd occasionally glanced at my memories, but never with purpose. Never looking for answers.

"It couldn't hurt to try," she said.

"You're right, it couldn't." This time, I paused. "Are you going to tell me what's really wrong with you?" I asked quietly. "I'm worried."

"I'm old, sweetheart. Like my book's pages, I have more of my days filled than unfilled."

I looked at her as we sat in the still night and I knew that if this were something simple she'd tell me.

Which meant it wasn't something simple.

You'd think that working for a science nerd I'd have already learned that nothing in life was simple. But I don't think I really had.

Until now.

Miss Ida. Charles. A life's vocation.

Nope. Nothing was simple at all.

I thought about my conversation with Reese. Maybe I didn't have to have all the answers. I just had to choose my next chapter.

And I'd done that.

My next chapter was here with Miss Ida.

I'd worry about what would come next after I finished this one.

Part Two
The Well-Traveled Road

Chapter Eight

"Figuring out where I don't belong is a lot easier than figuring out where I do belong."

The next day, Miss Ida seemed to sway as she walked and would have fallen without the walker.

She laughed it off, but my concern was growing.

I wished there was someone else I could call. Someone she would listen to. I decided to ask Bette Lee to come for a visit sooner rather than later.

Miss Ida was almost too compliant when I suggested a nap that afternoon.

As she slept, I sat in the living room and thumbed back through my memories, hoping to find something that would ease the sense of concern that was growing day by day.

I'd written in under half my pages, but after listening to Miss Ida yesterday, I realized I'd have to do better. I'd write more. I'd fill up at least a couple books in my lifetime, maybe more.

I knew I'd never write the way she did. Sometimes she wrote short, pithy entries, but sometimes her writing was almost lyrical.

Years ago, she was sad one day and I asked her what was wrong. She said it was the anniversary of her father's death. She'd opened her book and turned to a dog-eared page.

"I read it every year. It was my own eulogy for him of sorts," she told me. "What I'll remember most about my father."

She read from the page, *"My father was a man of few words, but the words he did say I harvested and stored away. Most of the time, he spoke with a smile that seemed to start in his eyes and gently work its way down to his lips. How those blue eyes twinkled when he saw me or mama. And I remember how he danced. He never took my mother out, but when we listened to the radio after dinner he'd reach for her and twirl her about the kitchen, the Fred to her Ginger. And we'd laugh.*

"Of all the things I'll miss, I'll miss his laughter the most. He didn't guffaw or even chuckle. His laugh was a deep rumble in the center of his chest that seemed to reverberate through whatever room he was in. And today, in his honor, the memory I will take forward will be his laughter. I suspect as I go about this next chapter of my life—a chapter that won't include him—I will sometimes feel the rumble of his laughter deep in the center of my soul. That's a memory that's worth preserving."

Every year on the anniversary of her father's death, I'd asked her to read me that entry. And in an odd way, I too mourned for the man with rumbling laughter...a man I'd never met. Before I left for college, I told Miss Ida that I had written that memory of her father down in my book.

Miss Ida had liked that her father's memory would live on in me.

I found it now and reread it. An echo of her memory of her father had become my own.

Maybe that's where our memories really began to intertwine...with her father. Since he gave her the book, it seemed right that we both carried a piece of him with us.

My observations weren't nearly as eloquent as hers. Maybe Miss Ida had a natural poetry in her soul, or maybe I was a product of the one hundred and forty characters generation...everything moved quickly and to the point. I'd never really taken time to play with beauty of words in most of my memories.

I glanced through some of my entries.

Apple pie...ala mode.

Kayaked with Charles at sunset. Breathtaking.

Made the Brain curry. His expression is worth remembering.

No, the entries weren't poetic, but the entry about the Brain and curry was enough to make me laugh all over again. He'd taken a bite and immediately spit out the curry and tried to wipe his tongue off with his napkin. Through his sputtering fit, he managed to tell me that I should never make curry again.

Ever.

He'd insisted I make him a PBJ instead that night.

I'd said something about so much for broadening his horizons.

He'd scoffed and said if I needed to broaden them, I was welcome to buy strawberry jam instead of grape jelly. That was broad enough for him.

Remembering the curry made me miss him. Brian was not only my employer, but he was my best friend. I texted him, even though it was earlier than I called most days.

I smiled when I looked at his nickname in my contacts.

Hey, Brainiac. How goes the day?

Nerdman: *Tell me again why I keep teaching freshman sciences?*

Because of Tim.

Nerdman: *Right.*

Tim was a freshman who'd spoken Brian's language. They'd become friends, more than mentor and *mentee* or teacher and student.

There have to be other diamonds in the rough out there.

120

I didn't need to see him to see his look of frustration.

Nerdman: *Not in this class. I don't even think any of them qualify as coal...something that has the potential of being a diamond someday.*

Nerdman: *Did you call to simply listen to me complain?"*

Maybe.

I miss you. I just wanted to see how you're getting along without me.

Nerdman: *I lost my watch.*

Brian was one of the few holdouts who wore a watch to tell time, rather than just check his phone or wear a fitness tracker with a watch face.

Before I could start listing places to look, he texted back.

Nerdman: *I found it.*

That was progress. He had a habit of wandering around in a daze when he was mulling over something. When he *lost* things, they were never in a logical place.

Great. Where was it?

Nerdman: *In the freezer. I'm not sure why I put it in the freezer.*

Your mind works in mysterious ways.

Nerdman: *That was the biggest news here. How about with you?*

Me? I think being here is good for me. Might give me time to figure out what next.

Nerdman: *Talked about this a lot lately. I love having you here, but I think we both know this isn't where you belong.*

Figuring out where I don't belong is a lot easier than figuring out where I do belong.

Writing the thought made the truth of it more concrete.

Generally Brian's texts ping back before I've hardly hit send. He preferred texting to phone calls. So when my phone was text-free for a few minutes, I noticed.

Nerdman: *I have this friend who tells me that I can't always bludgeon my way to an answer. Sometimes I just have to go with the flow. Maybe you should go with the flow, too.*

I snorted, knowing I was *the friend* in question. I thought back to my Choose your adventure analogy and realized I gave good advice.

I never said go with the flow.

Nerdman: *Whatever.*

Nerdman: *And wherever you end up, remember...*

Nerdman: *You're not allowed to quit completely.*

I laughed again.

You can't get rid of me. I'm like a good fungus. I stick.

I texted him a copy of his day's schedule.

Bye, Brain.

He didn't respond. In the Brain's mind, he'd solved my problem by reminding me to chillax. And he'd solved his own concerns by reminding me I couldn't quit completely.

To be honest, I suspected having me be a virtual assistant suited him better than me there in person. In person, I made comments about his hygiene, or forced him to eat. It was harder to discern if either thing was an issue when I was managing his life over text.

I'd have to make it a point to video chat on occasion.

I picked up my book and went to first pages and some of my earliest memories.

I smiled when I saw one written in red ink. It read, *Cotton candy and rickety fair Ferris wheels.* I'd made the F in Ferris a capital because I knew that Ferris was the name of the inventor, George W. Ferris. I don't remember where I'd learned that. I wondered if I'd known back then.

I'd drawn a small heart over the *I*'s.

And I remembered more than why the F was capital...

I'd known John Gardner my entire life, but that night was our first official date. I'd liked him since my freshman year, but Bette Lee didn't allow me to date until I was sixteen.

I'd been allowed to go out with John in groups though. But this time, it was just the two of us. He had his license and was driving. I'd hoped for something totally romantic, but we went to the Wattsburg Fair.

Now, I didn't mind the fair. I loved walking through the livestock barns.

But I remember thinking it wasn't a usual first date.

Still, I hadn't complained.

I'd bought a new shirt and had a pair of older sneakers. They were new enough to look okay, but old enough that I wouldn't mind if they got muck on them in the barns.

We'd been sharing cotton candy as we rode around and around on the Ferris wheel. It squeaked and clinked, sounding like at any second it might fall apart.

Then it screeched to a halt with our car at the top.

"Look at that," John said.

For a second I looked out ahead of me, but all I saw was the barns and people milling about the fairway. Then I looked at John, who was looking at me.

"You have cotton candy on your lip," he said as he leaned forward and kissed me.

We'd kissed before, but this one was different. There, at the top of the Ferris wheel with a cone of cotton candy between us, we kissed and I believed I'd found exactly where I was supposed to be. Forever. With John Henry.

Unfortunately, forever didn't last beyond high school.

But looking back, I knew that at that moment, I'd felt as if I was exactly where I was supposed to be.

I realized something as I had the thought.

And as if on cue, my phone pinged and it was a text from Charles. I realized I'd never changed his nickname in my contacts. We'd met at a mutual friend's party. He'd ask for my number, then given me his and I'd called him *The Suit*. It wasn't simply he'd worn a suit to the dinner, but that he'd struck me as a buttoned up sort of personality.

He was, but over time, I'd forgot to notice how his starched personality didn't always mesh with my less rigid one.

I was remembering now.

The Suit: *I'm driving to Erie tomorrow, if that's okay?*

Yes. That would be good.

The Suit: *We need to talk.*

Yes, we do.

My realization moments ago was still fresh in my mind.

The Suit: *I'll see you around lunch then.*

He'd been abrupt since I left. This text conversation sounded like something I'd expect from the Brain, not Charles.

I was pretty sure I knew what he was going to say to me. And if he didn't say it, I was pretty sure I was going to have to.

Yes, it was easier figuring out where I didn't belong.

Easier to figure out, but not easier to do.

Miss Ida's Book of Memories

Having someone here who I love and who loves me makes everything easier.

Chapter Nine

Sometimes love isn't enough.

I spent the next morning looking back over my *Charles pages* in my book. The first few years, they'd been filled with small sweet memories. The day he'd taken me to the Henry Ford Museum. We'd held hands as I read all the placards that told about each piece. He even managed to look interested as I oohed and aahed over the Dymaxion House that Buckminster Fuller had designed.

It wasn't until later that I realized he had not enjoyed the trip as much as I had. When I asked him why he didn't hurry me along, he'd said, "Being in love means sometimes you do something just because the other person loves it."

I'd quipped, "And sometimes you just live through it."

He'd laughed and said, "Yes. And pray they don't want to do it again too soon."

I'd written, *Doing something because the other person wants to. Buckminster Fuller.*

I did go back a few years later, but I didn't drag Charles along. I went with the Brain who spent more time reading placards than I did.

As I thumbed back through those pages, I realized that slowly, Charles and I had stopped trying to do things just because the other person loved it. We went out on dates and spent evenings together, but a lot of those evenings involved both of us working on other things, not concentrating on each other.

We didn't try to share things any more. He needed me in a way that was very similar to the Brain.

Things went smoother for him when I was around. He'd said as much.

I was convenient.

But to be fair, he was convenient for me as well. There was a sense of security knowing he was there to see a movie with or go out with.

We both deserved more than a marriage-of-convenience.

I'd known what I needed to do all along, but as I heard Charles' car pull in the drive and I put down my book, there wasn't the slightest bit of doubt anymore.

"Hi, Dee," he said as I opened the door. "Where's Miss Ida?"

"She's having a morning in bed. She's not feeling well. I made a call to the visiting nurse and asked her to stop by again today. So I'm sorry, but we're stuck here."

"I came to see you," he said. "It doesn't matter where we are."

That was sweet and almost romantic, but one look at his expression said that romance wasn't his reason for the visit. "Would you like to come in?"

"Why don't you come outside," he said. "Unless you can't leave Miss Ida?"

"I'll leave the door open so I can hear her when she calls."

We each sat on the opposite sides of the bench, leaving a wide valley of space in between us.

"Dee, you're not coming home any time soon, are you?" Charles asked.

"Not too soon, no. There's something wrong with Miss Ida. Something she doesn't want to tell me. I'm trying to give her time to process whatever it is before I push her into sharing." And maybe, just maybe, I was giving myself time to adjust to what I was pretty sure wouldn't be good news.

"If it was nothing, she'd have told me, so it's something." Something that wasn't good.

127

"I'm sorry," he said.

"So am I."

"Even without that, you're not chomping at the bit to get back, are you?" He sounded sad as he asked the question, as if he knew the answer.

I sighed. "No. The Brain and I are doing fine with this new system. I suspect he's right and it's time I look for something else to do."

"Do you miss me?" Charles asked, pivoting the conversation in an entirely new direction.

"Of course," I said without thinking.

Charles shook his head. "No, really, take a minute. Do you really miss me?"

I thought about how Bette Lee had missed Big Henry and knew that I didn't miss Charles that way.

I think I missed the thought of us, more than us. I wasn't sure that would make sense to anyone but me, but I also knew it did make sense to me.

Instead of saying it, I said, "It's been a hard week, Charles. You've seemed angry with me ever since I said I was coming home and postponing the wedding."

"The wedding you don't want," he said sadly.

"The wedding I don't want," I agreed, just as sadly. "It was one of the things I wanted to talk to you about. It's not just that we can't agree on the wedding. I've spent some time looking back through my Book."

"You and that book." He shook his head. My Book of Memories was just one more thing he didn't understand about me.

I nodded. "I remembered so many sweet moments. That first day when we met. Our first date. Even then it was apparent that we have such different styles—we've always known that."

He nodded. "We made our differences work for us, rather than against us at first.

"But lately..." he said slowly, letting the sentence hang there, big and bold. "But lately, rather than meshing those styles we've clashed," I

128

finished. "Neither of us has been very good at compromising, so someone always feels like they've lost. I really don't want the wedding that you and Frannie want."

"I've known that, but I thought you'd come around," he said.

"I don't think I'm very good at coming around." I tried to laugh, but it came out wooden to my own ears. "So what are we going to do?"

It was cowardly, because I could see he knew what we needed to do as much as I did. I was just making him say it.

And not forcing the issue with Miss Ida was equally cowardly.

I liked to think I was brave and I didn't like being confronted so clearly with the fact that I wasn't.

"I was thinking about our trip to the Henry Ford Museum," I said as a way of putting off what I knew I needed to do.

He groaned. "Seriously, how many refrigerators does one man need to look at or worse, read about?"

I laughed, though it wasn't a Miss Ida's father sort of laughter, but a small sound that seemed better than tearing up. "I had so much fun looking at everything there."

He sighed. "I know. I didn't."

I nodded. Maybe that trip should have told us everything we needed to know, but maybe neither of us was ready to listen.

I was pretty sure we were both listening now.

"You're such a big part of my memories. And I do love you," I said, not sure if I were trying to convince Charles or convince myself.

"I know. I don't have a book, but you're part of everything. When I look at my house, or office, I can see your influence. And I have missed you, but you're right, I've been angry. I thought I was angry that you chose your friend over me, but I think it's more than that. I'm not angry with you. I'm angry with myself. I love you and I want us to work. Things..."

"Things go more smoothly for you when I'm there," I filled in, echoing back his own words.

He nodded. "But I'm not sure that's enough. We both want different things, and I'm not talking about the wedding. I'm talking about my political career and social networking and..."

I nodded. "We both have different styles. I'm a hermit, you're a social butterfly." I laughed sadly, mainly to keep from crying. "I meant that in the manliest of ways. You want to change the world on a national level. I'm happier working on a smaller scale. Hearing that the Brain is getting himself to class and eating on a somewhat regular basis is a huge change for the good. You think macro, I think micro."

Yes, the Brain had rubbed off on me, I thought sadly. "We're not a good fit and love isn't enough to overcome that."

"I know. I think I've known for a long time and tried to ignore it because I do love you."

"We're like jigsaw puzzle pieces that are close to fitting, but even though you can smack the pieces together, if you look at the picture you can see they don't quite line up." So I said, "Maybe it's time to admit that we don't fit."

"I do love you," he said slowly.

"And I love you. But something else I noticed when I was looking through my book. We stopped *trying* to fit at some point. I went to your events reluctantly."

"And I stopped going to your stuff all together," he said.

I tugged at the engagement ring I hadn't wanted and had never liked. As it slipped over my knuckle I felt a sense of relief mingled with sadness. Even though I knew what I was doing was the right thing for both of us, it hurt.

I handed it to Charles. "I do love you," I whispered.

"I love you, too. But I think if we went through with this, we'd eventually resent each other. That's the last thing I want."

I thought about Miss Ida and how she missed Albert. He'd been gone longer than I'd known her, but the way she talked about him made it seem as if he'd just left. He was that much a part of her.

Charles had never been that to me. And he'd never been what Big Henry was to Bette Lee. And I was pretty sure I'd never been either of those things for him.

"If you think about it, we both love a lot of people. We love our parents, our families and friends, but that doesn't mean we should be married to any of them. I think marriage requires a special kind of love," I said, weighing this new revelation. A kind of love we didn't have.

Charles was quiet a moment then said, "If you loved me the way I want to be loved, I'd come first."

"And if you loved me the way I want to be loved, you'd never make me choose you over the other people in my life," I said.

He stood. "I should go."

"Charles, you just drove five hours to break up with me in person. I think that deserves at least lunch." I took his hand in mine. "We've both admitted that we love each other and we're friends. As someone who loves you and is your friend, let me ask you to lunch."

"I'm not sure if this would be easier if we had some big fight," he said.

"I don't think it's ever easy to let someone go," I said. "But if you think it would help, I'd start a fight." I gave him a fierce look.

Obviously it wasn't too fierce because he laughed. "It's probably better we don't fight. You'd probably break something if you tried. Fighting isn't something you do well."

131

I thought about all the times I'd just let things go, thinking I was making things easier. "Maybe that's something I need to work on," I mused.

Maybe if I'd fought harder in our relationship, we wouldn't be here. I chose to let things slide until there was so much momentum I couldn't stop our relationship from slipping away.

He looked at me and nodded. "Maybe it is time you learned."

I had a whole list of things I'd discovered I wanted to work on. Fighting, being brave, finding my path and my passion.

I took Miss Ida a sandwich. Charles didn't ask to say hello to her. And I didn't insist.

"Are you okay?" she asked me.

I nodded. "Sometimes doing the right thing is hard."

She took my hand and gave it a squeeze. "You've always been stronger than you've known. Even if it's hard, you'll do what's right."

I went back out to Charles. We ate and visited. It was awkward at first, but slowly, it became less so.

I glanced at this man I'd agreed to marry and was now agreeing to let go after such a short time apart.

I knew the decision was the right one.

As he left, I kissed his cheek and waved goodbye with a smile on my face, and it was only after his car disappeared from sight, I realized this might have been the last time I'd see him. And if I did see him again, it would be on different terms. We'd be people who used to be a couple.

Like me and John Henry.

I thought about where I'd thought we'd be. In my fantasies we'd had a small house, filled with kids and laughter. I'd always been fuzzy about what I'd be doing, or even what he'd be doing, but that small dream of a family was as real to me as Miss Ida's.

I realized that Charles had never dreamed any small dreams. His dreams were big and he was committed to seeing them through.

Our dreams had never meshed. And now, all the dreams I'd had for the two of us—a family, a home, and a lifetime together—were gone.

I didn't have any new dreams to replace them with.

I went out to the front porch and felt moisture on my cheeks. I realized I was crying.

And suddenly, the pain I'd thought I'd feel earlier hit me. Even knowing that our relationship wasn't right for either of us, saying goodbye to all those plans and dreams hurt.

Saying goodbye to Charles hurt.

Silent tears trickled at first, and then started to stream down my face.

Soon, there were hitches in my breath. Maybe they were sobs.

I cried for what I'd left behind...no, not actually what. I was crying for the dream I'd lost. And I cried because I knew that I wasn't brave, but somehow I was going to have to find the strength to start again. I cried because I wasn't sure I could.

I closed my eyes and wrapped my arms around my legs. I rocked back and forth, trying to find comfort for myself.

"Dee?"

I looked up and saw Reese. He didn't say a word as he sat next to me and wrapped his arm over my shoulder. Then he scooped me up and pulled me onto his lap.

He still didn't say anything.

I wanted to tell him I didn't need his comfort. I wanted to be strong enough to tell him I could mourn for my loss on my own.

But in the end, I simply laid my head on his shoulder and continued crying.

He swayed from side to side as he simply held me. His hand brushed my hair, offering comfort, but demanding nothing, not even an explanation.

When I finished, he said, "We need to be clear about something."

"Yes?" My voice sounded hoarse to my own ears.

"This wasn't a date." He smiled as he said the words and I realized he was trying to cheer me up.

It worked because I started laughing. And that was a relief.

"Do you want to talk about it?" he asked.

"I broke up with my fiancé," I said, more to say the words out loud than as an explanation. After all, how could I explain my sorrow to him when I wasn't sure I understood it myself? I knew my heart wasn't broken. I was pretty sure it wasn't even bruised. But knowing that Charles and I weren't meant for each other didn't make letting him go hurt less.

Knowing something needed to be done didn't make doing it any easier.

And maybe, a small part of me wondered if letting go of my dream hurt more than letting go of the man. Wondering that made me feel very small.

Reese didn't push. "Fine. Then how about I order takeout for dinner and invite myself over for a movie. Miss Ida loves Star Wars. We could watch the new one."

"She does?" I asked.

"You two might be close, but obviously you don't know all her secrets," he said with a laugh. "I had a Star Wars themed Halloween last year. She told me how much she loved the movies. I've been meaning to bring the new one over for her."

I was touched that Reese remembered she liked Star Wars and even more impressed that he'd planned to bring it over for her.

"You are a very nice man," I said. I realized how far removed he was from the Mad Dog Reese I remembered from school.

"And you are a very nice lady," he said.

I must have made a face because he said, "Do you know what I remember about you most from school?"

I shook my head, and as I did so, I realized I was still on his lap. I moved back onto the bench and waited.

He didn't seem to notice I moved. He simply went on, "Harriet."

I remembered. She was a freshman and I met her in French class when I was a sophomore and found out she'd had a series of surgeries on her leg at the local Shriner's Hospital. She had one last one scheduled at the end of the school term.

I'd organized a fundraiser in her name for the Shriners, and then put together a visitors' schedule, so she had someone from school drop by to see her every day that summer. I suddenly really wanted to touch base with her and see how she was. On the heels of that thought, I realized that when things settled down it would mean Miss Ida didn't need my help and I'd be back in Detroit.

"I haven't thought of her in years."

"I visited her that summer. She said she'd never felt so popular and that she owed it all to you. If I'd stuck around, I'd have asked you out."

I smiled and shook my head.

He nodded. "I thought you were amazing then. And I still do now."

And he looked at me as if I weren't a red-eyed woman who'd literally just cried on his shoulder. I felt awkward and so undeserving. Helping out with Harriet had been easy. It was like organizing a cupboard, only better. Harriet was a sweet kid who deserved the support.

135

Wanting to change the subject, I said, "Let me go see if Miss Ida's up to a movie."

I went back to her room and knocked softly. When she didn't answer, I opened her bedroom door slowly.

The hinges squeaked and she stirred. She sat up and smiled when she saw me.

"I was having the most wonderful dream. Albert brought me a cup of tea and said, '*I remembered how you made it.*' He was such a special man."

I smiled. "Speaking of special men, we have an invitation for dinner and a movie by a special guy."

"I'm not sure I'm up for that, dear."

"And that's why he's special. He's bringing in take-out and has the new Star Wars DVD. Rumor has it you're a fan."

She grinned. "It turns out I am. I didn't realize it until a few years back. But I'm still not sure I'm up for getting out of bed."

"Leave that to me."

We had a Pad Thai picnic in Miss Ida's room. Then Reese and I carried the TV and DVD player back and set it up on her dresser. We sat next to each other on Albert's side of the bed and watched the movie with her.

Afterward, she said, "I love seeing girls kick butt in movies. Back in my day, women were expected to wait for a man to rescue them."

"But that's not how you did things. Remember that grabby date? You could be a kick butt heroine." I was teasing, but in truth, Miss Ida had always been my heroine. She was the kind of woman I wanted to be when I grew up.

Reese offered to carry the TV and DVD player back out to the living room, but I said we'd leave it here for now. I settled her in and walked Reese out to the front room.

"Thank you for everything tonight," I said at the door. "Not just dinner and the movie."

"You know some people call dinner and a movie a date, but I think we'll just call it two friends getting together. But..."

"But?"

"I have an invitation to a party for an old friend at the Art Museum a week from Friday. It was a plus one. Would you like to go?"

"Would it be a date?" I asked, teasing.

"That's the thing about plus ones...you can define them however you like. So what if we start as just two neighbors going to a fancy party and see where that gets us?"

I laughed as he leaned down and kissed my cheek before he walked back across the street to the Nick's old house.

"I never answered you," I called.

He turned around. Under the light from the streetlamp I could see his grin. "Yes you did."

I reached up and felt my cheek, sure that he'd left some sort of brand behind.

I remembered the movie and realized that I had something I'd wanted to do.

I texted the Brain.

> **Would you mind if I called your editor to see if she might have other clients who could use my services?**
> Nerdman: That's a great idea. I'll tell her to expect your call tomorrow. Night.
> **Night, Brain.**

I'd worked with his editor in the past. She was nice. Even if she didn't need someone translate geek-speak into English, she might know someone who did need someone.

It wasn't a career, but it was a start.

Miss Ida's Book of Memories

I love Star Wars because the Force always win. Even if it doesn't seem like it at first.

Chapter Ten

Today I'm borrowing Miss Ida's words for my memory. "Just like you can choose what memories you take with you, I think you can choose other things. And I choose hope over despair." I choose hope.

On Sunday morning, John Henry was at the front door at nine with coffee for himself and two green teas—one for me and one for Miss Ida.

"Why don't you come join us on the porch?" I invited her as I took her a cup.

I didn't ask merely because she'd be a buffer, but because I genuinely enjoyed her company. I worried that she was spending too much time in her house cut off from people.

"I think I'm going to sit here and drink my tea, but you go out and enjoy catching up."

"We're talking later," I warned her.

For a moment, I thought she was going to tell me that she was fine and there was nothing to talk about, but she surprised me and nodded.

It was progress.

I leaned down and kissed her cheek, then took my tea out to the porch with John.

He talked about football. School ended soon and he had football clinics, then summer practices starting.

His excitement was palpable.

And despite the fact I would never be a football fan, I enjoyed his enthusiasm.

I realized I felt a bit of that same excitement when I thought about calling the Brain's editor.

"Your turn," he said suddenly.

I tried to think of something to say.

"What's wrong with Miss Ida?" he asked, helping me.

"I'm not sure. She's not talking and I've given her time, but I think her time's almost up."

"It's hard to balance her right to privacy and the fact you love her."

I nodded at his insight. "That's just it. I'm glad you see it too. I wondered if I was making things up to give myself an excuse to stay."

"Why do you need an excuse?" he asked.

"Exactly," I said. "I don't."

"So how are Bette Lee and Big Henry?" he asked, tossing me another conversational bone.

I caught it and gave a rousing monologue on my parents. We both ended up laughing.

"I missed this," John said.

"What?"

"Talking to you about not much of anything and laughing myself silly. Whenever I thought of you, that's what came to mind...the laughter."

When I thought of John what had come to mind? Not just the way he broke up with me, but the time he'd cheated on me with Maryellen Scandig. And the time he'd stood me up for a date because he'd forgotten or...

I might not have added any of those incidents to my Book, but they'd left an imprint regardless. We might be able to choose what memories we memorialized and kept with us, but all the bad ones don't just disappear. They leave their imprint. Maybe by concentrating on the good memories we took away some of the bad one's power, but we couldn't obliterate the impact all together.

I wondered if I hung on to all my grievances against John because of the way he'd broken up with me, or was I just reminding myself what I didn't want in a man?

I was obviously silent too long, because John started filling up the quiet space with more stories of his job and team again. Those stories faded and he abruptly said, "I remember taking you to see sunsets on the beach. You loved them. Maybe we can go see another while you're home? The last one we went to see, there were seagulls flying across the water as the sun finally hit the horizon and you drew in your breath and held it, as if you were afraid to spoil the moment. And I kissed you then..."

Before I could say anything, he kissed me—on Miss Ida's porch with a cup of tea in my hand.

Technically it wasn't cheating because Charles and I had broken up. I'd returned his ring.

But John didn't know that.

He'd cheated once before...once that I knew of.

Suddenly I knew that John Henry was a path I was lucky I escaped.

Even though the way he broke up with me hurt, it was absolutely for the best.

All those thoughts flew one after another across my mind in a split second as I pushed at John and pulled back.

Unfortunately for John, I still had my tea in my hand.

More unfortunate, it didn't stay in my hand as I pushed. It sloshed all over him as it fell.

Most unfortunate of all, it was still quite warm—the to-go cup was well insulated.

He howled and stood up.

"Sorry," I said.

He looked furious. "All you had to do was say no."

"I did say no last week. Remember?" I reminded him.

"Still—"

"Still, I think it's time for you to leave," I said standing. "And I think it would be best if you didn't come back."

"Listen, Sadie Mae—"

I didn't want to listen. "John, it's time for you to go."

And without waiting to see if he left, I turned and went back in the house.

"Well, you showed him," Miss Ida said laughing. "You're still *sassy*."

I could probably find my sassy page in my book pretty easily. But I didn't need it. I fell back into the memory.

One Saturday, as I sat having tea with Miss Ida after cleaning—I don't know what I'd cleaned that day. Another memory lost to time. But I do remember sitting with my teacup and cookies when Bette Lee came to the door. She told me that John Henry had called and I was supposed to call him back on the landline because Bette Lee didn't believe I needed my own cellphone.

I'd said, "He can wait while I finish my tea."

And Bette Lee said, "My aren't you a sassy one today." I wasn't sure if she approved or not,

Miss Ida had chimed in, "And *sassy* looks very good on you."

I knew exactly where she stood on the topic of my sassiness.

I laughed at the memory. "Thank you. But really, what kind of man kisses a woman who's engaged?"

"Technically you're not engaged any more," she pointed out.

"I know that and you know that, but he didn't know that."

I thought about Reese's gentle peck on my cheek and party invitation. I realized I was intrigued. And I knew that no matter how we designated the plus one, it was a date. I'd called Julie, Miss Ida's most recent helper and she said she was happy to come sit with Miss Ida for the night.

We hadn't seen much of her since I was home to help Miss Ida. She was graduating from Mercyhurst Prep and was swamped, so it worked out well. She seemed like a nice girl. I knew she'd keep an eye on Miss Ida, who was still chuckling.

I knew what I needed to do.

While I was still feeling sassy, I said, "Miss Ida, I've been here a week and a half." It was hard to believe that's all it had been. So much had happened during my short visit.

I continued, "It's time you tell me what's really going on. I think maybe you needed time to adjust, so I didn't push."

She gave me a look that said she disagreed, so I corrected, "Well, I didn't push as much as I wanted to. But it's time. And don't try to tell me its just old age. You and I know it's not. And I deserve better than that."

"Sadie, I—"

I could see her trying to throw me off the scent again, so I said, "We've already established that I'm in a sassy mood today. And in case you haven't noticed, I'm not going anywhere. So you might as well tell me."

"I have begun to suspect you're not leaving any time soon," she said. I couldn't tell if she was annoyed by the fact, or relieved. Maybe it was a combination of both.

"Bless your heart. It's sweet that you ever thought I might," I said, giving my best Bette Lee impression.

"Your mother would be proud," she said with a smile, but then grew serious and added, "But it's not your job to take care of me. I'm just a neighbor. An old neighbor."

"No, it's not my job—it's my privilege. Taking care of each other is what family does."

"I don't want you to stay because I need you," she said.

"Miss Ida, I think I want to stay because *I need you*. I need to be here."

That statement was a truth that didn't really sink in until I said it out loud. I needed to be here in Erie with Miss Ida.

I'd already figured out a few things. I suspected there was a lot more for me to discover. "You've taught me so many times what's important. Every day when I write in my book, I think of you. Because of you I look for the best in my life. Some days, my memory is just a list of happy things. Ice cream cones, a walk on the beach, finding beach glass, reading a good book..."

I didn't have her way with words, but I needed her to understand. "Bad things happen too, but you've taught me to leave those behind and concentrate on the better things. Whatever is wrong with you...we'll get through it and still find good moments for our books." More memories that would tangle. "No matter how bad it is, you won't be alone. And maybe that counts."

"I wrote something to that effect in my book last night." She was quiet a moment. And finally, softly and slowly she said, "After I fell, they did tests and found an aneurysm."

I wasn't a medical person any more than I was a scientist, but I knew enough about both things. And I knew aneurysms weren't good. They were weaknesses in blood vessels. That's all I knew, but by this time tomorrow I'd know more.

"Are they going to do surgery?" I asked.

She shook her head. "No. The doctor said the surgery is dangerous and given my age, he didn't anticipate *a good outcome*. That's how he said it. *A good outcome.* I'm pretty sure it's doctor-speak for I'll be dead, or worse."

I didn't ask what was worse than death, because I could think of any number of things that would be.

"I had an uncle once who was in a coma for two months and when he came out, he had some fancy word that meant he couldn't find words. He asked me to get him a ball once. I couldn't figure out what ball. Turns out, he wanted a drink of water. He had a son, my cousin, Junior. Junior could spit farther than he was tall. And he was over six feet. Can you imagine how much practice it would take to spit six feet? In all my years, I don't think I've ever spit on purpose. Except that time I ate a fly."

"You ate a fly?" I asked on cue, knowing she needed a minute to regroup before I pounded her with questions.

"Not on purpose. I was telling Albert a story and a fly flew right in my mouth. I didn't swallow, thank heavens, but I did spit it out. Albert, he laughed and laughed. I told him that it wasn't funny. I worried I had fly breath. He kissed me and assured me that I didn't."

She smiled as she remembered. "Then he told me I did however have pickle breath. He'd just bought us both a dill pickle from the grocery store."

"Miss Ida, what is the outcome if they don't operate?" I asked softly.

"Ultimately the same." Miss Ida humphed. "*My age*, he said. Why if I were younger, I'd have smacked him for commenting on my age. Bette Lee would have given him the what for."

She meant it as a joke. I could see it how much she wanted me to laugh, but the best I could manage was a weak smile. "Can the nurse talk to me later?"

Miss Ida nodded. "Yes. I'm sure Doran can explain better than I can. I should have just told you from the beginning. I don't know why I didn't."

"Maybe you just needed a minute to adjust. I get that," I said. "But I think we should get a second opinion."

"Why? If he's right, it might kill me. But honey, when you get to be my age—and I do realize the irony

145

of commenting on my age after just complaining that the doctor did—but when you get to be my age, just about anything could do you in. I read somewhere that people who are using the facility sometimes strain and give themselves a heart attack. I'd rather die from my brain exploding, than die on the toilet."

I smiled then, which I knew had been her intent. "Miss Ida."

She laughed. "Bette Lee wouldn't approve of toilet talk. But here's the thing, honey. Everyone dies. Sadie Mae, I've had a good life. I've been loved and I have loved. I only have one great regret."

I saw her look at Barbara's painting with so much longing it hurt me. I couldn't imagine how much it hurt to lose a daughter.

I knew that Bette Lee would look like that if she lost me. I didn't need to ask her or try hard to imagine it. She would never get over the pain of losing me. Just as I knew that I'd never fully recover from losing her.

I looked at my friend and realized that sometimes people needed permission to talk about their pain.

"Can you tell me what happened to Barbara?"

All of my mother's rules about not asking personal questions seemed absurd now. Miss Ida was sick and I was the closest family she had left.

"I don't know," Miss Ida said softly, pain punctuating all three syllables. "I pray for her every night. I wish I could do more, but that's all I have to offer her now. I left you a letter about her. If she comes looking for me after…"

She didn't say the words, but I knew she meant after she was gone.

"…I want her to have someone. And I knew, without asking, you'd be there for her, just like you've always been here for me."

I nodded. "Tell me?"

She pointed at the antique secretary in the corner. "There's a small photo album in there."

I got the album and as I carried back, I saw an envelope poking out. Miss Ida took that first and handed it back to me. "This is for you. You're the executor of my estate. I should have asked about that, too, but I didn't. Bette Lee would bless my heart and chalk it up to me being a cheeky northerner. I know, I'm talking about your mother a lot tonight, but she is a one of a kind woman. She's so sure about what's right and what's not. And we both know she'd think just dumping my estate on you was cheeky, but in actuality, I knew you'd say yes. I knew I could trust you with this."

"You can," I assured her. "Bette Lee would also say that being a family means doing what needs to be done. And Miss Ida, you are family."

Miss Ida nodded and patted my hand.

We sat for a moment, then she looked at her memory book. "There are only two days that I didn't write an entry in my book. One was the day Albert died. The other was..."

She opened the photo album to a picture of a fat baby with dark brown hair and a drooly grin. "That's my Barbara. Barbara Marie."

"Sometimes I feel as if I know her just a little because of the paintings..." I loved the ones of Miss Ida, but the other wall still disturbed me. I rarely looked at it, much less studied those paintings.

"I cleaned out all her personal items years back. They're in boxes in the attic. I thought about painting over the walls, but the pictures there gave me comfort. Sometimes I go sit in there and wish things were different."

She flipped to the back of the small album. There was a girl, probably in her early twenties, looking at me now. Miss Ida traced her dark hair with a finger. Barbara's shining greenish blue eyes lit up with a smile that reminded me of Miss Ida's.

"I don't know where she is or what happened to her," Miss Ida said sadly. She blinked her eyes hard, as if holding back tears. Her voice wavered as she continued. "For a long time I couldn't decide if knowing would be better or worse. I've decided that not knowing is better. Maybe that's why I tried not to tell you what was wrong with me. Not knowing can be better, because if I don't know for sure, I can have hope. I cling to that hope. When I'm gone, if you ever see Barbara, please tell her that. I prayed for her and hoped for her every day of her life."

I shook my head. "I still don't understand."

"I lost her a long time before that last day. Albert and I had her late in our marriage—late in life. I've often wondered if we spoiled her too much, or maybe we were so in love with each other she felt left out?"

I felt another surge of connection with Barbara. I'd often thought that Big Henry and Bette Lee were complete in and of themselves. Oh, I knew they loved me and if something happened to me there would be a hole in their lives, but they didn't just function as a couple, they functioned as one unit. Miss Ida and her husband sounded as if they had as well.

"Maybe we were too strict, or not strict enough?" She shook her head, as if she was still trying to decide where she went wrong.

Softly, she said, "I can't pinpoint the exact day we started to lose her. It seems to me I should be able to look back through my book and say, yes, it was this day. I should be able to point to it. Maybe I concentrated too much on what was good in my life and ignored something I shouldn't have."

She paused and flipped to the front of the book to a page that was dog-eared and showed signs of wear. There was a small piece of paper wedged between the pages, tucked into the binding so that it wouldn't fall out easily. "She did this when she was ten. I always knew she liked art, but this was the first time I realized how talented she really was."

It was a horse, running along a beach. A wave lapped at its hind right leg, but it had thrown back its head and kept going. I could feel the wildness of that horse. No one had ever put a saddle or bridle on it. No one could ever tame it.

"We'd read Walter Farley's Black Stallion books and she drew this. I swear, I could hear the sound of that wave crashing into the shore. And at that moment, I was determined to see to it Barbara had all the training she needed to foster her gift. When I look at this picture, I remember that at that moment, she loved me. At that moment, we were so close. I don't know how I lost her."

There was such abject pain laced around every word. I could almost see the pain and the confusion like a palpable aura. I didn't know what to say to help. I reached out and took her hand in mine.

"I do know she was a junior in school the first time we heard she was drinking. Her father and I grounded her. We were never drinkers, so we didn't keep alcohol in the house. We talked to her about why she shouldn't drink. We told her it was illegal. We took things away from her. But still, she drank and ran with a wild bunch. I don't think we met most of them, and the ones we did meet we didn't approve of. Albert said as much, which only made her more determined."

Miss Ida shook her head and tears glistened in her eyes, but they didn't fall. I suspected they had fallen in the past. Maybe with time, she'd mastered containing them.

"We did our best," she said again, her anguish in the words palpable. "Our best wasn't good enough though. We failed her. She said she couldn't live like a prisoner and left home when she was eighteen. I've pulled out this picture so many times. It seems prophetic to me now. I've realized that no one could tame our Barbara anymore than this horse could be tamed."

"Miss Ida..." I didn't know what else to say. I squeezed her hand. It felt fragile and cold in mine.

It seemed ephemeral.

"After she left, she came in and out of our lives from time to time, mainly whenever she needed something. We tried to help her, Sadie Mae. We tried to save her," she said, begging me to believe her.

"Miss Ida, I'm no expert, but I don't think you can save someone else. At least not until they're ready to be saved."

"There came a moment when Albert and I both realized that. Barbara came home looking so sick and dirty. She took a shower and put on some clean clothes I'd bought because she almost always came home in that state. I went to the kitchen to make tea and when I came out she was gone along with my father's pocket watch. It used to hang there." She pointed to the table where the glass cloche with its empty hook had always sat.

"I cried like I've never cried before. I cried until Albert came home. That was the moment we both realized we couldn't save her, no matter how hard we tried. If there was any remnant of my Barbara there, she'd never have taken something that was so dear to me." She reached out and touched the globe and I wondered how many times she'd done that as it sat there in its watchlessness.

"I'm sorry."

"Barbara knew that watch wasn't worth much money. But it reminded me of my father. I think we treasure things more for the memories they carry than for any monetary value. She stole the watch and it was the last straw."

I thought about the things I valued the most. My collection of Heinlein collector books that Big Henry and Bette Lee surprised me with just a couple

Christmases ago. My Book of Memories. That first book Brian wrote. He'd dedicated it to me. Each was indeed tied to memories.

Miss Ida nodded. "The last time I saw Barbara was a few months after Albert died. I opened the door and...I wouldn't have known her if I met her on the street. She was dirty and drunk. I didn't have to be a drinker to recognize that.

"She said, '*Hello, Mother. May I come in?*'

"It struck me that she still said *May* not *Can*. Her proper English seemed at odds with how bad she looked. I shook my head. I'd been dreading the day, but I'd promised Albert. He'd been so upset about my father's watch. He's the one that put the empty dome here. A reminder to both of us to be strong. We had to realize we couldn't fix Barbara. She had to fix herself. She had to want to be fixed. I knew what I had to do—I had a card tucked in the frame of her painting by the door. That picture showed different paths.

"That card was a path I was offering her. A better path than she'd been on.

"I opened the door and handed it to her. 'Here's the name of a rehabilitation hospital. I've left word that if you ever check yourself in, I'll cover the bill. But that's the last money you'll ever get from me.

"She said, '*I don't want your money. I want a shower and a bed, maybe a cup of tea...*'

"She smiled at me as she asked about the tea. For a moment, I could see the little girl who had countless tea parties with me. The talented girl who'd drawn that horse and the mural in her room... But it was just a moment. On its heels I saw the woman who'd stolen my father's watch. I could forgive her for breaking my heart, but not Albert's. She'd been daddy's girl and rather than treasuring the status, she'd exploited it.

"I shook my head and locked the screen door. 'No. I promised *your father before he died* that I

151

wouldn't let you in unless you'd straightened yourself out.' She didn't even flinch when I said Albert was gone."

And that was that. The tears Miss Ida had so valiantly held back flowed like a river of pain. She cried as if the day were happening right now, instead of in the past.

I leaned over and held her, like Bette Lee used to hold me when I was younger and in pain. Like Reese had held me when I cried over Charles.

"I'm so sorry," I said over and over.

I felt Miss Ida pull herself upright and I let her go.

She took a tissue from her pocket and wiped her eyes. "Barbara swore at me that day when I handed her the card. She said things no child should ever say to their mother. She never said she was sorry to hear her father was gone. There's no fighting with someone who's drunk or high or whatever she was. I simply shut the main door and dead-bolted it. She ranted and cried on the porch for a while and then it got quiet. When I went outside she was gone and I haven't seen or heard from her since."

"I don't remember her." I tried to come up with something, but there was no whisper of a memory.

"She was older than you," Miss Ida said. "And she was gone long before you started cleaning for me." She paused a moment and added, "I know I did the right thing. It was the only thing I could do."

I knew she meant it as a statement, but it sounded more like a question. I didn't have an answer for her. So I simply squeezed her hand.

"If she'd gone to the hospital and tried, I'd have done anything I could to help her. But I couldn't make *her* want to get better. I couldn't make *her* want to lead a worthwhile life. I went to some meetings and they told us that alcoholism is a disease. But it's a disease no doctor can cure. There's no surgery for it. There was no treatment that would work until *Barbara* wanted to get better. Until she did, there was nothing I could do. Nothing Albert could have done."

"I'm so sorry," I said again.

They were the most in adequate words, but I didn't know any better.

"So am I," she said with such utter heartbreak that I felt myself start to cry.

I treasured Miss Ida's friendship and I couldn't imagine squandering not just that, but her love. I couldn't imagine being Barbara and seeing Miss Ida's look of disappointment as she handed me a card for a rehab. My heart broke for my friend.

Miss Ida reached out and tenderly brushed away my tears. "Don't cry, sweetheart. I've cried enough for both of us. I pray for her every day and I choose to live in hope. Just like you can choose what memories you take with you, I think you can choose other things. And I choose hope over despair."

I looked at my neighbor, my friend, my family. Her body might have aged and become frail, but she still had the most amazing, strong spirit of anyone I'd ever met.

She patted my hand. "The letter in there says most of this. When I die, you inherit everything. There's no stipulations or requirements. But in the letter I asked if Barbara ever does show up, you help her. If she wants treatment, help her get it. And if she comes, tell her that turning her away was the hardest thing I've ever done. I did it because I loved her more than anyone else in the world. I've prayed for her and thought of her every day of her life. That didn't change. Tell her that sometimes love means doing what's best for the other person, not what's easiest for yourself."

I hugged Miss Ida then. "I'm so sorry," I whispered in her ear. I was on the verge of tears again, though I'd never met Barbara.

"So am I. Though I hope that someday she finds a way past her addiction and finds a worthwhile life. I've hoped the hospital would send me a bill, or she'd call. But nothing."

She opened up her book of memories and pointed. I could make out the tape that held the page in place. "A few visits before she'd been home she'd walked into the living room and found me writing the day's entry. She grabbed my book and ripped out a handful of pages. *'You want to rewrite history with your happy memories. Well, Mom, I'm not happy. You can't just whitewash my life and make it whatever you want. It's messy. I'm a mess. I know that. Why won't you help me?'*

"I am helping you, I told her. *There's a place. They can help you—"*

"But I don't want that kind of help, Mother. I want money, Mom. With a little money I can make it and..."

"Not another cent," I told her.

"Mom."

"I love you, Barbara. But we can't do this any more. You can't waltz in and out of my life only when you need money for your next high."

"Mom."

"'You've broken your father's heart.' She was so angry when she left that time. "After she left I wrote, *Sometimes love means letting go.* I let her go, and while I know it was the only thing I could do, I broke my own heart that day. She'd already broken Albert's. He loved her. Oh, Sadie Mae, that man thought the sun rose and set on that girl. I was never jealous because so did I. That last day on the porch, she started to scream at me and shouted that I'd never loved her. That I'd never believed in her."

"Miss Ida..." I didn't know what to say.

"That was a lie. I did. I hired a private investigator years ago, you know. He said the last record he found of her was in Arizona. She'd been arrested for public intoxication. After that, nothing."

"We could try again."

Miss Ida shook her head. "As much as I'd like to, I don't know I could survive if I found out she was dead, or she was drinking still. Even though I want to know, it's better not to know and have hope."

"You still have hope? After all these years?" I asked   softly.

"Always. I love her. And I think that hope is part of that. Because I love her, I couldn't allow her to throw her life away. I couldn't stop her, but I couldn't support it. Every day, I go back and look at my memories. I remember when she was ten and rescued a robin that had fallen from its nest. She called a vet, who told her that normally the parents come back for it. She waited for hours on the porch, making sure that baby bird wasn't bothered by feral cats. The parents kept feeding the bird. For two days she watched over that fledgling right along with the parents. Finally, it flew into the tree and she knew it was okay."

"She sounds like she has a good heart," I said.

"She did. And somewhere under her addiction, I'm sure she still does. I was so mad that she let alcohol take over, filling up all the spaces that had once been filled with love and friendship, hope and a future. I couldn't help but think, what if she'd never had that first sip of alcohol? I think about all the things she could have been and could have done and I'm so angry."

"I'm sorry, Miss Ida," I said again. And I was. Deeply, profoundly sorry.

She patted my hand. As I looked at her hand on mine, I realized that it looked like one of her teacups...translucent and fragile.

And I was afraid her Barbara wouldn't get better in time to say goodbye.

I was afraid Barbara wouldn't come back and fulfill all the lonely years of Miss Ida hoping.

155

Miss Ida's Book of Memories

Barbara and I finished *The Black Stallion*. She's sat scribbling on a scrap piece of paper as we talked about it. When she got up, she left the paper. I was in awe as I looked at what amounted to a doodle. I could smell the ocean and feel the wild freedom of that horse.

Chapter Eleven

"Hope is..."

We'd had the same nurse coming since Miss Ida had come home. Doran seemed nice enough, but she'd been distant around me. I suspected it was because Miss Ida had told her not to tell me what was wrong.

This visit, Miss Ida gave her permission to talk to me.

The pale blonde nurse radiated competence and compassion in equal measure. Now that she had Miss Ida's permission there was no distance as she patiently explained what was happening to my friend.

Doran said that the aneurism was growing and due to its location and Miss Ida's age there wasn't anything they could do. The aneurism was what was causing Miss Ida's vertigo and her headaches. Doran talked about outcomes when it ruptured.

When, not *if*.

"How long?" I managed to ask.

Doran looked at me with kindness. "Days, weeks, months… We simply don't know."

"What can I do?" I asked, feeling helpless.

I could organize a pantry, or even the Brain's life, but no amount of organizing was going to fix this.

Doran reached out and took my hand. "Be here with her. I talked to her about getting her affairs in order having a DNR—do not resuscitate order—made."

I thought about the envelope Miss Ida had given me and her story about Barbara. That's exactly what she was doing—putting things in order.

"I'm sorry," Doran said.

"Me, too. She is an amazing woman."

"I've worked as a hospice nurse for years. Some people fight against the idea of death. Some meet it with a calm acceptance. And a very few look at it as an

157

adventure. They're not seeking death, but they're not afraid of it. Ida has talked to me about her Albert. I think knowing he's waiting for her makes this easier on her. Easier for her than it will be for you. I think that's probably the greatest truth that I've found about death. It's easier to die and move on to your next great adventure than to be the loved one who's been left behind. Just remember, you won't be alone. If you have more questions or just need to talk, call me. I'm scheduled to come back Wednesday, but if you need me sooner, I'm a phone call away."

She patted my hand before releasing it, but unlike Miss Ida's, her hand was warm and strong. "I'm glad she finally told you. I wasn't permitted to say anything to you without her consent, but you needed to know. I'm afraid I've been a bit of a nag, trying to encourage her to tell you. I can see how much she means to you."

I smiled. Doran was about as fierce as a kitten. "Thanks."

"And just know that you mean as much to her. She's told me all about you. It's not everyone who would be here for a friend like that."

"It's not everyone who would understand a friendship with such a difference in ages."

For a second, Doran seemed far away. "I had a patient once who I just connected with. Mary Ann. I don't know how to explain it other than to say I didn't know her very long, but she made such a huge impact on my life." She patted her stomach. "I'm so hoping the baby is a girl. If so, I'm naming her Mary Ann. If she's half as wonderful as her namesake, I'll be lucky."

"Congratulations," I said. There was something comforting in talking about a birth in the midst of talking about a death. "I wouldn't have guessed you were pregnant."

"Great. That means I just looked fat. Paul—my husband—says I look *radiant*, but I think he's biased."

158

"I think he's right. I hope it's a girl," I said. It was nice to have someone who understood my relationship with Miss Ida. "Thank you."

"I meant what I said, you call me if you need me," Doran said. "Call me whenever you need me."

"I will," I promised.

After she left, I sat for a long time in the plaid chair next to the small table with the lamp and empty glass dome. Beyond that was the flowered chair. I'd seen Miss Ida sitting there since my first visit all those years ago. I knew she was old and I knew she was sick, but still, it was hard to imagine a time when Miss Ida wouldn't sit in the flowered chair.

After she told me about Barbara and gave me the sealed envelope, I'd known that she was preparing for her own death.

But before Doran said the words and told me what was going on medically it hadn't felt real.

Now it was real. Too real.

And suddenly I understood what Miss Ida meant when she talked about Barbara, about the fact not knowing allowed her to hope.

Now that I knew about Miss Ida—though we still had time—I knew there was no hope. There would come a time when Miss Ida wouldn't be here. She wouldn't sit in that chair, or make a perfect pot of tea, or write in her book.

She'd have no more memories.

All that would be left were my memories of her.

And I wasn't sure that would be enough.

As I cried, I realized that selfishly, my tears were more for me than for Miss Ida.

Doran was right. Miss Ida would have Albert at her side again. I'd be here alone.

Not alone. I'd have my parents and the Brain, but I wouldn't have her.

I cried some more.

I didn't want Miss Ida to hear me, so I took a shower and cried until the hot water gave out.

I dressed and rinsed my face in the cold tap water, hoping that the evidence of my tears was obscured.

When I thought I was presentable, I knocked on her door, but she called from the living room, "I'm out front, Sadie Mae.

Miss Ida was sitting in her chair. For now, she was still here. I had to remember that. I had to remember to treasure whatever time we had left.

"Miss Ida—" I started.

She held up a hand to stop me. "Sadie Mae, don't look so sad. Nothing's changed."

"Miss Ida," I tried again, but couldn't find any words. I didn't know how to tell her how much she meant to me.

"I've thought about this," she said. "I mean it, absolutely nothing's changed. I'm here. I'm breathing. I'm smiling. I'm boring you with my stories. That aneurism has been there for a while. It may rupture and I understand the implications when it does, but—and this is a big *but*—but from the moment we're born we start walking down the path to our deaths. I don't want to sound macabre, but it's true. Some people take a long time to get there, some get there sooner. But it's where we all are headed. And none of us knows precisely when or precisely how we'll get there. It looks like we know my *how*, but then again I could walk across the street to Reese's and get hit by a car. Or a bus. Or an airplane could drop out of the sky and land on my house. Or..."

"Miss Ida," I scolded, torn between laughter and sorrow.

"Sadie Mae," she said in the exact same tone.

"Fine. I see your point," I allowed.

"And my point is, you have a life and I don't want you to feel you have to stay here. Neither of us knows when I'll die. You don't need to sit Shiva now."

"I swear, Miss Ida, that's not why I'm here. I think I need to be here. I feel like Barbara's painting. I've started to figure out where I don't belong. I'm hoping through process of elimination I figure out where I do belong. As long as you don't mind me staying."

Miss Ida took my hand. "You are welcome here as long as you like. It's your home."

She was right, it was. More than Detroit had ever been. Now that I was un-engaged, I had no reason to hurry back.

No reason to go back at all.

I could stay here as long as I wanted.

I held onto that idea, letting it grow and blossom.

I could stay.

Miss Ida shot me a look, wondering what I was thinking. I wasn't ready to talk about it, so I simply said, "Thanks. Now how about some tea?"

"That would be lovely."

I took the last two cookies from the cottage cookie jar and set a tea tray while I waited for the water to get warm.

As I set the tray on the small table, Miss Ida put down her pen and flipped through her book. She stopped on a page and smiled.

"This is a particularly good memory. You mentioned my cookie jar the other day. I bought it because it reminded me of my grandmother's house. She lived in a tiny house behind Mom and Dad's farmhouse. I would go over and visit most afternoons and she'd serve me tea from a brown betty like mine, and she'd always have a plate of cookies to offer me. She didn't have a cookie jar. She had a tin that she kept them in. It was probably shiny silver at one time, but that was long before I came along. It was dulled with years, but that was the only dull thing about it. She always had cookies in it. My favorites were the gingersnaps, but I liked them all. I think about her every time I make tea. And when you started coming to visit on Saturdays, you reminded me of myself, visiting her. You were such a balm."

"I've thought about you every time I make tea in my brown betty. I've told the Brain about our Saturday rituals and bought a teapot for his house, too. He laughed the first time I made him real tea, but over the last year or so, he's become a tea snob. He won't order it at restaurants because he finds the teabags they bring out an insult to real tea."

"Our memories seem to intersect over teapots," Miss Ida said with a laugh.

"And cookie jars," I said. "I remembered yours with such fondness that I bought a similar one for myself. I bought a cookie jar for the Brain, too. Only I bought him a Death Star."

Now that I knew she was a closet Star Wars fan, I knew she understood and smiled as she laughed. "He must miss you."

"Maybe. But not the way you think. We're friends and I know he enjoys my company, but I'm not sure he's actively missing me. He's someone who gets lost in his work. He probably doesn't even know that he misses having me around to pull him out of it, but he does."

"So he needs you, too," she said.

"Yes."

"Maybe it's time to stop worrying what I need, or your Brain needs, or before you broke up with him, what Charles needed. Maybe you need to think about what you need? Maybe that will lead you to where you want to be. Maybe it's not about finding your path...but creating one. Forging ahead," she said.

I mulled those words over the rest of the day.

We didn't talk any more about her aneurysm or the fact she could die.

Maybe we were both letting the situation settle in. And as it did, I kept feeling stabs of pain. I'd always known that Miss Ida was mortal, but it was easy to forget. She had such a large spirit.

That night, after I settled Miss Ida in bed, I went out to the porch. Rather than sitting on the bench, I sat down on the lawn and stared north at the darkening sky. I couldn't see the lake from here, but I knew it was just a couple miles north.

They sky was in between daylight and dusk. It felt like every time I blinked, it was a bit darker.

"Miss Dee," Lulu called from her window. "Can I come over for a minute?"

"Sure," I called back, feeling a bit lighter knowing she was going to visit.

She came running out the side door moments later, carrying the book I'd bought her.

"I saw you sitting out here looking for the stars."

That wasn't exactly what I'd been doing, but I could see why my star-crazed neighbor would think that.

"I wrote down, *Miss Dee's looking for the stars, but it's too early. Stars come out after it gets dark. Sometimes it's hard to wait.*"

She looked up and grinned. "I hate waiting. Mom says I don't have any patience. *Patience is a virtue*, she says." She did a good job mimicking her mother. "I don't know what a virtue is, but I guess I don't have it, because I hate to wait. When you're a kid you've got to wait for everything. When I ask my mom why she and dad got a divorce, she says, *Wait until you're older. You'll understand. It wasn't you, it was just that we didn't work.*" She frowned. "I don't get it and I don't think getting older will make me get it. I don't understand why people leave."

Right there. Lulu had summed up my feelings.

I didn't understand why Miss Ida had to leave.

"Lulu," Heidi called from next door.

"I gotta go. You just wait though. The stars will be out soon. And the moon. I don't know why people sleep through the night. There's always so much going on after dark."

I laughed. "I'll keep that in mind next time I can't sleep."

"Lulu," Heidi called again.

"Gotta go." She took her book and scampered back across the lawn between the houses.

It seemed as if Lulu had barely gone inside when I saw Reese crossing the street, but when I looked up the stars had indeed come out and it was quite a bit darker, so time had passed.

"For a quiet neighborhood, it's anything but quiet," I said by way of greeting.

He sat down next to me. "You look pensive tonight."

"It's dark. You couldn't see how I looked from across the street."

He laughed. "Maybe not your expression, but the way you're holding yourself screamed, *pensive.*"

I wanted to tell him about Miss Ida, but I felt that would be breaking her confidence. She would tell people when and if she was ready.

I changed the subject instead. "How was your day?"

"Busy," he said simply.

"What does a day in your life look like?" I asked, realizing I didn't have a clue exactly what he did all day.

"I switched shifts with a friend, so I was on first shift today. I was in a car by myself. I drove through some of the more difficult neighborhoods. I parked by one of the grade schools and pulled over cars going over the fifteen miles an hour speed limit. I went on two domestic calls and..."

He shrugged. "When I list my day like that it sounds odd. I guess today, like most days, I just tried to make a difference where I could. A lot of our job is catching people who've made bad decisions and broken a law, but my favorite part of the day is reaching out to people and encouraging them to make better decisions. Just parking near a school makes drivers slow down. It makes kids behave. I make a difference just by being there." He laughed. "Maybe that's a good life lesson... sometimes just being there is enough."

"I hope it is for Miss Ida, but..." I hesitated. I knew that Miss Ida appreciated me being here, but I knew she was still hoping for Barbara. It had been years since Barbara left. Maybe she was still drinking. Maybe worse than that. But what if she was better and just afraid to come home?

Miss Ida said she lived in hope. What if...

"Reese," I asked as the idea crystalized. "What if I need to find someone? How would I do it?"

"What kind of someone?" he asked.

"Someone who left Erie years ago and might have been in trouble. Someone who might still be in trouble." I didn't say it, but someone who might be dead by now, if she was as bad off as Miss Ida said.

"Its not something I can do at work. We can't just look people up in the system without some just cause," he said.

I shook my head. "No, I didn't mean you. I meant me. Is there someway I can look someone up? I mean, I know I can do a basic Internet search, but if that doesn't work..."

"I have a friend who used to be a cop. He works as an investigator for the DA now. He might be able to help you find this person."

"Would it be expensive?" I asked. I was comfortable. The Brain paid me more than I thought I was worth, but he insisted I was worth every dime. So I had a bit of a nest egg.

"Ned's a good guy. I'm sure you can tell him what you can afford and make sure he doesn't go over it."

I nodded. I wasn't sure if I should go looking for Barbara. It might be opening Pandora's box. And yet, the thought of Miss Ida waiting and hoping broke my heart.

"Thanks," I said. "If you could get me his info, I'll think about calling him."

"Is there anything else I can do?" he asked. Not in a way that made me feel he wanted to solve my problems, but like a friend. He was willing to help if he could.

"You could sit here with me for a while and just watch the stars. I love this time of night. I saw a bat flit by. I know some people hate them. And while I don't think I want one flying into my hair, I enjoy watching them fly around. I like to watch the stars. Lulu was here before you and she told me that I had to wait for it to get dark and then I'd see the stars. I thought it was a nice commentary on life in general."

"It is," was all he said.

As we sat side by side, Reese's hand brushed mine. And I realized that I'd really like to reach out and hold onto it.

I'd just broken up with the man I'd planned to marry and found out one of my best friends could die at any moment, and I was thinking about holding another man's hand.

I wondered what kind of person that made me.

It was quite a bit later that I said, "I should go in and check on Miss Ida."

Reese nodded, then stood up and offered me a hand up. "Thank you," he said.

"For what?" I hadn't done anything.

"For just being here. For letting me sit with you. For taking care of an older woman who needs you. For

166

being kind to little girls who love the stars. I'm glad you came back to Erie, Sadie Mae."

He turned and crossed the street before I could respond. I called out, "Good night," and he waved his hand back at me.

I tiptoed back into the house and opened Miss Ida's door. She was motionless. I told myself she was surely sleeping, but I waited a moment just to be sure she was breathing.

She was.

I went across the hall.

As I sat in Barbara's old room and I looked at the wall that I didn't tend to study. Just as the west wall was Miss Ida's memories in pictures, I was pretty sure these were Barbara's. There were a few pictures I thought might be self-portraits, but most of the pictures were of other things. A playground's rusty swing that appeared to be in motion. There was a bottle of what had to be alcohol under it. A car with steamy windows, and a single hand on the back window. It had a Titanic sort of look, but for some reason felt disquieting. I found a rainbow that wove its way through some pictures. There was a pot of gold at the end, and what looked to be a bottle sitting in it.

My phone pinged. I welcomed a reason to stop studying the pictures.

It was Reese. I'd simply used Reese as his name, but I'd added a picture in my contacts of a cartoon dog with whirly eyes. Mad Dog was my thought every time I saw it.

He sent Ned's number.

Reese: *I want to help with whatever this is, however you need me.*

Thank you.

I glanced at one of the last pictures on Barbara's wall. It was similar to the picture of the paths in the woods next to Miss Ida's front door, only these woods were dark and sinister.

Although these pictures were dark, even the woods were dark, the fact that she'd drawn it and realized there were paths made me feel as if she were asking someone to come find her in the middle of those dark woods.

And right or wrong, I made a decision.

The next morning, I called Ned's friend.

That Friday, I made dinner for Miss Ida, then went into my room—Barbara's room—to get ready for my plus one. Reese said this was a black tie event.

I noticed he didn't tell me that before I agreed to go.

I'd gone to a small local boutique and found the dress. "It's a Carrington Rose original," the woman had said.

I shrugged. "Sorry, I don't know much about designers."

She'd laughed. "That's okay. She's local. Brilliant and oh-so talented, but local."

She'd said the sentence with just the right tone.

I'd grinned. "Let me guess, you're Carrington?"

She'd extended a hand. "Carrie to my friends."

I'd run my hand over the soft, flowing fabric. "It is lovely."

"It looked great on you, though I'll need to take it in some places a bit."

By some places she'd meant my chest did not fill out the ample material. As if she could read my mind, Carrie had added, "I tend to leave that generous because it's easier to take it in than add to it."

She'd been funny and willing to put a rush on the alterations.

I'd picked it up this morning.

I slipped the dress over my head now and zipped it up. It looked as if it was made for me. The color was odd. Sometimes it looked tan, and sometimes there was a decided green undertone. Carrie had assured me that women with peaches and cream complexions like Bette Lee couldn't pull off green, but with my courtesy-of-Big-Henry tea-colored complexion and dark brown hair, I could.

I put my hair in a simple bun, ignoring the pieces that slid out. I was trying to put on makeup when my phone binged.

It was the Brain.

I read his text and FaceTimed him back, rather than trying to text him. I propped the phone.

"Hey," he said as he answered. I saw him do a double take. "What are you doing?"

"Getting ready for a night out. Miss Ida's helper, Julie is coming to sit with her while I go out."

"On a date?" he asked.

"Sort of." I didn't try to explain the plus-one status.

Brian looked perplexed.

"Charles and I broke up," I reminded him. "I'm allowed to date."

"I know, I know, but this was fast."

I didn't feel fast. But when I did the math, I knew that it was. Reese had become a friend and moving from that friendship to a date... Maybe it should have felt scary, but it didn't.

I slipped an earring in place. "I FaceTimed because it seemed more efficient than texting. The paper I sent said..." I answered his questions about what I hadn't understood in the new section he'd sent me. "If I don't get it, then college students won't either."

He sighed. "You're right. If you were in my class, I'd give you an A."

I knew from experience that was high praise. "Thanks. Maybe someday I'll I'll take you up on it."

He laughed. "Please don't. You'd go all bossy and ask a million questions. I'd never get the material covered."

I laughed. "I know you're right."

169

He gave me an odd look again. "Have fun on the date. I'm going to come visit your Miss Ida and this Reese someday soon. I want to check him out."

"Bless your heart if you think you have a say."

He recognized me imitating my mother and said, "Good night, Bette Lee."

"Night, *Brain*." I put a heavy emphasis on his nickname and he sighed as he disconnected.

Someday I was going to convince his sister to fill me in on that story.

The doorbell rang. I slipped on my shoes and I hurried out to get it. It was Julie.

"You look great," she said as she came in. She walked over to Miss Ida and hugged her.

"Thanks," I said, nervously straightening the dress.

"You do," Miss Ida echoed from the chair.

Julie sat opposite her. Before I could say anything, I spotted Reese walking across the street in a tux.

He looked like he was made for wearing tuxes. It was classic black and fit to a tee.

"Wow," he said as I opened the door.

"Wow yourself," I replied.

He stepped inside. "Hi, Julie. Now, don't you worry, Miss Ida. I'll have her home at a reasonable hour."

Miss Ida laughed. "See that you do, young man. And see to it you behave like a gentleman. When you meet her father, you'll be very glad you did. Big Henry is...well, big."

"Should I be nervous?" Reese asked.

"Big Henry's as intimidating as a teddy bear," I said.

Miss Ida scoffed.

"Thanks for the heads up," Reese said. He kissed her cheek. "We won't be late, but really, don't hesitate to call if you need something."

"I won't."

I wasn't sure if Miss Ida was saying she wouldn't need anything, or she would holler, but Julie caught my eye and nodded, so I knew that the young girl wouldn't hesitate to call.

Reese took my arm as we crossed the street and got into his car.

The drive to the Art Museum was a quick one—most everything in Erie is a quick drive compared to other cities—which was good because we were silent. Not in a companionable-friends-can-be-quiet sort of way, but in an awkward-first-date sort of way.

We parked on Perry Square and walked to the museum.

"They have a new addition," he said. "It was a few years back. You're going to love it."

And I did.

Party guests had spilled into the outside courtyard, with its mix of greenery, walkways and brick walls that butted against the wall of glass and the new entry.

The space tied beautifully into the older sections. We had a drink and Reese wove among the guests. It felt like half of Erie was in attendance. He introduced me to each new person, but after a while, the names and faces all blurred together.

Finally we came up to an older lady with a ready smile. "Dee, this is my favorite partner ever and our next mayor, Harry. Harriet, my good friend, Dee. We went to school together and she's recently moved home." He casually threw an arm over my shoulder, as if to indicate I wasn't just a good friend. I saw that Harry recognized it. Her eyebrows rose ever so slightly.

"Maddox, you have good taste in women." Her voice was husky and deep. It was a voice that held authority and self-confidence.

I grinned. "He let's you call him Maddox?"

She laughed. "No one ever *let* me do anything. I just call things as I see them and—"

"And that's why she's going to make such a great mayor," Reese quickly filled in.

We both ignored him. "What did you call him back in high school?" she asked.

"We barely knew each other back then," Reese quickly filled in.

"I suspect since this is your party, you should mingle, but maybe some day soon we should have dinner and compare stories," I said with a laugh.

"I think I'd like that," Harry said. Someone called her name and she smiled. "It was really nice meeting you, Dee. Thank you for coming."

Party guests had access to the exhibits, though most guests were simply mingling in the courtyard and entry area of the museum.

"Don't you have any one else you have to see?" I asked as Reese steered me into a gallery.

"You're the only one I want to see."

"I thought this was just a plus-one?" I teased.

"You and I both know it wasn't ever that." He took my hand as we walked through the gallery. I pointed to a painting. It was primary colors...colors you would see in a basic eight pack of Crayolas. It reminded me of school.

As I looked at the abstract shapes, I was pretty sure I could see an apple. A desk. The lined paper the teacher used to hand out for writing class.

"I like this one," I said.

Reese shook his head. "I don't understand it. If someone's going to paint something, I want to know what it is, not have to guess."

"I like that sort of art, too. But I like paintings like this. It gives the observer an opportunity to become a creator as well."

Reese cocked his head and wrinkled his brow, as if to say I was nuts.

"No, think about it. I'm not an artist, but I have to imagine that it's like when the Brain writes a book. He has a message he wants to share with the reader. Sometimes he has a hard time making the science accessible, and that's where I come in. I see what he wrote. I ask him to explain the science to me, and then I go back and try to clarify his vision."

"So the two of you write the book?" Reese asked.

"No. I don't write. I just clarify. When a writer's working on a book, it belongs entirely to them. They have something to say and a vision to present and the manuscript is their medium. Then they turn it over and the book's written, rewritten, edited and packaged. I'm just a small part of that process."

"And then?" Reese asked.

"It's sent out in the world. Once they're finished, the author loses all say in it. That book becomes the readers'. Each new reader comes into it and takes what they need to out of it. Maybe they're reading it for a class...they take what they need for that teacher or that upcoming test. Or maybe they're reading for fun. Maybe they're reading to learn something new, or experience something new, or approach the world from a new point-of-view. Every reader's perspective and experience in that book is unique to them. Sometimes what the reader takes from the book is very different than what the author intended."

"You've given this some thought," he said.

I laughed. "I had an English teacher who taught the classics. She'd make statements about what the author intended. *He wanted you to feel... She wanted you to see...* And I'd always argue that my teacher had no clue what the author intended reader take from a book, she could only know what she *took* from it."

I stared at the painting. "I think it's like that with art. The artist has a vision when they start a

173

project. They have something they want the world to see. They work to take something internal and make it external—put it on canvas, or whatever medium they're working with. Once they're done, once that painting or picture or sculpture—whatever it is—goes out in the world like this, it no longer belongs to the artist, it belongs to the observer."

Reese just looked at me and looked at me as if he was studying a painting. I reached up and turned his face toward the painting.

"When I see this painting, I see the first day of school. I see an apple, a desk, a piece of paper...but more than that, I'm taken back to elementary school. I remember that feeling of walking into a classroom."

He stared at the painting another moment, then turned back to me. I knew he was going to kiss me before he leaned my way. And I knew that I was not only going to let him, I was going to kiss him back.

So I leaned forward and closed the gap between us.

I realized that maybe life imitated art. Like an unread book or an unstudied work of art, each person we meet would somehow impact our lives. Sometimes in a very cursory way, but sometimes in a profound way.

There in Reese's arms, surrounded by beauty, I knew he was becoming important to me.

I thought of Barbara's painting.

And wondered where this path would take me.

Miss Ida's Book of Memories

There was an article about "Elder Orphans" in the paper today. I looked at Sadie Mae and knew that I would never be that. But my heart broke when I thought of all those who don't have a Sadie Mae in their life.

When she started to read that section, I said, "Thank you."

"For what?" she asked.

"For being here with me."

"Miss Ida, I wouldn't want to be anywhere else. It's what family does."

She reached across the table between our chairs and took my hand.

I wanted to tell her that it wasn't what every family did. I wanted to tell her how very special she was. I wanted to tell her that I loved her not only because she was *her*, but because she truly didn't see anything special in the fact she was *her*.

And the fact she doesn't realize how special she is, only makes her more special.

I finally said all that with just three words, "I love you."

She smiled. "Love you, too."

I hope someday she reads my entire book and realizes just how special she is.

Chapter Twelve

"There was an article in the paper today about Elder Orphans...older people who have no one left to care for them. Miss Ida read it said thank you. I wanted to promise her that she'd never be alone. That she'd never have to worry. She said, "I love you." I said, "Love you, too." I thought that summed up all the things I wanted to say and so much more."

After Doran came the following Wednesday morning, I drove Miss Ida downtown to an attorney's office. I was in the waiting room when the Brain's editor called.

Amy and I had talked a few times. She sounded excited as she explained that they'd signed a new author. "He's Brian-esque and could use a bit..." She hesitated.

"Of common people?" I supplied.

She laughed. "Yes. I've read Brian's manuscripts before and after you worked on them. I think you could be just what we need."

We discussed terms. She suggested I get an agent or literary attorney and said she'd send me a sample of the book and a contract.

I was sitting in the afterglow of the call when my phone pinged, announcing I had a text message.

It was from Ned. He'd found Barbara and sent me her phone number and address.

I stared at it.

I hadn't expected to hear anything this soon. I wasn't sure if I'd hear anything at all.

Barbara Hall lived in Dallas, Pennsylvania. I'd never heard of it, but Pennsylvania was a big state. I Googled it and found it was less than six hours from here.

I could leave right now and be there before dinner.

I could go tell Barbara Miss Ida was sick and needed her.

Thoughts of losing Miss Ida mingled with pictures on Barbara's wall.

I knew I needed to see Miss Ida's daughter for myself before I told her I'd found her. That meant I needed to go to Dallas, Pennsylvania.

I was coming up with plans when Miss Ida came out with a large manila envelope. She was quiet the rest of the day, which suited me because I was still trying to decide how to do what I needed to do.

After dinner, Miss Ida asked me to sit in the plaid chair next to her floral one. She took the envelope from the end table and handed it to me. "Inside is my will and copies of all my important papers, including that DNR Doran talked about. When it's my time, I hope there's not a question of doing anything. I hope I'm just gone. But if there is, don't. I'm ready."

"I'll take care of everything," I promised. It was the hardest promise I'd ever had to make. "When it's time, I'll make sure they let you go."

"And there's this." She handed me a smaller envelope addressed simply to Barbara. "I put that letter for Barbara in the envelope, too. If she comes after I'm gone, I want her to know that I love her and that didn't change."

"I will see to it that she gets it."

"I want you to take my book when I'm gone. Read it before then, for that matter. I don't think anyone else would want it, but I know you'll understand that it's not just a book of memories, it's the essence of me. I hope you'll occasionally open it up, read a memory and think of me."

"Miss Ida, of all the things you might ask me to promise, that one goes without saying. I will always remember you and think of you. Every night, when I write in my own book, I think of you. And no matter what's happened to Barbara, I know she's thought of you, too. Every night I've been here, I've gone to sleep next to a mural of your memories that she painted."

"Sadie Mae, I've lived a long and happy life. That's not to say I haven't known heartache, but this book is proof that I've known great happiness. And most of the happiest moments I've saved here, weren't big moments. They were small ones. Albert bringing me flowers. A sunset on the beach. Barbara throwing her arms around me and saying she loved me forever and back again. And you. You're a big part of those happy memories." There was a hitch in her voice as she said the words.

"I'll try to honor all your wishes," I promised, though the words felt as if they were cutting me.

She patted my hand. "I knew you would, dear. You've been such a friend to me."

Her hand rested on top of mine and I realized how cold it was. Miss Ida had always felt larger than life...as if she burned more brightly than other people. But that fire was ebbing.

Softly—so softly it took me a second to realize she was speaking—she said, "I've come to think my father might have been wrong. He said we could choose to save only the good memories, and there was a truth to that, but not the whole truth. Some of the bad memories are so profound they remold us into something new. After I lost Albert and then Barbara left, I changed. For a time, I went through the motion of finding a good memory. You'll know those days when you read them. Hot oatmeal was one. I think you really have to be grasping at happiness straws to write *hot oatmeal*. But then one day, I heard a bird singing in the tree outside my window and before I knew it, I wrote it down. And the next day..."

She paused and shook her head. "All those good memories couldn't obliterate my losses, but they eased them. And I adjusted to my new dimensions. Eventually, I found a way to live with them. And every day since, I've tried to find something happier than hot oatmeal to write about. But if Barbara ever comes, I hope you'll tell her I loved her. Sending her away was the hardest thing I've ever done. I've missed her every day and I've prayed that she's built a new life for herself and that it was a good one. And if she did, I understand why she didn't come back, but...well, tell her that and that I never stopped loving her. Not for one minute of one day."

I knew my decision to find Barbara was the right one.

I prayed it had a happy ending.

After Miss Ida went to bed, I went outside to the front lawn. Moments later, Reese was walking across the street.

"Fancy meeting you out here," I said.

"I hope it's all right."

"I like our evening meetings," I confessed. More than liked them, they were becoming a part of my day that I looked forward to.

"What's wrong?" he asked as he sat down next to me. "Is it Miss Ida?"

I didn't answer because I hadn't exactly sorted everything out, so instead I said, "Tell me about your day?"

He gave me a searching look, then nodded. "I had one of those moments that makes me glad I'm a cop.

I got a call right after lunch. We had a missing special-needs child at the bayfront. I went down along with every other cop who could. I looked around for someplace a five-year-old might hide and noticed that the dinner cruise boat was docked. She was on the top deck. I called in that I found her. April was watching the seagulls. She said she'd brought some bread to feed them and wanted to get close to the sky for them. She reminded me of Lulu and the stars."

I nodded. I could see that.

"I took her to her mother and I don't think I've ever seen someone so angry, relieved and happy all at once. And I'm pretty sure that she's going to be grounded and coddled in turn for a few days." He smiled. "It was a pretty good day. We witness so much crap, but there are moments like this, when a call gets a happy ending. It makes up for the others."

I reached out and took his hand. "I think saving a child makes for a very good day indeed."

"I remember when I came on the job and everything was bright and shiny. I had a feeling that I could save the world. And then one day I realized I couldn't. But on days like today I remember that feeling and realize that I might not be able to save the whole world, but today, I saved this one little girl. And that's enough."

Maybe that's how I had to look at being home with Miss Ida. No, I couldn't save her, but I could make these happy, special days.

Tomorrow, I'd do something special with Miss Ida. Something to make her smile. And that would be enough.

"Thank you," I said.

"For what?"

"For being here. For saving one little girl. For..." For being you, was my thought. I was thankful that Reese was simply here and simply himself.

And that too was enough.

I knew I couldn't leave Miss Ida while I did what needed to be done, so I called reinforcements.

The next day, I did what I did best—I started planning and organizing.

I called Bette Lee. Julie was a fine caretaker if I had errands or needed an evening out, but if I was going to be gone for days, Miss Ida needed more care.

Bette Lee agreed, just as I knew she would. She talked about the trip they'd been planning and they'd already decided to visit Erie, but I knew that she was coming because I asked.

I realized that I was truly blessed, because not only did I have people in my life who would throw everything aside to help me, but I *knew* I had people in my life who would throw everything aside to help me.

There was a difference.

I found a hotel and booked a room for two nights.

I went shopping and filled the refrigerator and the pantry.

And I made tea for us in the afternoon.

"Are you going to tell me?" Miss Ida asked conversationally as she took a sip of her tea.

"Tell you what?"

"What has you all aflutter?"

"My parents are coming to visit," I said.

"Yes, but that's not it." When I didn't say anything, she said, "Albert always said I didn't need to say the words for him to hear my worries. Did I ever tell you that he knew I was pregnant before I did?"

I shook my head.

"We'd long since given up on children. Albert always said that when two people were so in love, maybe there wasn't enough room for someone else. He told me I was more than enough. And he was more than enough for me, but that didn't stop me from hoping. I was late, only a few days and he came home with flowers. Daisies and baby's breath. And I knew that he knew. I remembered hugging him and thinking that my life was perfect. Still I worried. I was an older mom. One nurse called me geriatric. I know that's an accurate description now, but at the time I was so offended. I worried my way through my pregnancy. Albert kept trying to calm me down and tell me no matter what we'd be fine. I wish I'd listened and realized that all the worry in the world won't change anything. I still wrote in my Book and still found happy moments each day, but if I hadn't worried, I might have had more to choose from."

"So what you're telling me is don't worry?"

"Worry never changes anything. If worry could change anything..." She let the sentence fade. I knew she was thinking that if worry could change anything, then Barbara would be here.

Softly she added, "You have make the best decisions you can and then accept whatever happens."

I reached out and took her hand in mine.

I spent the rest of the day trying not to worry. I'd set things up for Miss Ida while I was gone, and any worry wouldn't change what I'd find when I found Barbara. I'd just have to do my best and live with the consequences.

After Miss Ida went to bed, I went out and sat on the grass. A bat was circling overhead. I could see the dark shadow fluttering above me, presumably hunting for insects.

I'd seen them at zoos and they were actually kind of cute up close in person. I'd read a story years ago by my favorite children's author, Pip. She talked about a bat who longed for the stars. The rest of his family simply flew around each night, hunting insects. But he—Ephraim—was different. He noticed the stars and wanted nothing more than to go see them. He forgot to eat and simply sat in the grass every night to look longingly at the stars.

It might be a bit below Lulu's reading level, but I made a mental note to pick up a copy for her.

I flopped down, my back cooled by the evening grass and continued looking up. I could see hundreds of stars, but I knew if I left the city and went out to the country I'd see more. Many more.

I thought of Barbara. Did she ever stare at the stars?

The murals in her room and the painting by the door seemed to point to the kind of person who would.

Did she ever stop drinking? If so, why hadn't she come home?

What would I find?

I tried to shut down my worrying but was saved from my own thoughts when someone said, "A penny for your thoughts."

I didn't need to tear my eyes away from the night sky to know who was standing next to me. "They're not worth a penny."

Reese sank down on the ground next to me. "Please tell me."

And I realized that maybe I couldn't stop worrying on my own, but maybe if I shared what I could with Reese it might not be so bad. I trusted his judgment.

"Your friend, Ned, found..." I didn't know how to explain Barbara.

"The person you were looking for?" Reese supplied.

I nodded. "And I'm going to find her, but I'm not sure of the outcome. I know what I hope for. And I know that there's a chance I've read too many fairytales and I'm being unrealistic. Because there's probably a better chance it won't have a fairytale ending."

That's the worry that haunted me. What if I was starting something that hurt Miss Ida? How could I take the chance? But she was waiting in hope...and she was dying. How could I not at least try?

"I'm not sure exactly what we're talking about...who we're talking about," Reese said.

"I'm not sure it's my place to tell this story," I said.

Sharing with Reese didn't feel like gossiping, even if it wasn't my story to tell.

"Then here's my opinion in generic terms, not that you asked. But my mother would tell you that never stops me."

I laughed. "I think I remember seeing her at school a couple times. She seemed nice."

"She is. I'll introduce you next time she comes to town. But about your problem. You're afraid of the unknown. You're afraid to take a chance and lose."

"If it were just me..." I stopped myself. "No, that's a lie. You're right, I am afraid of the unknown. I like things organized and quantified. I can organize someone's life or pantry, but things like this...just taking a leap of faith? Yeah, I'm no good at that."

"I'm not sure anyone is," Reese said. "But sometimes you have to be brave."

"So what you're saying is buck up?" I asked with a smile as I used my father's phrase.

He laughed. "Yes."

"You sound like a cross between Big Henry and the Brain," I grumbled.

Reese grinned. "I'll take that as a compliment."

"I'd already decided to do it, but I'm fretting. Mom and Dad will be here tomorrow. They're going to stay with Miss Ida while I go on my little adventure." I hoped beyond hope I was making the right decision.

"You're going by yourself to find whoever Ned found for you?" Reese asked.

"It's only a six hour drive," I said.

"Do you know the person in question?" he asked.

"You sound like a cop with all the questions." I was teasing, but not really. All of a sudden, I saw him as

184

a cop, not just a friendly neighbor. I was pretty sure he was good at it. He had a calm, caring but firm sort of aura.

"I am a cop," he said simply, echoing my thoughts.

"No, I don't know the person," I admitted. "But I don't expect trouble."

"No one ever does," he said with a sigh. "When are you going?"

"Friday, if Mom and Dad get here tomorrow and I'll take off the next morning."

"Fine. I'm off Friday and Saturday this week, and I have some comp time to burn so I can be there on Sunday, too. I'll talk to my Lieutenant, but I can make it work."

He'd lost me. "Pardon?" I asked.

"I'm inviting myself along on the trip," he stated.

I couldn't decide if I was insulted that he thought I couldn't handle this on my own, or touched that he wanted to help. "Reese, I'm a big girl. I can handle a six hour drive."

"I'm sure you could, but this...this isn't just looking up some old high school crush. I can see how torn you are about whatever it is. And I know you've been sticking close to Miss Ida for a reason. If you're leaving her, even for the weekend, then it's important. No one should have to be alone for that. If you let me come along, I promise I'll stay at the hotel or a coffee shop while you meet whoever you were looking for."

"That's it? No questions asked?"

"Dee, I'd be lying if I said I don't have questions, but I..." He shrugged. "You'll tell me what you can when you're ready."

We sat for a long time and simply looked up at the night sky. And I realized at some point that Reese had put his arm around me.

Shortly thereafter, I realized how much I enjoyed the sensation.

I finally said, "I should go inside."

He stood and I immediately missed the feel of his arm on my shoulder, but then he offered me a hand up. I took his hand in mine and felt comforted again.

We stood, hand in hand for a long moment, and then finally he leaned down and kissed my forehead.

"Good night," I said.

"Good night. I'll talk to you tomorrow after I've made all the arrangements," he said.

I was nervous about finding Barbara, but suddenly I felt better. Reese hadn't forced me to answer questions I couldn't answer. I wasn't sure how to explain what I was about to do. If I messed this up, I could be hurting someone I loved.

I ran through all the possible scenarios.

I found Barbara and she was still drinking or taking drugs.

I found Barbara and she'd died.

I found Barbara and she was better, or trying to get better.

I knew I wanted a fairytale ending, and I knew that this was the real world and not a fairytale. I didn't want to do something that made matters worse for Miss Ida.

But the reason that happily-ever-after was such a common ending to stories is that sometimes that was how a story ended.

Happily.

Miss Ida spoke of hope.

I *hoped* I'd made the right decision.

I *hoped* for a happily-ever-after.

I hoped.

Miss Ida was right. Those were powerful words.

The sun had barely risen when I woke from my precarious sleep to a sound.

A deep thud.

I sat upright in bed and tried to figure out what the noise was.

"Miss Ida?" I called as my sleep-deprived mind cleared enough to come to a conclusion. I sprang out of bed and hurried to her room.

"Miss Ida?" I called again as I silently prayed, *Please let her be okay. Not yet. Please let her be okay. Don't take her yet. Please—*

She was sitting on her floor next to the bed.

"What happened?" I offered her a hand, but she shook her head and patted the floor next to her.

I sat down. "Are you okay?"

"In my dreams, I am not an old dizzy lady. I'm the young girl who was crying on her father's shoulder on the swing. I'm that young girl who met Albert in the theater. I'm a young mother, springing out of bed because the baby was crying in the next room. When I wake up, for a few moments, I forget I'm old and dizzy and a burden on my friends."

I shook my head and put my arm over her shoulder. "Never that."

"When I try to bound out of bed, that's when I remember again I'm old. The realization hits me with a thud. Literally sometimes."

She laughed. There was no bitterness. No joy. It was a laugh that said all you can do is accept what life has handed you.

"Maybe I shouldn't go away this weekend," I said.

"Sadie Mae, you are the young girl I dreamed I was. Go have an adventure. You've given me wonderful babysitters—and I know that's exactly what they are. Otherwise, you'd be staying to visit with your parents. Still you know Bette Lee won't let me get away with anything."

I got to my feet and helped her up slowly, as gently as I could. "Miss Ida, maybe when you wake up your body reminds you that its tired, but when I look I see..."

"What do you see?" she prompted.

"I see that young girl when I look at you. She's still there living in a world of hope and possibility." That's the truth. I could see Barbara's paintings of a younger Miss Ida. When I looked at my friend, that's who I saw.

Maybe some people would think a friendship between someone in their eighties and someone in their twenties was odd, but I was coming to believe that no matter how our bodies fail us, or how wise we become as we age, somewhere inside our younger selves are still there.

Miss Ida would always be her father's daughter, Albert's wife and Barbara's mother. And in that light, our friendship made perfect sense.

"That younger version of me does live in hope. Because she's reminded every time she sees you that hope and possibility..." She stopped and simply patted my cheek. "I love you, Sadie Mae."

"I love you too, Miss Ida," I said simply.

I realized a long time ago that blood didn't make family.

Miss Ida was family.

The Brain was family.

And though I didn't want to leave her, I knew I would because Miss Ida had given me many gifts—my Book of Memories and hope and her friendship.

I'd find Barbara if I could. I would hope that it would turn out for the best.

I thought about the picture by the door as the coffee perked. I went out to the living room and studied it by the glow of the lamp.

There in the faint light, I could see a thin line, barely there in the upper right hand corner. I was sure it was a path. It would be full of brambles and obstacles on it, but I hoped somewhere down that unexpected path, I'd find Barbara.

And I'd bring her home.

Miss Ida's Book of Memories

My memory today isn't something that happened to me, it's something I dreamed. I was in the kitchen making tea in my brown betty. I reached for the cookie jar and put chocolate chip cookies on a plate. They felt hot in my hand, as if they'd just come out of the oven, not the cookie jar. I guess that's how things work in dreams. I put them on the tray next to a box of paints. I was happy because Barbara was going to love them. I'd found a paintbrush that was small and fine. I remember repositioning it on the paints. I wanted it to be just right.

Barbara came in and squealed as she looked at the tray, just as I knew she would. I asked her why she painted so small and she told me, "I paint so small because my feelings are so big. Love you."

And then she ate a cookie and drank tea. I did too.

In my dream, I was as happy as I've ever been.

Chapter Thirteen

"Life is full of certainties.
The sun rises every morning and sets every
evening.
Autumn follows summer.
And my mother would always be my
mother.
The certainties are easy for me to deal with
because
they suit my need for order.
It's the uncertainties that I have a tough
time with."

"Miss Ida, Bette Lee and Big Henry will be here soon," I reminded her.

She smiled. "I haven't seen them in so long." She got that faraway look that told me she was remembering.

"They're bringing the RV. Do you mind if they park it in the drive?"

She laughed. "They can park it in the yard for all I care. I'm just happy that if you're going to call in babysitters, you called in such nice ones."

"Miss Ida—" I said ready to protest, but I knew she knew. "It's only for a couple days. Reese and I are going away for the weekend."

When he offered to come along, I hadn't realized how nicely he'd given me a cover story.

Miss Ida looked concerned. "Isn't it too soon? You know I like Reese. But you just broke up with Charles."

"I know and I agree. We're getting separate rooms. But truth be told, he suits me. He doesn't think a weekend spent crawling through antique stores and eating at mom-and-pop diners is a waste of time. He listens to me and talks to me not at me. I'm comfortable with him."

And as I said the words to Miss Ida, I realized how true they were.

"That's how I felt about Albert. We never did anything daring or even overly exciting. We didn't travel the world, or even travel far from home. But we were together. And that made all the difference. Finding someone who can make planting a garden exciting is a rare find. He suited me as well."

She closed her eyes and leaned back in her flowered chair. I wasn't sure if she was dozing, or simply dipping back in her memories again and remembering those simple times with Albert.

I cleaned the house, though it didn't need much. Miss Ida and I were both neat by nature. But I scrubbed all the floors and the smell of Murphy's Oil Soap reminded me of that first day with Miss Ida.

Bette Lee and Big Henry arrived in the late afternoon. They parked their RV in the driveway and I smiled as I walked across the lawn.

"Sadie Mae, you are as pretty as a picture and a sight for these old eyes," my mother called as she got out of the RV. She looked as fresh as a daisy even after driving for twelve plus hours.

"Bette Lee, you will never be old."

She kissed my cheek and her subtle, flowery perfume wafted. "That was the perfect thing to say, darlin'. Your mama must have raised you right."

Her accent had become more pronounced since she moved down south.

Big Henry walked around the front of the RV and wrapped me in a fierce hug. "Your mama says you finally dumped Charles."

"I don't think I dumped him. I think we mutually agreed we weren't meant for each other. Afterward, I made him lunch, so it was pretty painless for both of us."

"Even if it wasn't a match made in heaven, letting go of someone is hard," Big Henry said. "I'm proud of you."

I was an adult and had managed my own life for years, but it still felt good to have my father say that.

He added, "And I'm proud that you're here helping Miss Ida." He kissed my cheek and released me from his embrace.

"Thanks, Dad."

He looked at me and grinned. I rarely called my mother or father Mom and Dad.

"So let's go see Miss Ida," Bette Lee said.

Neither asked about her health. They just chatted about their upcoming trip through North East's wine country on their way to the Finger Lakes in New York. "Big Henry lives in fear," Bette Lee trilled. "I built a wine cellar."

"You built?" I teased. I thought I had a good imagination, but for the life of me I couldn't picture Bette Lee with a hammer in her hand.

"I hired the man who built it," Bette Lee said. "And now that the wine cellar's built, we're going to travel through Pennsylvania and New York, stocking it. It'll give Big Henry a taste of home."

"I don't drink wine," he said.

"Now, darlin', you know that since we built the wine cellar you're going to learn to drink wine and like it."

I smiled because I knew that before I visited next, Big Henry would learn to be a wine aficionado. Like it or not.

"So how's our girl treatin' you, darlin'?" Bette Lee asked Miss Ida.

"She's whipping the house into shape and doting on me. Why she's been cooking."

"Uh oh," Bette Lee said.

"Hey," I protested.

Miss Ida grinned. "Well, there might have been a small incident with burnt toast that led to one neighbor yelling at us, and another neighbor coming over to check on us."

"At least I haven't overstated my abilities and tried paffles," I said.

Miss Ida smiled as Bette Lee asked, "Which neighbor did the checkin'?"   "Reese," Miss Ida said. "The boy she's going away this weekend with."

"Separate rooms," I piped in. I could feel my face warming.

"Do tell," Big Henry said to Miss Ida. "What do you think of him?"

"He is truly the best neighbor. After he moved in, he took over mowing my lawn and snowblowing for me in the winter. Although, I was a bit annoyed with him when he tattled because I fell."

Bette Lee smiled. "Maybe you should look at it that his tattling brought our Sadie Mae here to stay for a while. And from what I've heard, getting away from Detroit made her consider what she was doing with Charles. So in essence, Reese saved our Sadie Mae from marrying the wrong man and now she's spending a weekend with him."

"Separate rooms," I said again, though no one was really listening to me.

Miss Ida sighed and looked at Bette Lee. "Now, you've taken all the wind out of my sails."

The three of them continued chatting as if I wasn't there. I finally left them to it and went to make dinner. I might not be the world's best cook, but I could make a shepherd's pie.

After dinner, Miss Ida was done in. I helped her get ready for bed and once she was tucked in, I said, "I'm leaving early tomorrow, but you know you can count on Bette Lee and Big Henry."

"I know dear. You worry too much. I would have been fine on my own. I still feel guilty you've put your life on hold to take care of me."

"Miss Ida, I love you," I said. Maybe loving Charles hadn't been simple. I did love him, but not the way a wife needed to love a husband. But Miss Ida? I'd loved her since that first day. It was just that simple and easy.

"And being here is coming home. I'm so thankful. I feel like I'm exactly where I need to be right now. And Miss Ida, between you and me, I haven't felt that way in a very, very long time."

I kissed her cheek. "I'll be home Saturday or Sunday."

"I'll be fine. I suspect Bette Lee will be a tough babysitter."

I suspected she was right. I went to the door and she called, "Sadie Mae?"

I stopped and turned back. "Yes?"

"I love you, too."

"Goodnight."

I went out to the living room and found just my father.

Big Henry said, "Bette Lee went out to the RV already. She wants to get to bed early. She'll come here when you leave. But I waited to say goodnight. You know, your mother had problems getting pregnant and when we finally managed, I hoped for a boy. A little Henry. But the moment I saw you, I fell in love. And every day, I've been so thankful that you are my daughter."

"What brought that on?" I asked. This was not Big Henry's usual buck-up speech.

"I'm so proud of you, that's all. I don't know if I say it enough."

I hugged my father. "I love you, Big Henry."

I walked outside with him and Bette Lee stepped out of the RV. "I'm so glad you came to take care of Miss Ida."

"A very wise woman once told me that that's what we do...look after our neighbors. But Miss Ida's more than that now. It wasn't a hard decision to make. I appreciate you coming all this way to help me out. I just don't want to leave her alone."

"I understand that. Just looking at her, I can see she's slipping. Where are you and your new friend going?"

"We're going to look up an old friend." I couldn't lie to Bette Lee, but I wasn't willing to tell her too much. I thought that was enough.

"I thought you might head to Detroit."

It was the first time I really thought about going back to Detroit and realized there was nothing there for me now. I'd have to decide what to do with my house. And just like that I realized that I wasn't going back to Detroit. No matter what happened, it wasn't home.

It had never been home.

"I'll still have to go up from time to time to check in on the Brain. I can handle most things via text, but I suspect that an occasional visit will be warranted. But I'm staying in Erie for now."

I said the words and realized that for all my angsting about so many things, this was an easy decision. I was home and I was staying.

Bette Lee didn't ask about the house or anything else. She simply nodded.
"Well, have a good time, but not too good a time."

I smiled. "Reese is just a friend. Separate rooms, remember?"

She smiled in such a way that said she wasn't buying it.

I simply said, "Thanks again for coming. I knew you would. I don't think every daughter can say that, but I did know you'd throw everything aside to be here for me."

She continued to chuckle. "It will be nice to stay in town for a few days. I want to meet Heidi and Lulu."

"You'll love them, Mom. I like knowing their living in our home."

"Silly girl," she said and mussed my hair. "They're not living in our home. They're living in our old house. Our home is us. Wherever we are. Your home was in Detroit, but it's in Erie again. Ours is in Virginia. That means you have a home there, too and we have a home here again with you. Home is the people you love."

I'd just thought that Detroit wasn't home. And I realized that though I'd felt a sense of nostalgia visiting Heidi and Lulu's house, I hadn't felt like it was home. Miss Ida's felt like home. My mom was right, it was Miss Ida herself, not the house.

I nodded. "You're right. I haven't spared hardly a thought for my house. I'm home here. Thanks, Bette Lee."

"Darlin', I'm always here for you." She went back into the RV. I could see the lights glowing through the curtains. It was nice knowing my parents were right there in the drive.

Rather than go inside, I sat down in the middle of the front lawn.

The moon was full, but partially covered by a cloud, but it was enough to brighten the night sky. Other clouds partially hid the stars from view.

There were lights in the RV, in Miss Ida's, in Mr. Gerry's.

I looked at Reese's and there was a light in the front window there as well. And as if my thinking about him was enough to call him, I saw him walking across the street.

He sat down next to me.

"Big Henry and Bette Lee made it so I'm free to go," I said, then added, "You're sure you want to come? I'm perfectly able—"

He cut me off. "I'm sure. I'd hope to come over earlier to meet them, but I got tied up at work."

"You can meet them when we come home."

He nodded, then asked, "Why do you sit on the lawn when there's a perfectly good bench on the porch behind you?"

I thought a moment about how to answer so I didn't sound nuts. "When you were little, did you ever spin in circles, then fall on the ground? It felt like you were still spinning and you couldn't quite get your sense of balance so you had to lay there and wait to find it again so you could stand without falling?"

I could see him nod in the faint glow of the moonlight.

"When I went to school, I remember learning about gravity in science class. The teacher told us that the earth spun like that all the time and that's why there was gravity. She told us that we'd been spinning every moment since we were born, even if we didn't know it. So, I sit on the ground to remind myself that I'm always spinning, even when I don't realize it. I've been spinning my whole life and I can handle it. If I take a minute and catch my breath, I can stand without falling."

Reese leaned over and kissed me.

It was a quick peck. Nothing that romance heroines would rhapsodize about. It was a soft introduction, making me wonder what would happen if I leaned closer and deepened the kiss.

I didn't.

I pulled back and said, "Reese, I'm not ready yet. I don't want you to think this weekend is—"

"I don't."

"Separate bedrooms," I said, not sure if I was reminding him or myself.

He cut me off again. "I don't think that this weekend is about us. It's something else entirely. And I promise to be on my best behavior. Separate rooms and everything. But tonight's not this weekend. And I'd very much like to kiss you again."

"I'm just...not yet. I'm not ready. I just broke up with a fiancé half a minute ago."

He nodded. "I get it. Any idea when you will be ready?"

Thinking about Charles, I realized just how *not* affected I was by our breakup. But maybe I just didn't realize how deeply I was hurting and it would hit me later. I certainly didn't want to be in a rebound relationship when that happened. So I shook my head. "You'll be the first to know."

He nodded and sat next to me quietly for a long time.

I broke the silence and asked, "Do you know the poem about paths in the woods?"

"Frost?"

I nodded. "I feel like I'm in the woods right now. I took the easy path with Charles and even calling it off wasn't hard. Then John came back in my life."

He froze for a moment as if digesting the idea of me and John. He moved a fraction of an inch away from me as he said, "And you see the path your should have taken."

I reached out and put my hand on his. "No, I see the path that was a dead-end. One I was thankful I didn't take. John and I were over the day he left for college."

He shifted back toward me. "Where does that leave you now?"

I thought about Barbara's picture. "This weekend's a small hardly-there path in the woods that I'm taking for someone else. When I get back, I'll have to think about me. I've put the past behind me and I've turned around from the path I was on. I'm back at the edge of the woods, trying to decide where I want to go next. Miss Ida said that maybe I don't need to look for a path, but rather I need to forge one for myself."

"Am I one of the paths?" Reese asked.

"No, but maybe you're *on* one of the paths I could take," I said. I realized the truth of it.

I thought about Miss Ida and Albert.

Bette Lee and Big Henry.

Old Henry and Bea.

Maybe how long you knew someone didn't matter.

Maybe it was knowing they...fit.

I suspected Reese could fit me very well.

He smiled. "I'll take that. About the trip. Did you explain to your parents?"

"This is between you and me. I told Bette Lee, Big Henry and Miss Ida we were going away for a weekend and left it at that."

"Okay. I think that tomorrow, when we're underway, you should think about leveling with me. I'm a cop. I can keep things to myself."

"Like a priest in the confessional?" I tried to tease, but it fell flat.

Reese didn't seem to notice. "Just like that. Dee, a friend not only keeps secrets, but shares burdens. I'd like to think we're friends."

I didn't just like to think it, I realized that we were indeed friends. Maybe friendship, like love, happens in its own time. I'd known people for years and would still classify them as acquaintances. And yet, I'd met people and almost instantly connected. I wasn't sure I could explain why, but I knew it as truth. At least my truth.

So I nodded. "Tomorrow then. Is five o'clock too early?"

"I'll be ready," he said. For a moment, I thought he might kiss me again, but he didn't. He simply stood and walked across the street.

At five the next morning, Reese was waiting in Miss Ida's drive, a small suitcase next to my car, and two to-go mugs in his hand.

I'd programed the address Ned had sent me into the GPS the night before, so it was just a matter of turning it on and heading out.

"So?" Reese said simply.

I knew there wasn't going to be any *simple* about my answer.

"It's Miss Ida's daughter, Barbara. She's been gone a long time. I'm not sure she'll come back to see her mom. Frankly, I'm not sure Barbara *should* come back to see her. But I need to know... She needs to know that Miss Ida's..."

"Dying?" Reese asked softly.

I nodded as I turned onto Old French Road and headed toward the interstate.

"Why has she been gone?" he asked.

"She's an alcoholic." Even if she was sober, she was an addict because it was something you learn to manage ...something you had to overcome on a daily basis. It was something that was never truly cured.

He asked the question I knew he'd ask—the same question I asked myself over and over again. "You think it's wise to go see her then?"

"I don't know. If she's sober, I want to give her a chance to see Miss Ida before its too late."

We were both silent after that. Thinking of a time when Miss Ida would be gone hurt. I realized that I'd never faced an intimate loss.

Old Henry and Bea passed away when I was young, and though it hurt—though I'd loved them—

201

they lived in Dubois and I'd only seen them a few times a year. Losing them hadn't left a hole in my life.

Losing John Henry had...but looking back, I'd gotten over the pain in short order.

Losing Charles?

I'd miss his presence more than I'd miss him. I loved him, but not the way I should. I felt guilty at the thought, but it was true. I wasn't sure I could explain that to anyone if I had to, but I didn't have to, so I didn't worry about it.

But losing Miss Ida would leave a huge hole in my life. And even though she'd been gone so long, losing her mother would have to leave a hole in Barbara's, too.

"And if she's not sober?" Reese asked.

"I don't know," I admitted. "I just know I have to go."

I wasn't sure. I was taking Miss Ida's letter. If Barbara was sober, I was going to give it to her. She'd have to decide if she was going to come see her mother or not.

I remember what Miss Ida said about their last meeting. Barbara had never gone to the rehab and she'd never been home. Still Miss Ida prayed for her and Miss Ida hoped for her.

I hoped, too.

I hoped beyond hope I was doing the right thing for the right reason.

Miss Ida's Book of Memories

Sadie Mae told me she loved me. I knew that. But it was very nice to hear the words.

Part Three

The Less-Traveled Road

Chapter Fourteen

"When you follow a path into the unknown sometimes you find someplace unexpected and beautiful..."

We found Barbara's house.

It was a tiny cottage. I didn't think it could be more than a thousand square feet. It had white clapboard siding and a porch that seemed unproportionally
large against the tiny house.

"I'll wait here," Reese said.

I walked onto the porch and knocked. My heart was pounding and my palms were sweating.

"She's not there," an older woman hollered from the window next door.

"Do you know where I can find her?"

"No. She keeps to herself. Frankly, she's gone more than she's here. But I do know you can find a lot of her paintings downtown. I bought a few last year. They might know where she is."

I thought of Charles saying I collected old ladies like old ladies collected cats and I smiled. "Could you give me the address?"

The older woman told me it was just a few blocks.

We pulled up in front of a small building in the middle of a row of businesses in Dallas, Pennsylvania. Reese pointed to it.

I felt a sense of hope. If Barbara was still painting then maybe she was better.

The gallery was small, but I guessed when you painted miniatures, you didn't need a large display space.   The large front windows that had prints displayed. I stood for a long moment, studying them.

"They look like the painting at Miss Ida's," Reese said.

I nodded.

All of them had a tiny letter B in the right corner.

We walked in the door and to the left there was a small desk and a shelf of jugs and jars. I barely registered the woman sitting there. I was drawn to the small paintings and sketches that lined the walls.

I heard the woman ask Reese if we were here for something specific and I heard him reply that we were looking for Barbara Hall's work.

I didn't need the woman to confirm that these were Barbara's.

Bea's.

The neighbor said Barbara painted and went by Bea.

I thought of Old Henry's wife. Bea had been short for Beatrice. She'd been a tiny woman who seemed far too tiny to be married to Big Henry, who was the size his name would have implied.

I spotted a painting that was a forest scene akin to Miss Ida's.

I'd studied Miss Ida's, so I noticed subtle differences, though I was pretty sure most people wouldn't see them. This one was smaller. The paths were slightly lower in the print. But it was definitely painted by Barbara.

And it definitely spoke of looking for a place to belong.

There was so much longing in the picture I felt tears well up in my eyes. I'd read somewhere that good art could move you. If that was the measure, then this was very good art.

I looked at the picture next to it. A rocky beach. Lake Erie?

I looked closer. There, where the rocky sand met the tree line, a snake like path. Down a bit further, a smaller path.

The next small painting was a mountain scene. A river wound its way down from the left upper corner to the right lower corner. Around the river, I could see paths beaten into the mountain grasses.

I saw other paintings of scenes that reminded me of Erie and the Lake. And some seemed to be other areas of the country. More mountains, plains, canyons…

But all of them had paths etched into the scene. Whether they were bold and blatant, or subtle and almost hidden.

Some were just a suggestion of a path. A secret path that led to…?

Where were all of Barbara's paths taking her?

I came to the end of the display. The last painting I knew. It was my childhood yard. There was the mulberry tree. It was smaller in this picture, but it was definitely my childhood yard. The mulberry, the silver maple, the chestnut tree…

It was a different perspective than I'd seen them as a child. This was the view I had now through Barbara's old bedroom window. A view I'd come to know.

"You like them?" the clerk asked.

I finally looked at the woman. She had a rainbow colored headband holding back brown dreadlocks. There was a small silver stud in her nose, and I could make out the tattoos climbing from her wrist up her forearm and disappearing beneath her sleeve. She wore a flowing cream-colored shirt and a pair of holey jeans. But when I looked beyond all that, I saw her brilliant blue eyes and I suspected I knew who I was talking to.

"I came here to see them," I said slowly.

She looked surprise. "You know the artist?"

"In a way." I added, "Does the collection have a name?"

"The Long Way Home."

There was longing in the woman's voice and suddenly I knew I was right.   "Barbara?" I asked.

She looked surprised, then confused as she nodded.

Reese who'd been silent, looked at her as well.

I could see Miss Ida's clear blue eyes in this woman's face. As I studied her, I saw the first threads of silver weaving through her hair.

"Who are you?" she asked.

I pointed to the picture of my yard. "Sadie Mae."

"The little girl next door?" she asked, smiling.

I nodded.

"What are you doing here?" she asked.

When I answered, "I came to find you," her smile faded.

"Why?"   I heard her trepidation in that one word.

"It's a story that might take a while. Could I buy you dinner tonight?" I asked.

She nodded. "The bar next door has food. It's simple, but good."

My stomach sank at the mention of the bar. Was she still drinking? She looked clear enough, but that didn't mean she wasn't drinking and doing whatever else she did.

I glanced at Reese and he gave the slightest shrug, as if to say he wasn't sure either.

"I'm not," she said as if she heard my unasked question.

"Not?" I repeated.

"I've been clean four years, five months and sixteen days. No drugs, no drink."

"But you eat at a bar?" I couldn't help but ask.

"Yeah, but of all the places in the world that I could go to get a drink, that's not it. Diz Jones wouldn't serve me alcohol if it was the only thing to drink and I was dying of dehydration."

I wasn't sure who Diz was, but I liked him already. "Oh."

"Mom isn't..."

I knew what she was asking. "She's much the same as ever," I said, reassuring her Miss Ida was still alive.

"Does she know you're here?" Barbara asked softly.

I couldn't tell which answer she was hoping for, but I shook my head, and she looked simultaneously relieved and sad.

"What time are you done?" I asked.

She stood. "Right now."

"Won't your boss mind?"

"I'm my own boss, so no." She pulled a key from her pocket and put it in the register, as if to lock the drawer.

"Before you close, could I make a few purchases?" I asked.

She stopped. "You don't have—"

"I want to." I pointed to the picture of my yard and the one of the paths through the woods that reminded me of Miss Ida's.

She took them out and wrapped them carefully. I pulled out my wallet, but Barbara shook her head. "They're yours."

"They will be after I pay," I insisted. "These are worth more to me than you could possibly charge me."

She rang me out and Reese chose a picture as well.

Barbara locked the shop and we walked next door to Diz's Place.

The bar was quiet. I was pretty sure two in the afternoon wasn't the most popular time at a bar.

One older couple sat at the bar itself, and there was a table of some younger kids near the window.

Barbara led us to the back table, which was probably the quietest corner of the bar.

A giant of man with copper colored skin, business cut hair and a ready smile, reminded me of a much younger version of Big Henry as he came out of the back carrying plates. He spied us, dropped the plates with the couple and hurried over to us.

"Bea what's up?" he asked, concern in his voice.

"If you have a minute, come join us, Diz. Sadie Mae is an old neighbor who came looking for me."

He shot her a look that asked if she was all right. She gave the merest nod.

They reminded me of my parents...with just a look or a nod, they could carry on an entire conversation.

"I'm Dee now," I said.

"Dee and Bea." She gave a small laugh that said she was nervous.

Diz called somebody named Ham in the back and said to take over, then he joined us. "Can I get you guys something to drink?"

"I'm so sorry," Bea said. "I should have asked."

I shook my head. "We're fine for now."

"Is Mom okay?" Bea asked bluntly.

I shook my head. "I'm sorry. I should have led with that. She's fine."

"Still at the house?" she asked.

I nodded. "I've been gone a long time, but Reese lives across the street in the Nick's old house."

"Oh, those boys were beasts," she said. "You, on the other hand, were a very quiet kid. I babysat for you a few times."

"I don't remember." I sometimes thought I had the smallest flicker of a memory of Barbara, but it was wispy and impossible to pin down.

"You were little," she said. "Barely school age. We cut out paper snowflakes and you decorated the front window with them. Your mom seemed to like them. She put them up for a few years after."

"I remember them. They got too fragile to hang up, but Mom still has them. She had a fight with Big Henry when they moved. He was trying to downsize and she insisted on keeping her *treasures*." I realized as I said the word, most of those treasures were things I'd made her.

"I'm sure she didn't raise her voice when they fought, just like I'm equally sure she won," Bea said with a laugh. "Your mom seemed all soft and sweet, but she had a core of iron."

"Still does. And whenever she gets into it with Big Henry, she always wins. I think he tries to fight out of habit, more than any expectation of winning."

She laughed again. It seemed like her default response. Laughter. That reminded me of Miss Ida, too.

"About your mom," I said, needed to tell her why I'd come.

Her expression grew serious. "I'm not sure I'm ready to hear what you're going to tell me yet. So let me start."

I nodded. I understood. Until I said the words, Miss Ida could remain as she'd always been in Bea's mind.

I thought about what Miss Ida had said and knew that until I said the words, Bea still had hope.

"Did Mom tell you about the last time I saw her?" Bea asked.

I nodded, not willing to share more than that.

Bea reached in her pocket and pulled out a laminated card. She passed it to me. It was the name of a rehab clinic. "She gave me this and told me not to come back until I was clean. For years, I blamed her. If she'd have let me in and helped me, I'd have been able to stop using. I'd have been okay. That was the lie I told myself. It was easier to blame my mother than blame myself. But one day, I woke up in a house I didn't recognize, sleeping next to a man I didn't recognize. I didn't even know what state, much less what city I was in.

"I gathered up my clothes and was about to leave when the man woke up and said—"

"*Don't go*," Diz supplied. "*Rumor has it I make a great omelet.*"

She smiled and took his hand. "I stayed for the omelet and then...just stayed. I sobered up. Not overnight and I've slipped, but here I am."

"The gallery?" I asked.

"Diz owned that building as well. At first he simply let me use it as a studio, but then he suggested I open it as a gallery. I'm not getting rich, but I make enough to pay rent and support myself."

"You do beautiful work. Miss Ida still has the painting of the woods, like the one I bought. I fell in love with that picture. It seemed to echo how I was feeling about my life."

"How?" she asked.

"Like I'm standing in the field, looking at the woods, looking at paths and trying to decide what one to take."

"I based it on the poem by..."

"Robert Frost," we said at the same time.

She smiled and nodded.

"Your mom's let me read some of her memories and she's told me other ones. There's a theme...she loves you. So many days were filled with you. When she was pregnant, when you were born. Your first steps and milestones, but so much more than that. The day you wrapped your arms around her neck and said, *I love you more than pickles*. She wasn't sure where you'd heard that, but she laughed and said she loved you more than ice cream and then you both argued for the rest of the day about what was the ultimate *more than*."

"I maintain that infinity was the most," Bea said quietly.

"She loves you that much. She's been waiting for you. She told me she prays for you every day and that every day since you left that last time she's lived in hope."

"I wanted to go back clean and sober and say, *Look Mom, I'm not a loser.*"

"She never thought you were a loser. She thought you were lost." The words were connected, but so different from one another. "You were lost and Miss Ida would have done anything to help you find your way home."

"She did do it. She let me go. She refused to bail me out. If she hadn't, I don't think I'd have ever stopped."

Diz, who'd sat quietly until now, reached out and took her hand. *"Everything you've done has led you here..."*

"And here is a good place," she finished. It was obviously something they said a lot.

And though I didn't know Bea well, I felt we had a connection through Miss Ida. A connection that let me ask, "If you're better, why haven't you come home?"

"Because I'm afraid." She shook her head. "That's the truth, but it's only part of the truth. Every day, I'm tempted to drink or use. I thought it would get better, but it doesn't. Every day I'm tempted and I realize that I could slip again. Every day..."

Diz took her hand. "Every day you could, but every day, you don't."

She nodded. "But what if I went home and slipped again? I'd hurt mom so much. Still, I've learned to value honesty. And it's more than that. I'm so afraid of what I'll see in her eyes. Did she tell you about the watch?"

I wasn't sure how to answer, but she was right. Honesty. "Yes."

She stood and reached in her pant's pocket and pulled a plain gold pocket watch out of it.

"Is that it?" I asked.

Bea shook her head. "I've looked for it. While I was looking I found this, and it was close that when I found it I thought it might be. It wasn't, but I bought it. I carry it because..." She blinked quickly, trying to hold back the tears. "Have you ever done something so awful that you know nothing will ever make up for it?" Her voice was almost a whisper. "Something that you wish you could take back?"

"Bea," Diz said. His voice was laced with suffering for her pain, but more than that, it was laced with love.

"The last time I went home, I saw disgust in my mother's eyes. I disgusted her because of what I'd become. I couldn't fault her, because I disgusted myself. Even in the throes of addiction I knew what I was doing to myself was wrong. I simply couldn't stop it. I tried. I'd wake up and tell myself that I was done. I was never going to drink again. Then hours later, I'd take just a sip. Then another and then...

She shook her head. "I disgusted myself, but it was worse knowing I disappointed my parents. And even worse than that was knowing they still loved me. My parents gave me the world. They gave me their love and everything I wanted. When she saw I loved drawing, Mom found me classes. She came to every school art show. She practiced spelling words with me and read to me from her book. And knowing her stories, I knew..."

Bea couldn't blink fast enough to hold back the tears any longer. She sobbed deeply. They seemed to consume her entire body. "I knew what that watch meant to her because it was her father's. I knew that it wasn't worth much money, but I was angry and I wanted to hurt her, and I knew as I walked out the door that I hurt her. I knew..."

She sobbed over and over. I put my arms around this woman I didn't know, but felt that maybe I did a bit through her art. "I know that you don't know me, other than some faint memories of me as a child, but I've gotten close with your mom and I know that you matter more to her than a watch. When we talked about it, she said that memories matter more than items. And you know your mom...she's full of memories. She has a whole book of them."

At that, Bea smiled through her tears. "She does. I think I took the watch because I wanted her to hate me as much as I hated myself."

"It didn't work," I said simply.

"I've stayed away because I'm afraid that it did. I'm afraid that I'll go home and see how I've broken her heart all over again. I'll see disgust and recriminations in her eyes."

"When you go home, you'll see only love. And pride that you overcame your addiction."

"I didn't. I want a drink every day and every day I don't. But I could."

"But you don't," I said, repeating Diz's words. "She looked for you. But you'd dropped off the radar."

"She looked for me?" Bea asked.

I nodded. "She hired someone."

"How did you find me?" she asked.

"I hired someone better." I nodded toward Reese. "It pays having a cop around who knows people."

All my worries about whether or not I was right to meddle disappeared. I was here because here was the right place to be. "Four years, five months and sixteen days is good enough," I said softly. "She wants to see you. She loves you."

Bea cried again and Diz reached out and pulled her into his arms. He didn't say anything, he simply held her. He let her cry herself out and I felt tears in my own eyes. Reese reached over and put his hand on mine.

I flipped it over and squeezed his hand.

"I've wasted so much time," Bea finally said.

"No. Like you said, everything you've done has led you here and here is a good place. In a way, everything we've both done has led us both here right now. I'm here to bring you home. Bring Diz and come see Miss Ida. Let her see that you're okay. That's all she wants. That's all she ever wanted. She never forgot you and she's always loved you."

"I thought of her every day. Hold on. I've got something up at Diz's place," she sprang from the table and ran through that kitchen door.

Diz looked at me, and smiled. "It was good of you to come find her."

"I love Miss Ida. I wanted her to have the peace of knowing Bea was okay. I hoped she was."

"She's more than okay," he said. And in his eyes I could see the love. So much love.

Bea came back with a thick book. "I have five more of these, but this one is my most recent."

She slid it across the table to me and Reese.

I opened it and there, on the first page was a picture of Miss Ida.

It was the Miss Ida I remembered meeting that first day. Her hair was in a bun and Bea had captured the twinkle in her eye that reminded me of Mrs. Santa Claus.

Page after page of pictures. Some were of people. Many were of Miss Ida.

But there were places, too. Some reminded me of the paintings. There was a wide range of locations. Mountains, plains, oceans, lakes.

Then there, on one page, was the watch. Hanging from the now empty dome on Miss Ida's table back at home.

"Mom had her book of memories. Each observation, no matter how mundane was almost poetic. I could never find the words to say what I wanted to...what I needed to. So I started drawing small sketches. Of where I was and who I met."

I kept flipping through the pages. "Your mother would love these."

They were small, like her art in the gallery. But they all contained such intricate details. A man with shaggy eyebrows and tattoos up his neck. If I met him on the street, I'd know him.

"Why do you paint so small?" I asked. I hadn't realized that it was a burning question until I said it.

Bea shrugged. "I don't know. It started with a mural in my room. I wanted to fit Mom's stories on the wall, and there were so many stories. I knew I'd need room. As I worked on it, I realized I enjoyed it. I liked trying to capture the bigness of a story, or a feeling of it in one small space. Sometimes I think I paint so small because my feelings are so big and that's the only way I can contain them."

I looked through the sketches and Bea told me stories about each one. At some point, I realized Diz and Reese had left the table and moved to the bar.

And still we talked.

I told Bea about going to work for Miss Ida and our friendship.

She told me about places she'd been and people she'd met.

Finally she sighed. "It's probably time for you to tell me what's wrong with Mom. I'll be honest, I wish you didn't have to. In my mind's eye, she's still..." She flipped through her book and flipped to the first sketch of Miss Ida.

"She has an aneurysm. And..."

Bea paled as I laid out Miss Ida's prognosis.

"She could go anytime?" she asked.

I nodded. "She gave me a letter to give you if you came after..."

"After she died?"

217

I nodded. "When and if I saw you. Well, I'm seeing you now." I took the envelope from my purse.

I watched as more tears formed in her eyes as she read the letter. Wordlessly, she passed it back to me, nodding, indicating I should read it.

Barbara,

I had a dream last night.

Your father came to me and took my hand. We went into a school auditorium. It looked like the one at your grade school. You were in a play called Stone Soup. Do you remember? I still have the stone your teacher gave you in a box in the attic.

In my dream, you came out onto the stage, but instead of your stone, you held a piece of paper and said, "Mom, I want you to be proud of me."

Then I was on the stage with your dad and we were both hugging you. And you hugged us back. And you were our Barbara again. And Sadie Mae was in the front row watching us, clapping and crying. I beckoned her up to join us, and the four of us hugged.

When I looked in the audience, I saw my family there. My parents. Aunts and uncles I hadn't thought of in years. My grandparents.

In my dream, I had my family with me and I was at peace.

When I woke up, the dream was so vivid, and the peace...the peace was still with me.

***Is** still with me.*

If you ever read this, then the dream was true and you're better. And that is all I've ever wanted. It's all your father ever wanted.

I worry that you will get better and come home and I won't be here waiting for you. If that happens, know we always loved you. That last day, when I said you broke your father's heart, I worry that you didn't realize that hearts heal as well as break. If you're better, his has healed...even now. And I worry that you think my shutting the door on you was an indication that I didn't—

don't—love you. If you think that, you are wrong. So wrong. I loved you then and I love you now. And I forgive anything that needs forgiving, and I hope you can forgive your father and me for all our failings as well.

All we ever wanted was you to be whole. We wanted you to build a happy life.

If you have this letter, then you've met my Sadie Mae. Don't think she was a replacement for you. She was an addition to you. Just as a heart that breaks can heal, a heart that loves can always love more.

And I have loved.

I love you both. I think she'll be your friend, and maybe even your family, if you'll let her.

Be well, my Barbara. Be happy. And remember that though we were imperfect, your father and I always loved you.

I love you still. I always have, and I always will.

Mom

Tears ran down my cheeks and I brushed them away. But brushing wasn't enough. I pulled a couple napkins from the metal holder at the end of the table.

Barbara pulled a few as well. "She didn't mention the watch."

"Because it doesn't matter," I said. "She forgave you."

"She just wants me back," she whispered.

"She does." I added, "I think that she keeps your painting by the front door as a reminder that you have to choose your own path, but she's hoping your path will bring you home to her."

Bea nodded. "I have to make a few arrangements, but I'll come home."

"Good," I said.

"Why did you take a chance on me? I might have still been a drunk."

"I'd like to say if you were, I'd have walked away without saying anything. Maybe I would have, but I

219

think even then I'd have given you the letter. You deserve to know."

"That she's dying?" Bea asked, saying the last word slowly, as if accustoming herself to their weight and heft.

"That she loved you...loves you," I corrected.

Bea nodded. "You're staying with her?"

"As long as she needs me. She's right though, I don't want you to think I ever wanted to take your place. She was my employer, then my friend and now she's family. I love her and I know she loves me, but that doesn't mean..."

Bea took my hand. "I know. And I hope she's right and we can be friends."

"I hope she's right and we can be more. I hope we can be family."

We went up to Diz's apartment and spent the evening with Diz and Bea. We shared Miss Ida stories, and our own stories.

I sat on the couch next to Reese. At some point I realized his arm was over my shoulder. It felt right there.

Diz went down to the bar and brought us up dinner.

And still we talked as we ate, and after.

When it was getting late, I said, "We need to go. My parents are with Miss Ida, but I want to get back tomorrow." I'd told them Sunday, but I didn't want to leave her any longer than I had to.

I'd done what I came to do. I'd found Barbara, given her the letter and asked her to come home.

"We'll be right behind you. Sometime tomorrow late afternoon or evening," Diz said. "I just need the morning to line up people to cover my shifts."

"I'll see you both then." And I hugged them.

We drove to the hotel in silence. Reese put the car in park and turned it off, then asked, "Are you okay?"

"I am. I really liked Bea. I wasn't sure..." The sentence hung there a moment, and then I said, "I don't think I realized that I was angry at her. I mean, really mad. I've seen her talent at Miss Ida's and I know Miss Ida. How could she let anything—drinking or drugs—get between her and her mom?"

"It's a disease," Reese said. "I'm not excusing it, but I've seen so many people who've ruined their lives because they can't shake it. Addiction digs its hooks into you and it takes incredible strength to get out from under it."

"That's what I found. She's talented and she's so strong. I saw so much of Miss Ida in her. And Diz? He's so totally head-over-heels for her. I think the two of us can be friends."

"Me, too." He opened the door and got both our bags.

"I can carry mine," I said.

"I'm pretty sure your mom would expect me to be a gentleman. When I meet her tomorrow you can give me a glowing report."

I laughed. "She would and I will."

The clerk gave us key cards and we went to our rooms. They were next door to each other. I went inside and realized they were adjoining rooms. I heard a soft tap at the door. I opened it and saw Reese smiling. "I just want to be clear, I didn't request this."

"I should be equally clear that neither did I," I said.

He nodded. "But if you need me, I'm just a door away."

I nodded. "Good night, Reese. And thanks for coming with me. It was nice not to be alone."

"I'm always here for you, Dee."

For a moment, I wanted to ask him into my room. I wanted to take him to bed, but I knew that though we'd known each other since childhood, we didn't know each other well enough for that.

221

I shut the door, got ready for bed and fell asleep almost immediately.

And I dreamed.

In my dreams I was standing on Miss Ida's front porch with Reese. He held my hand and I waved with the other one as Bea pulled into the drive. We went into the house and Miss Ida wasn't there. We searched everywhere and I cried, "We're too late."

I cried and sobbed in the dream.

The sound of someone knocking woke me up.

For a moment, I was confused. I had a huge void in my heart, knowing I'd let Miss Ida down. I realized I was crying.

And slowly, as I woke up I knew that Miss Ida wasn't gone yet. It was just a dream.

I heard the knocking again.

It was the door to Reese's room.

"Dee, are you okay?" he called.

I got out of bed and opened the door. "Sorry if I woke you. It was just a bad dream."

And though I knew that's what it was, I couldn't shake the feeling of loss from my dream.

Without saying a word, Reese opened his arms. I stepped into his embrace and instead of loss, I felt a sense of discovery.

I turned my head and placed my cheek against his chest. I felt it rise and fall with his breath. I heard the steady sound of his heart's beat. I drank in the scent of him. It smelled of the outdoors...woodsy with an undercurrent of spice.

He held me for a long time, without saying a word.

And for the first time in my life, I was tempted to invite a man I'd only known a blink of an eye to bed.

I knew I wouldn't follow through on the temptation. That wasn't how I was made. But still, there was wanting.

"Would you like to come in and just talk?" I asked, needing to be sure to keep the boundaries in place, more for myself than Reese who'd never been anything but a perfect gentleman and friend.

"Yes."

The hotel only offered one plush chair and one desk chair, so we sat on the edge of the bed.

"Do you want to talk about the dream?" he asked.

"I dreamed we were too late. You and I were on the porch when Diz and Bea arrived. We went inside but couldn't find Miss Ida. It was too late."

"Why don't you text your mom and check on Miss Ida," he prompted.

"It's kind of late."

"Your mom doesn't strike me as someone who will mind."

And so I did.

Just checking on Miss Ida.

Bette Lee: Doing fine. Played Scrabble tonight. She tried to use QUETZALS. I challenged her. It is a word.

I texted, **Bless your heart.**

And followed with, **Thanks. Love you. Night.**

"She's okay. Miss Ida kicked Bette Lee's butt at scrabble." I decided to look up quetzals. Two ten-point letters made it a keeper.

"I played Scrabble against her once. She cleaned my clock."

Reese still had an arm around me. I wasn't ready to have him let go. "Tell me about after you left school."

"I hated school. I didn't find any of the classes interesting, much less challenging. I took my GED and when I passed it, I dropped out and enlisted. It was the best decision I ever made. I've been speaking at high schools a lot, and I've encouraged the kids to think outside the box. But you get that."

"Me?" I asked. I wasn't sure what he was talking about.

"I admire that you don't work a nine-to-five. You've forged your own path."

"I didn't forge anything. I fell into it." Maybe that was the truth, but there was more of the truth. "I talked to the Brain's editor. She said she thinks she has a freelance position for me."

"That's great," he said.

"It is. I'm pretty sure I was never meant for an office job."

"Me either. It's one of the things I love about being a cop. Every day is different. Some days are hard. I see humanity at its worst. But then there are days when I know I've made a difference. I changed a tire for a woman last week. It was a little thing, and it certainly didn't stop a crime, but it was a tangible way of helping someone. When I speak at schools, I'm reaching out to kids. We talk about issues that matter to them. And I hope when I leave, they see I'm not just my uniform, I'm a person. If they ever get pulled over, I hope that helps frame the cops they meet in a new light."

We talked. Sitting next to each other in the bed. It wasn't sexual in the least, and yet there was a closeness that I marveled at.

At some point in the wee hours, I fell asleep. I woke up, still held in Reese's arms. He was sleeping. He wasn't really snoring, but I could hear his breathing.

I stayed still, hoping not to wake him, but I felt him stir.

"Good morning," I said.

"Good morning yourself."

"We should get on the road." I knew I needed to go back. But if I could, I'd have stayed in this hotel room the rest of the day, curled up next to Reese, sharing stories and bits of ourselves.

"Yes. But when everything settles down, I'd really like to spend more time with you. Dating. Just hanging out. I...like you. I feel like I'm back in high school, but there it is. I like you and want to spend time with you."

"Ditto."

He leaned over and kissed my cheek. Again, it was as chaste as chaste could be, and yet I felt...

I tried to sort out what I felt, and finally just admitted...I felt. And whatever I called the feeling, it felt good.

Miss Ida's Book of Memories

Albert and I went out on our sixth date. We watched the sunset on a beach at the peninsula. He simply held my hand, but I felt more connected to him than I've ever felt to anyone.

I think I'm falling in love.

Chapter Fifteen

"I had a second dream last night. This one about my parents. We were walking near our old house. There was a marvelous old brick house that I called the castle when I was little. I raced to it in my dream, just like I raced to it when I was young. "My castle," I shouted triumphantly. Bette Lee and Big Henry caught up to me and I said, "I'm gonna make this my home when I'm bigger." My mother knelt down and said, "Your home will never be a place...this is just a house and even if you live there, that's all it will ever be. Home is people. Your father's my home. You're my home. We're your home. And someday, you'll fall in love and he'll be your home, too." I remember the castle from when I was young. It was pre-Book of Memories. So I'm not sure if I remembered this moment in my dream or simply made it up. But whichever it was, Bette Lee was right."

I saw Big Henry sitting on the porch as we pulled into the driveway.

"Mr. Hanson," Reese said as he got out of the car. He walked over to my dad and shook his hand. "It's nice to meet you. I'm Reese. Maddox Reese."

"It's nice to meet you as well," Big Henry said as their handshake continued.

They stared each other down and at some point found what they were looking for. They both nodded and released their handshake.

Bette Lee opened the door. "So this is your young man," she said.

"My friend," I clarified. Reese shot me a look that said it was more than that, and I looked back at him as if to say I knew that but wasn't ready to broadcast it especially to Bette Lee. He smiled at that and said, "Mrs. Hanson, it's nice to meet you. I remember you from PTA back in the day. You were always very kind."

"And I remember you, young man. You were a scamp, but you were always very polite and sweet." My mother made the word *scamp* sound like an endearment. "And you've been a good friend to my Sadie Mae. I hope we can have dinner when we come back through town."

"I'd like that," he said.

And just like I'd had an unspoken conversation with him, I was pretty sure he was doing the same with Bette Lee and I wondered just what they were saying to each other without words.

Whatever it was, my mother hugged him. "We'll be back soon and I'll collect on that raincheck."

She let Reese go and he asked me, "Want me to come in?"

Part of me very much wanted to say yes, but instead I shook my head. "No, but will you be home if Diz needs someplace to hang out later?"

"Yes." He leaned over and kissed my cheek. It was platonic, but it made me want to lean over and kiss him properly.

I didn't, but I'd have been smiling if I weren't about to face Miss Ida.

My parents were grinning as Reese walked across the street.

"So why are you home early?" Bette Lee—never one to beat around the bushes—asked.

"I found what I needed, so there was no point in staying away," I said.

"Do you want to talk about it?" my father asked.

I shook my head. "I'll tell you and Bette Lee all about it later. I have to talk to Miss Ida first."

He nodded. "Then we're going to head out. Bette Lee wants to go antiquing in New England. We'll be a week or two, but we'll stop back here before we go home if that's okay?"

"Or sooner if you need us. We'll have Reese over to dinner so your father and I can get to know him properly," Bette Lee added.

I knew that Big Henry would wait. I was hoping Bette Lee would as well. "I'll tell you all about it then."

He nodded again as he stood up and swept me into a hug. "I'm proud of you."

"For what?" I asked from his tight embrace.

"For being here. For helping Miss Ida. Someone raised you right." With my head pressed against his chest, I felt his chuckle as much as heard it. And I thought about Miss Ida and her father. I squeezed mine harder.

"Yes, you both did," I said.

He smiled and shook his head. "You and I both know it was Bette Lee."

"Yes it was," she said from behind me.

"Big Henry helped," I assured them both.

He laughed outright this time and again I felt it rumble deep in his chest.

"I love you," I told him, my voice muffled against his denim shirt.

"You, too, darlin'."

It took me a minute to realize there'd been a whisper of Bette Lee's accent in that sentence. And despite my nerves about Bea, I managed a smile as he released me from his hug. "Bette Lee's turning you southern."

Bette Lee grinned. "It took a lot of years, but your father's finally coming around. He loves it down south."

"I love not shoveling snow in the winter," he said, but he was grinning which took the umph out of his qualification.

"You're sure you don't need us, Sadie Mae?" my mother asked.

"No. I can't tell you how lucky I feel knowing that I can call and you'll come. No questions asked."

Bette Lee pulled me into a hug this time. She smelled of magnolias and love.
"Sweet Pea, your father and I will always be here for you. We'll be back in a week or two, if that's okay," she said, repeating my father's request.

I might be an adult now, but hearing Bette Lee call me *Sweet Pea*, or any of her other endearments, still warmed my heart. "Yes, please. I'd love to have more time to visit. I want you to really get to spend time with Reese."

My mother didn't comment, but she did raise an eyebrow to let me know she noticed the comment.

"Then you can count on us coming back soon. We already said our goodbyes to Miss Ida. You call if you need us. We'll always come."

There are some things that can be counted on. The sun always rises in the east. Winter always follows fall. And I could count on my parents...always. "I know that. And I'd come for you both, Mom."

I rarely called her that, and I saw that she noticed. She smiled as she kissed my cheek.

She kissed me again and then got into the RV with Big Henry. They both waved as they drove down the street.

It might seem odd that they left so quickly, but I knew they were aware there was something going on and they were giving me space. They were trusting me to deal with it.

I took a deep breath as I went in Miss Ida's house.

She was in her chair. I kissed her cheek as I sank into its plaid companion.

"Did you and Reese fight?" she asked. "We didn't expect you home until tomorrow."

Rather than answer her question, I asked, "Miss Ida, you know I love you, right?"

She nodded slowly. "And I love you. What's wrong, Sadie Mae?"

"I did something. And I hope you forgive me. But I won't say I'm sorry." Before she could ask anything else, I blurted out, "I found Barbara."

She didn't say anything. She didn't ask questions or cry. She didn't look angry or ecstatic. She looked blank.

As if in slow motion, she brought her hands together, closed her eyes and then sat silently for a minute. I didn't have to ask what she was doing. She was praying.

I wasn't much for formal prayers, but I silently asked that the events I was setting in motion ended well. Then I waited for Miss Ida.

When she opened her eyes, there were unshed tears shining in them, which only served to amplify how blue her eyes were.

"Thank you," she said simply.

I felt a surge of relief. Miss Ida wasn't mad. "She's good. I mean, really good. She's been clean for four years, five months and sixteen days—seventeen

231

days now," I said doing the math. "She's coming home to see you."

"You told her to hurry because I might not be here very long," she said simply, stating a fact.

I tried not to think about a world without Miss Ida in it because it seemed to me that it would be a bleaker world. I knew that most people wouldn't know the name Ida Hunter Hall. But she'd made a big difference in my lives, and all the other lives she'd touched.

The world—my world—would be darker when she was gone.

"I hope we have a lot more time together," I simply said as I took her hand in mine.

"Sadie Mae, you need to know that if I went this very second, I would leave this world so much happier knowing Barbara was all right." She closed her eyes again, her hand still in mine. When she opened them, she said, "Tell me everything."

I did.

I told her about Reese's friend, Ned finding Barbara's address. About Reese's help. About the paintings and the gallery. About Diz. "They're both coming later today. Diz had to make arrangements for the bar."

"Bar?" she asked.

I knew exactly what she was thinking because I'd thought it, too. "That's what I said, but Bea—"

"Bea?" She knew who I meant and softly said her name again. "Bea."

"That's what she goes by now."

"My Barbara's Bea and you're Dee." She seemed to be weighing and measuring our nicknames. Finally she nodded. "I like that. It feels like a connection and when I'm gone, I want you both to have each other."

"I had the same thought. Bea said that Diz's bar was the last place on earth she could ever get a drink. He loves her you see."

232

It sounded like a simple statement. And maybe on some level that kind of complete love was simple. But given Barbara's history, I suspected there was an element of complexity to it.

Maybe all love was like that. Simple when examined by itself. But if you looked deeper, there were layers and complications to it.

"And she's happy?" Miss Ida asked.

"Yes. She's still painting. Oh, Miss Ida, she's so talented. Diz helped her set up a studio. I bought some. Reese did, too. I could see her talent in her works here, but her newer paintings have more depth. I'll show you..."

Miss Ida took my hand in hers, keeping me in my chair. "Just sit with me, please. And tell me everything again."

I did.

I told her about giving Bea the letter. I told her that Bea loved her. "It's there in every word she said to me. She felt guilty about the watch. She was afraid that she'd hurt you too bad."

"I love her more than a watch," Miss Ida said. She looked down at the globe. "Albert told me to keep it here to remind me that Barbara needed help. She's better now, so I don't need the reminder."

I got up and took the cloche into the kitchen. I'd put it in a top cupboard.

Miss Ida nodded as I sat back down. "She knows I love her?"

"I told her. Her love for you and your love for her was there in her Book of Memories."

Miss Ida looked surprised. "She keeps one? I gave her a book, but I didn't think she ever wrote down any."

I shook my head. "She doesn't write in them. She draws in them. She showed me one of her books. It's filled with pictures of people and places. She doesn't

233

see the world in words, but in pictures. I hope she brings one to show you. They're beautiful."

"I'd like that too, but knowing she's happy and she's sober is enough. That's all I ever wanted for her."

"I told her that. I told her that you thought of her and prayed for her every day. I told her that you loved her."

"Thank you," she whispered. She closed her eyes again, folded her hands.

I let her pray.

I hurried back to Bea's room. I picked up and packed all my things, then I changed the sheets. I wasn't sure if she'd stay here, but I wanted to be able to offer her room to her.

I slid the suitcase under the bed. I could grab it if needs be.

I thought about getting the paintings out of my car, but they could wait. Miss Ida was still in her chair, eyes closed and hands folded.

I said another small prayer of my own, asking for time for Miss Ida and Bea.

And we waited.

We made an attempt at lunch, but I don't think either of us managed more than a bite.

Bea had texted when they left Dallas. They were a few hours behind us. So when I heard a truck pull into the driveway I knew who it was.

"Is it her?" Miss Ida asked.

I nodded. "I'll let her in."

"I'd do it myself, but I'm not sure I can get up," Miss Ida said.

Diz was hugging Bea as I opened the door. "I'm going over to Reese's," he said.

I pointed to the small yellow house across the street. "He's waiting for you."

Diz chucked Bea on the shoulder. "You can do this," he told her. "I'll come meet her after."

I nodded as Bea came onto the porch. "I'll let you two—" I started to say, ready to follow Diz to Reese's.

Bea interrupted me and took my hand. "Please, don't go. Mom might need you."

I thought there was a chance Bea was saying she might need me as well. "Okay."

"You'll stay? Promise?"

"I'll stay as long as you want me to," I promised. I opened the door and she dropped my hand with a cry as she spied her mother sitting in her chair.

Neither said a word as Bea sprinted across the room and into Miss Ida's arms. They both cried as they hugged each other without saying a word.

Words would have been superfluous. Their love was palpable and so big it filled the small room.

I stood next to the door and tried to make myself small as they cried and hugged. Then they whispered softly to one another. Not as a way of excluding me, but because they were too emotional to speak any louder.

I'm not sure how long it went on, but neither seemed inclined to stop. I stood watching them, knowing that if I ever came home a prodigal child, this was how Bette Lee and Big Henry would greet me— with happy tears and whispered words of love.

I was an outsider. An intruder.

I didn't know what to do and wanted to give them as much privacy as possible. I thought about going to the kitchen, but I felt my movements would remind them of my presence and break the spell of the reunion.

I thought about one of Bea's paintings on the bedroom mural. A much younger Miss Ida sitting on a swing, holding a pink blanketed baby with such naked love in her eyes it was palpable.

Here, in this moment, that love was even more present.

It circled the two of them like an aura.

I'd thought that Bea's art was beautiful and moving, but the tableau in front of me was even more so.

Finally they broke apart.

"I've missed you," Miss Ida whispered. "Tell me everything."

As if afraid to move too far, Bea sank to Miss Ida's stool. "Come join us, Dee," Bea said. "You've heard most of this before."

And so I sat and became a spectator to their reunion.

Bea told her story with honesty. She didn't shelter Miss Ida. Instead, she said, "I could tell you I regret everything. And I do regret the pain I caused you, but I can't help but think if I hadn't done what I did and gone through what I went through, I wouldn't be here right now. And Mom, here is exactly where I want to be. I've built a life I love. The only thing that's been missing is you."

"I was here, waiting," Miss Ida said simply.

Barbara patted Miss Ida's hand. "I know. But after all those times that I came home full of promises that I didn't deliver on, I wanted to be sure this time was different. Not just for you, but for me. Does that make sense? All those times I saw you hope that this time was different. All those times I saw that hope die when I messed up again..." Barbara paused a moment. "I couldn't. I couldn't come back until I was well and felt confident. I know that there's no cure. I know that I'll always be an alcoholic. But right here and right now, I can look at you and say, *I won't drink today*. I have too much to lose."

"That's all I ever wanted."

"I have something for you." She reached into her jeans pocket and pulled the watch out. "I tried to find your father's, but I couldn't. This one looked close and for a moment, I thought I had it, but it wasn't his.

Still, I bought it. I know it's not the same, but I'm sorry. And I—"

Miss Ida reached for Bea's hand and took the watch.

"Sadie Mae?" Miss Ida said.

I knew what she was asking. I went into the kitchen and brought the cloche back out.

Carefully, as we watched, Miss Ida lifted the glass dome, hung the watch from the hook and replaced the glass. "It's perfect."

"I thought... I was afraid..."

"I forgive you, Barbara. I forgave you right after I discovered it was missing. You have always mattered more to me than a watch...than anything."

Bea reached into her back pocket this time and pulled out her phone. She popped the cover and pulled out a card. The business card.

"I kept it, Mom," she said. "You gave me this card and told me they'd always have a bed for me. I never went to them, but I knew I could. It became my talisman. I wanted to tell you that this card...it's the only reason I made it through some days. I wanted to come back to you whole. Or at least as whole as I can be. I wanted to look you in the eye and tell you that I'm better. I'm not perfect. We both know I'll never be that. But I'm better."

Miss Ida was too choked up to speak. Bea took the card back and once again put it in her phone case before she snapped it shut. She looked at Miss Ida and said, "Dee gave me your letter."

Tears were filling my eyes as I listened to them. They needed a moment. Or maybe I needed one. I stood. "I'm going to go make us some tea."

I hurried from the room before they could stop me.

As I filled the teakettle, I finally allowed all my tears to fall.

I thought about what Bea had said and I realized that I wouldn't change anything in my life. Not the years of confusion over what direction I wanted to go. Not my time with Charles. Not even John's *Dear Sadie Mae*-ing me.

Every step I'd ever taken had led me here. And here was a good place.

Other things...good things, came flooding back. Paffles. Burnt toast. Double rainbows.

I reached for cookies and realized even things like cookie jars and brown betties. All those moments and things and people...they all shaped me into who I was now. I was happy with who I was now...and where I was.

I thought about Reese across the street and realized that back on Vermont Avenue was exactly where I wanted to be.

When the tea was finished, I carried it on a tray into the living room along with two cups and the plate of cookies.

Miss Ida and Bea sat where I'd left them, still holding hands. I set the tray on the stand. "I think you two can manage without me."

"Will you send Diz over in a bit?" Bea asked. "I want Mom to meet him."

"Just text when you're ready."

I leaned down and kissed Miss Ida's cheek. "Thank you," she said.

Bea sprung up and threw her arms around me and hugged me without saying a word. Which was fine. No words were necessary.

I glanced at the painting as I stood in front of the door.

I might not know exactly where my path was going to lead, but I felt as if I were firmly on it.

I walked across the street and gave a quick rap on Reese's door, then let myself in. "Hello?"

"Come through. We're on the deck." I walked through the sparse living room through the dining room to the sliding glass doors. Reese and Diz were sitting on the deck, looking like old friends.

"Things are going well," I said without them asking. "I gave them some privacy. Bea said she'll text you soon. She wants you to meet her mom."

I took one of the other chairs. It wasn't until I sat down that I realized I'd automatically chosen the one next to Reese.

"I've heard so much about her mother," Diz said. "I encouraged Bea to call. Part of her recovery is making amends. She needed to face her mom. I think it was her last big hurdle."

"How long can you stay?" I asked.

"I've got coverage for the week. I can always go back and leave Bea here if she wants." He didn't look as if leaving Bea was something he was comfortable doing.

"She'd be fine," I said.

"I know she would. She's stronger than she's ever known. And she wouldn't believe me if I said it, but I need her probably more than she's ever needed me."

"Maybe that's what makes a good relationship. Needing someone and having them need you in return."

I thought about Bette Lee and how she'd missed Big Henry. She'd asked if I'd missed Charles that way. I hadn't. I'd never really missed John Henry that way either. But looking at Reese, I suspected I would miss him just like that. I'd come to count on him coming to join me on the front lawn.

The guys were silent in that not-uncomfortable way men could be. Their quiet felt like a balm.

I was talked out.

Cried out, too.

I'd done what I'd set out to do. I'd given Miss Ida back her daughter.

And this time with her...

239

I reached out and took Reese's hand. It felt right. Just as sitting here felt right. Being back in Erie, back on Vermont Avenue felt right.

I had that phone call scheduled with the Brain's editor next week and someone else from the company. Even if that didn't pan out, being here felt like the right move for me. Mercyhurst was less than a half-mile from the house. Maybe I could get up there for classes. I doubted they had Interpreting Geek-Speak majors, but maybe I should take some science classes.

That felt right, too.

A phone binged, and Diz pulled his out of his pocket. "They're ready for me."

"You're going to love Miss Ida," I promised him.

He nodded and left.

"So," Reese said.

"So."

He gave my hand—which I realized was still holding his—the slightest tug and pulled me toward him and then onto his lap.

I realized this was what I'd wanted right along. I wanted him to hold me and make me feel a part of something.

I'm not sure how long we sat there—my head on his shoulder, his arms around me—but I knew that he was part of what I'd been looking for.

Not in an I-need-a-man-to-complete-me sort of way, but rather in a found-the-piece-I'd-been-missing sort of way.

"I've made some decisions," I said, voicing things I'd thought but not given actual voice to.

"Oh?" he said.

I nodded my head against his chest. "I'm staying in Erie. I'm going to sell my house and move here."

"Good," he said simply.

"And I'm going back to school," I added. Really, until a few minutes ago I hadn't considered it, but I knew I wanted to.

"For?"

"Some science classes. I took a few back in college. It's how I met the Brain. But I want to know more."

He nodded. "Okay."

"And..." I paused.

"And?" he prompted.

"I'm taking you on a date. A real date."

He grinned. "I'd like that."

"I might not be exactly sure where I'm going, but I know that for now, I hope you'll be going with me."

He kissed me then. Really kissed me.

Or maybe I kissed him.

Either way, we were both there, both kissing and I suspect we might have done more than that if it weren't for Bea, Diz and Miss Ida.

I realized at that moment, I was exactly where I wanted to be.

Miss Ida's Book of Memories

I heard Albert get up, but I didn't move. I sat in the nursery rocking Barbara. I heard him in the kitchen and smelled the coffee when he started it.

He brought me back a cup. "You're going to spoil her," he whispered as he handed me the cup.

"You can't spoil someone by loving them too much. If I could, I'd hold her this close for the rest of our lives."

"When you love someone that much, you hold them close no matter how far away they go," Albert said.

As he left the room to get ready for work, I promised myself I would hold them both close for the rest of their lives.

Chapter Sixteen

"I've read romances where love is fraught with angst, anger and misunderstandings. But maybe sometimes the truest love can simply be an act of recognition. That moment when you're holding someone's hand and your heart says, 'There you are.'"

A couple hours later, Diz came back to Reese's. "I'm cooking tonight for everyone. I thought maybe I could convince Reese to take me to the store to shop so you can go back over with Bea and Miss Ida."

"I love that you're calling her that," I said. I didn't have to ask how it went. Diz's smile told me everything I needed to know.

"Well, despite the fact she offered, I couldn't call her Ida. And Mrs. Hall sounds too formal. I like your name for her. You don't mind if I borrow it?"

I hugged the big man. "No, I don't mind at all."

I laughed. Not because what he'd said was funny, but because I was happy. Happy this had all worked out. I don't think I'd realized how nervous I was until I wasn't nervous anymore. It was a convoluted thought, but it was true.

I wanted to give Miss Ida back her Barbara and I had.

It still didn't seem like enough for a woman who'd given me so much, but it was something.

I left Reese and Diz to go shopping and walked back across the street to Miss Ida's.

"Miss Dee," Lulu called, running out her side door and across the lawn with a piece of paper flapping in her hand as I reached the porch. "I made this for Miss Ida and you."

It was a picture. There was a woman with a rectangle in her hand and a circle of white hair. It only took me a second to realize the rectangle was a book. Next to that was a woman with brown hair and a book. And next to her was a young girl with blonde braids and a book. Flowers lined the bottom of the page, obscuring their feet.

"It's all of us with our Book of Memories," Lulu told me.

I realized that the flowers almost served to tie the three of us together. Very much like our memories intersected and tied us together.

I knelt down and said, "I am going to frame this."

"You are?" she asked.

"I am. I just bought some artwork and I'm going to put your drawing right next to it."

"Like I'm a real artist?" Lulu asked.

I nodded. "I think art is something that makes you feel. And when I look at this, I feel happy, so I think that means you are a real artist."

Lulu through herself at me and hugged me. "Thanks. I'm gonna go tell mom I'm an artist. I'm going to be the first astronaut artist ever."

She ran back into the house leaving me and my picture behind.

I was pretty sure I'd been right when I told her she was already an artist. I'd treasure this picture every bit as much as I treasured Bea's.

I walked into Miss Ida's. The living room was empty. "Hello?"

"Back here," Bea called.

I followed the sound of her voice and went back to her old bedroom.

"I hope you don't mind," she said. She was sitting next to Miss Ida on the bed. "I hadn't seen these in a long time."

"It's your room," I said simply. "I packed up my stuff and will leave it to you."

"No." She shook her head. "Mom understands. Diz and I are crashing in Reese's guestroom. My princess bed was fine when I was younger, but I suspect it wouldn't be overly comfortable for two adults. Maybe when Diz goes home, I'll spend a few nights here, if you don't mind."

"Whatever and whenever you want," I said. "I'm pretty sure Reese will let me crash with him."

Bea snorted and even Miss Ida laughed.

"Yes, I'm sure he will," Miss Ida said with an uncharacteristic knowing tone in her voice.

I felt myself blushing as I laughed along with them.

"I always loved this picture," Miss Ida said, pointing at a picture of her holding hands with a small princess with a requisite tiara, but also wearing an army jacket. Just under the khaki green jacket, I could make out a pink frilly skirt. "You told me that you wanted to be a princess. I spent days working on that dress. I went to three stores to find that tiara. And when I showed it to you, you said thanks and came out with the dress and Albert's jacket. You looked at me defiantly and said, *Daddy says that every girl's her daddy's princess.* There with your pink frilly dress and that army jacket, you were very much his princess and mine."

"I'm so sorry I didn't appreciate all your work," Bea said.

"No, that doesn't matter. You were being yourself. Doing things your own way. I should have known that a frilly princess wasn't your type of princess. You were a kick-butt-and-take-names sort of princess."

245

They laughed and continued reminiscing, but I noticed Bea's fingers tracing over that Halloween picture.

Miss Ida seemed to wilt and said, "I want to enjoy Diz's dinner, so maybe I'll go take a small nap first, if that's okay?"

"Of course," Bea said.

We both helped her across the hall and watched her settle on her bed. Bea kissed her forehead gently. "I'm so glad to be home, Mom. I'm sorry it took so long."

"Everything happens in its own time," Miss Ida said. "You're here now, that's all that matters."

I shut the door as we left Miss Ida's room and then walked the few steps to the living room.

Bea stood there. "Everything looks the same."

She walked across the room and touched the painting next to the door. "You said she kept it, but it's different seeing it here and knowing that all those years apart, she looked at it every day."

"She loves you," I reminded her.

"And I love her. I meant what I said, I don't know why I took so long coming home."

"I think she's right...everything happens in its own time. You're here now and that's what matters."

"I talked to Diz. He's going to have to go home next week, but I'd like to stay if that's all right."

"It is. I meant what I said, when Diz goes, move over here."

"And you'll move to Reese's?" she asked with Miss Ida sort of suggestive lilt.

I felt myself blushing again.

"Me and Reese, we're new and yet..." And yet what was between us didn't feel new.

"And yet, when you meet the right person, time loses all meaning. That morning so long ago with Diz..." She shrugged. "It was different and new and that was scary and yet it felt so right."

I made us tea and took cookies from Miss Ida's cookie jar.

We chatted like old friends as we sipped tea and ate cookies.

Maybe when you meet a kindred spirit time loses all meaning, too. Talking to Bea didn't feel like getting to know a stranger, it felt like catching up with an old friend.

It felt that way over dinner, too. We all laughed and talked as if we'd always been together. As if we'd always been...family.

After dinner, Reese took Diz and Bea back to his place to get settled and I helped Miss Ida get ready for bed.

She held my hand as I tucked her in. "Thank you."

I didn't pretend to be confused about what she was thanking me for. "You're welcome. I was so nervous. If she hadn't been..."

"Sober?" Miss Ida filled in.

I nodded. "I wasn't sure what I'd do. Ever since Ned sent me her information, I kept asking myself what-if? I never came up with a good answer for myself. I still don't know if I'd have told you I found her or not."

"What-if? We could play that game all night. What if you'd never come work for me? What if we lost touch and you weren't here now? What if you hadn't remet Reese and fallen in love."

"Love?" I weighed and measured the word. It felt too soon, and yet it felt right.

Miss Ida just gave me a look that was very Bette Lee-ish.

I shook my head. "Love. I think it might be too early to bandy that word around."

"There's no such thing as too soon or too late when it comes to love. I think I knew I loved Albert that first night at the movie theater. I loved Barbara the moment I found out I was pregnant. And I knew that I

247

loved you that first Saturday when you so obviously didn't want a job, but stayed for tea and cookies after the work was done. Love is one of the greatest mysteries in the world. Everybody wants to be loved and give love. There's never any rhyme or reason to who, why or when we love."

As always, Miss Ida was right. "I love you, Miss Ida." I kissed her cheek.

"And I love you, Sadie Mae."

I shut the door and went out to the front lawn. Tonight, more than ever, I needed to remind myself that the world was always spinning and somehow everyone managed to stand upright.

My phone pinged.

It was the Brain.

Nerdman: *Sounds like a lot going on. Do you need me?*

I always need you. You're my best friend. But I'm okay.

Nerdman: *Maybe I'll still come down for a day next week?*

Knowing being social wasn't one of Brian's strengths, I felt warmed by his friendship.

You don't have to, but yes.

Nerdman: *I'll touch base with a day.*

I put the phone in my pocket and stared at Reese's house. There were more lights on than most nights, which made sense since Diz and Bea were there with him.

I thought about her paintings.

For so long I'd been looking for my path. I wanted to organize my life like I organized a cabinet.

But there was something to be said about going with the flow. Because the flow had brought me here. And here was a good place.

My mother had insisted I work for Miss Ida.

She'd insisted I go to college.

And because I had no particular career in mind, I had an English degree.

Which led to my job for the Brain.

Which led to my staying in Detroit.

Which led to Charles.

Who taught me what I didn't want.

Which was ironic since he had goals and plans and a life mapped out. Even a wedding mapped out.

That should have thrilled me, but I hated it.

I felt constrained by it.

Fate led me back to Erie and Miss Ida.

I saw John Henry and the path I might have taken. In my organized worldview, we could have been perfect, but as I saw him now and looked back I realized that we wouldn't have been.

And that led me to...

As if answering an unvoiced call, Reese came out of the house and walked across the street.

He sat down on the grass next to me and leaned back. "I thought I'd find you here. The stars are coming out."

I leaned back again, my head resting against his outstretched arm. "They are. Why did you think I'd be here?"

"Today was a whirlwind. And you needed to remind yourself that the world is always spinning but if you take a minute, you can stand without falling."

I reached across my chest and put my hand in his. "I was thinking that I keep trying to plan my life. I love to plan and organize, but the things I appreciate most are the things I stumble upon. I feel that life should be on some kind of timetable, but..."

"But?" he prompted.

I rolled slightly so I could look at Reese rather than the stars. "I love you."

"I—"

"You don't have to say it back. I'm not asking for anything. I just realized that Miss Ida was right. I

249

feel like I've lived a lifetime in these last few weeks. It feels as if so much more time has gone by. Part of me—that cautious, organized part—would prefer I not say anything, but I'm tired of weighing and categorizing everything. I can't explain it, but it's there. Love. Miss Ida said she knew she loved her Albert that first night at the theater. I think I might have known I loved you that day you were at the door and I realized you were Mad Dog Reese from school. Right after that, I realized you weren't what I expected. And here with you right now, telling you I love you wasn't what I expected either. But there it is."

I rolled onto my back again and watched the stars. During my few second word vomit more had come out than even I knew.

I felt Reese stir and he rolled this time. He left one arm behind my neck and propped the other one on the ground, basically wrapping me in a loose embrace. "I love you, too. And it's not what I planned. It's not what I intended. But it's there. Every day I think I love you as much as anyone can possibly love someone else, and then the next day I see you and realize my feelings are even bigger. They're deeper. They're not going away."

He blotted out the entire star-scape as he kissed me.

Then he rolled back over, one arm still under my neck and my arm draped across my chest, holding his hand.

And at that moment, I knew I was on an entirely new and unanticipated path.

And I very much liked the direction it was headed.

Miss Ida's Book of Memories

I sat at the table tonight watching my Barbara and Sadie Mae laughing together, as if they'd always been friends. More than that, as if they were sisters. And Diz and Reese were there to fill in our family.

I remembered all the nights I rocked Barbara long after she'd gone to sleep. I swore I'd never let her go.

I never did.

As I looked around the table tonight, I realized that I was utterly and completely happy.

If this is my last entry in my book, just know that I have lived a life filled with love...and only the happiest of memories.

Bea's Book of Memories

A picture of a young woman's hand holding an older woman's hand.

Part Four

The Unseen Road

Chapter Seventeen

Four Months later

"Miss Ida said, I was loved. I have loved. Maybe at the end, those two sentences are all that matters."

I stood in front of the church. My palms were wet and my heart was racing. I wanted to do this right.

I looked out at everyone who'd come to honor Miss Ida. My parents were there. The Brain was as well.

His sister had called me two nights ago to extend her sympathies. She said Brian had been worried about me. "You've made such a difference in him, Dee. He's figuring out how not to always be the Brain. Sometimes he manages to be just Brian."

"About that?" I said. "What doesn't he want me to know about your nickname for him."

She'd laughed. "He doesn't want you to know that I didn't give that nickname to him. That's the name he used for himself when he was little. It stuck."

I'd laughed, despite my pain, when she'd told me. It had been that day's memory. I was reminded that even during the worst days, there's always a good memory somewhere.

I smiled again as I looked at Brian now.

He smiled back and I felt buoyed.

Doran was there. She looked ready to give birth to her *Mary Ann* at any second. The man sitting next to her had to be her husband, Paul. She leaned against him and he wrapped an arm around her shoulder.

Everyone from the neighborhood had come including Heidi and Lulu, and Miss Ida's helper Julie and Mr. Gerald from next door.

Then I looked at the front pew and saw my parents, Bea, Diz and Reese.

Always Reese.

We'd surprised all our friends and neighbors when we threw a surprise wedding at his Fourth of July picnic.

It was everything I'd ever wanted a wedding to be. We were two people who loved each other so much we couldn't wait to join our lives together.

Miss Ida was there along with everyone else I loved.

I made pink cake with coconut on the frosting, just like Miss Ida had told me her mother served at her wedding. When she saw the cake, she teared up and looked at me for confirmation.

I simply nodded and she smiled.

They were all here today as well, but this overcast, brisk September day wasn't the happy gathering we'd had in July.

Still seeing all our friends and family here helped ease the pain.

Seeing them, knowing they'd loved Miss Ida too, helped me calm down.

"On behalf of Miss Ida's family, I want to thank all of you who came today.

"I lived my whole life next to Miss Ida, but I never really knew her until my mother volunteered me to go work for her on Saturdays.

"Oh, I complained, but complaining to my mother is like spitting into the wind...it doesn't accomplish much of anything other than getting yourself wet."

Everyone chuckled and Bette Lee smiled through her tears.

"And Mom, in case I never said it, thank you. Miss Ida became more than a responsibility, she became my mentor and my friend. But more than any of that, she became family.

"Miss Ida was a woman who spent her life looking at the best in life. Every day she preserved her happiest memories. Her life wasn't perfect. No one's is. But she found moments to save and savor, even in her darkest times.

"Most of all, Miss Ida loved completely. Once she loved you, there was no undoing it. Nothing you could do or say could stop the force of her love. And I'm pretty sure that not even death can make her stop."

Bea was crying so hard that no amount of tissues could keep up. She wiped at her eyes and leaned against Diz.

"After I started cleaning for her, Miss Ida's memories intertwined with mine. I know that even though I can't see her now, that when I look through my Book of Memories, I will see her imprint on every page. And her love will be with us all just as surely. She might not physically be here, but she's written herself into the fabric of who we are. I know I will never forget her.

"Miss Ida and I...we had a May-December friendship that some people didn't understand. My ex once said that I collected old ladies like old ladies collect cats. He was wrong. I collect friends. And thanks to Miss Ida, I realized early on that friendship doesn't come with prerequisites.

"But none of that is a proper eulogy for my friend who taught me so much. She taught me to cherish the best things in my life.

"Even saying that seems inadequate. So last night, I turned to Miss Ida's Book of Memories. And of course, she found the words I couldn't. This is one of her last memories."

When I read it, I'd known Miss Ida had said exactly what needed to be said.

I looked at the paper I'd placed on the lectern:

"I was loved. I have loved

"Let that be my legacy.

"When you're young, the world is so big and so full of options. But as you get older those options shrink. So does the world. It narrows, but you don't mind because if you're lucky you've discovered what's important. What matters. If you're very lucky, you can see the answers as you look back through your memories.

"And I am a very lucky woman.

"They say you can't take it with you when you die. They're right about most things. You can't take the material things you've acquired. But love...you can take love with you. And you can leave it behind.

"So let love be my legacy. That's what Albert left me and it's what I'm leaving both my girls...my love.

"Think of me and remember that I love you both. And no matter what happens, know that I know you both love me.

"I was loved. I have loved.

"That's enough."

I took the paper with me as I headed back to the pew Reese and I shared with Bea and Diz.

I walked down the steps toward Reese, and trailed my hand across Miss Ida's cloth-draped casket.

Then Reese wrapped me in his arms and I finally cried. Not for Miss Ida. I knew she was with Albert and was happy.

No, I cried for myself. I wasn't sure how I would fill the void she'd left in my life.

The procession to the cemetery was a long one.

Diz and Bea sat in chairs near the casket. The Brain stood on one side of me, Reese on the other right behind them. My parents were behind us.

The clouds that had been hanging ominously overhead had cleared, leaving behind a bright September day.

257

It was a time in between. In between summer and fall.

They say if you don't like the weather in Erie wait a minute and it will change. Today I thought that the blue sky was a gift from Miss Ida.

Father Mike stood at the head of the flower-covered casket. Bea's arrangement said *Mother*. Mine was there as well. It simply read *Miss Ida*.

Other arrangements were behind Father Mike as he said the final prayers.

I knew one of the arrangements was from Charles.

He'd called and said how sorry he was. We talked awkwardly. It was odd that I'd once thought I could spend a lifetime with him. I listened to him talk about his life. Who he'd seen at one event or another.

He sounded happy. And I was happy for him.

I listened to Father Mike finish his prayers.

And then it was over.

We held the wake at Miss Ida's house, though the day was warm enough that it spread onto the porch and into the yard.

I found Lulu in the back room staring at Bea's mural. "This is just so cool," she said as she traced a picture of Miss Ida with her finger. "I wish I could draw like this. When I go to Mars, it would be cool to draw pictures. I know I could take them, but..."

Her words trailed off as she got lost in another picture.

"You could take lessons. You could take pictures with a camera, but they'll never tell the story the same way as something you draw can. Look at this one..."

I pointed to the picture of Miss Ida and Albert in front of the theater. "You can see how much she loves him already in this one. It was the night they met, but looking at the painting, you know they're meant to be together."

258

"How did they meet?" Lulu asked.

"Miss Ida had gone on a date with another boy. He tried to...kiss her. So she punched him and his nose bled all over her. She went out and Albert thought she was hurt. When she explained, Albert kicked the creep out of the theater and took her home."

I stared at the picture. "Sometimes you don't realize you've found a new path until you're on it. Miss Ida thought she'd gone to the theater to date the creep, but I really think she went there because she was destined to meet Albert."

Lulu nodded. "Just like you and her were meant to be friends, and you and me, and everyone here. Maybe it all started here." She tapped the picture of Miss Ida and Albert. "If they'd never met then none of us would be here."

I looked up and saw Bea and Diz standing in the doorway listening.

Bea came into the room. "You're right. If you think about it, there are so many paths we all can choose. It can seem like a miracle that you go through something bad, like a creepy date, only to find yourself in the exact right place with the exact right person."

Bea had Diz's hand in hers, and with her free hand she touched my shoulder and squeezed it.

I reached up and put my hand on hers.

She started telling Lulu more about the pictures and I left her to it. I made the rounds, making sure everyone in the house had food and drink.

And as I did, I heard bits of other people's stories.

"...she taught me how to make tea. Not bagged tea, but real tea leaves. She bought me my own brown betty last Christmas," Julie said, then sniffed loudly. "My mother laughed when I came home with it, but she says we've both become tea snobs because of Miss Ida..."

"...she scolded me for thinking she was too old and when I said I thought age made her more beautiful, she snorted and said, *age might make me wise, but I'm not sure I was ever beautiful. Albert used to say I was interesting. Maybe interesting is better than beauty.* I plan on holding onto that thought as I get older..."

"...her glider in the backyard broke, and when I surprised her and fixed it she cried. She said a glider was one of her favorite memories." It was John Henry. "She never told me why."

"I know," I said. And I told them the story of Miss Ida and her father. "He gave her her Book of Memories that day..."

We all shared Miss Ida stories. I'm not sure she realized what an impression she'd left on everyone she'd touched.

Bea came up to me later and pulled me into a quiet corner. "I've said it before, but I'll say it again, thank you for being there for my mom. I don't know what would have happened to her if you hadn't been willing to step in and take care of her."

"Thank you for sharing her with me. The house is yours, you know. She left everything to me, but only so I could keep it in trust for you."

"Diz and I have been talking about what we should do next. Part of me wants to come home. And he's got no real ties to Dallas other than the bar."

"I'm staying in Erie," I said. "I'd love to have you here."

She snorted. "Of course you are, it's home."

I didn't try to explain that Erie wasn't home, but Reese was.

She laughed and then said, "As for Mom's estate, if it's not too much of a burden, can we leave things the way she set them up for now?"

"Of course. When you're ready, it's all yours. But let's start with this." I handed her Miss Ida's Book of Memories. "She asked me to read it and I have. But it belongs to you."

She hugged me. "My mother spent her life believing in me. She left me her memories and she left me a family...a sister."

We hugged again and cried all over the book.

As Diz led Bea away, Reese came up to me. "Bea's lucky to have you. As lucky as Miss Ida was. As lucky as I am."

I kissed his cheek.

"What are we going to do now?" he asked as Diz and Bea drove up the street.

We'd been staying at Miss Ida's off and on. We'd moved a queen-sized bed into Bea's old room so we could stay close to Miss Ida. She'd protested, but I'd fought back and won. Bea and Diz had come into town off and on. When they were here we'd stayed at Reese's.

It might have seemed like a crazy way to live, neither here nor there, but I'd discovered that wherever Reese was I was home.

Bette Lee was right about that.

"We'll move to your house. In time, we'll all figure out what to do with Miss Ida's. I'll still manage the Brain's life, and I'm picking up some work for his publisher. Turns out STEM subjects are big now, and his editor said I have a unique ability to take geek-speak and turn it into something everyone can understand."

It was flattering, but I still felt as if I was missing something. "But I want more. I'd like to make a difference. Maybe I'll volunteer. Or maybe..." I paused a moment, then suddenly an idea I hadn't really known I was even entertaining came spilling out. "I read an article about elder orphans in the paper this summer. At the time, I remember thinking about Miss Ida, and my neighbor back in Detroit, Miss Carol. People who don't have extended family left as they get older. People who don't know where to turn for the help they need."

Reese didn't say anything. He simply waited for me to finish taking all my half thoughts and organize them into something coherent. "Elder orphans," I said again. The half-formed ideas becoming clearer. "What if there was a place here in Erie where people could reach out for help? Not only agencies, but real people. A Big Brothers and Sisters things in reverse. People who volunteered to adopt our elders who have no one?"

I felt excited at the thought.

I had realized that the article moved me, but I hadn't realized that this is what I'd been thinking until I said the words.

"I think it would be a wonderful legacy to Miss Ida," he said.

I sat down in the middle of the yard and looked up at the bright blue September sky. Huge, fluffy clouds moved lazily overhead, framing the small serviceberry tree whose leaves were still green, but there was a hint of orange to them.

"You're sure about moving into my place?" Reese said softly as he sat down next to me.

I took his hand in mine. "Wherever you are is home," I said. Reese—Maddox Reese—he was my home.

I didn't say it, but I held his hand and looked at the powder puff clouds in the autumn sky, I knew tonight I'd write about the day and this—simply sitting hand in hand with Reese—would be my best memory of the day.

I'd found the beginnings of my path.

I wasn't sure where it would lead, but I knew that Reese would be beside me as I found out.

I knew I'd found exactly where I belonged.

I'd found my home.

Miss Ida's Book of Memories

The day I lost my father, I thought I'd never be able to write in my book again. The next day, I went out to the old glider with my book. It was a hot August day. And muggy. I remember how muggy it was. My shirt clung to my back.

I could hear the cicadas singing and the sun was setting between the hollow of two trees.

I didn't cry. I'd already cried myself out. But my heart was broken. I wished my father would come out. He never said much, but he had a way of making me feel better no matter what. He'd say he loved me. That would be enough.

And in that moment, with the cicada symphony going as the sun began to set, I could almost hear my father say, *you are loved*.

And I realized that when you die, the one legacy you can count on leaving behind is love.

My father loved me. Death couldn't rob me of that.

My father loved me and I loved him.

I picked up my pen and started to write.

Chapter Eighteen

One Year Later

"In the end, the memories are all we have left. That's why sharing them matters. When I tell you a memory, I'm showing you the truest part of myself."

"You did it," Bea said.

"The logo's all yours."

"*Miss Ida's Foundation.* A clearinghouse of government departments and local agencies that can look after elder orphan's interest. And your adopt a grandparent program is wonderful."

"I have a meeting at Erie Insurance next week and some of the other bigger companies. I want to see if I can find volunteers through them to start. And I've talked to St. Mary's about residents who don't have a family and..."

Bea laughed. "You really do just charge ahead, don't you? I was reading Mom's book and she wrote about your love of organizing pantries. She said, *My Sadie Mae sees a mess and cleans it. She sees chaos and organizes it. She sees pain and she soothes it. She always charges forward, forging her own path.*"

"She did have a way with words," I said.

Bea nodded. "And you have a way of taking action."

I didn't say anything, but other than the *Miss Ida Foundation*, I never felt like I truly took much action.

Miss May, the new neighbor who was renting Miss Ida's house, came out on the porch and waved.

"She seems nice," Bea said. "She invited me over for tea and showed me that she'd left my room unchanged. Her twelve-year-old granddaughter loves staying in it. She asked if I'd come over tomorrow and tell her granddaughter about some of the pictures. About my mom."

"Oh, that's lovely," I said. "Becky spends most weekends with Miss May."

"You've mentioned her before," Bea said. "I thought I might take her a blank book."

And I knew she would. She'd pass on Miss Ida's story.

Ida Hunter Hall lived a life built on finding and cherishing the best moments.

She lived a life full of love.

And she was right, that love was her legacy.

It still impacted people.

And that was truly something worth leaving behind.

Dear Reader,

I always feel a connection to my characters, but I have a special kinship to Sadie Mae. Like her, I come from southern stock. Oh, I didn't know how deep my family's southern roots ran until I reached adulthood, but the more I find out, the more fascinated I am. We were in the Appalachian Mountains years back and as I watched a stunning sunset, I couldn't help but think that people in my family had watched the sunset from those very mountains.

Family.

That idea of family connections runs firmly through all my books, probably because it's a theme that runs firmly through my life...sometimes in unexpected ways. We found out a few years ago that my cottage south of Erie sits within spitting distance of a homestead of another branch of my family. I've spent decades driving over a road that was named after them. I drove right by the plot of land they lived and worked on. I feel as if somehow, my owning property there brings a part of my family story full circle.

I feel tied by blood to the mountains and to that small bit of land I own.

But for me, family is more than blood. There have been people in my life I share no common ancestor with, but they are people who've left a mark on me. John Nauss was one of those men. He was a friend of my grandmother's. We spent every weekend with her when I was growing up. And "Papa" John came over every evening. He wore soft flannel shirts, had deep wrinkles embedded in his cheek. Every Christmas he gave me a poinsettia and every Easter a hyacinth. He was truly as much my family as my grandmother was.

I think he's one of the reasons that I've known since childhood that family is more than blood.

I think that's why Sadie Mae struck such a chord with me. She feels her family roots deeply, but she recognizes that family is more than roots...it's the branches we send out into the world. Branches that shelter and invite others into our lives.

I hope you enjoyed her story. This was definitely a book of the heart. I wrote that opening scene a couple years ago and put it in my *do-something-with-it* file. When I skimmed through that file and reread it, I suddenly knew the rest of the story.

This isn't the first May-December friendship I've written about. For me, they ring true because those friendships have been so important in my life. My grandmother's best friend, Jean, has always been a part of my life. When I started writing, she was one of my earliest supporters. She read every book I wrote and always told me what she thought of it.

When we moved into my current house we gained a new neighbor. Marge lived just across our large yard. Over the years, she became a friend and then family. Our memories have indeed 'tangled' now.

I thought of Papa John, Jean and Marge as I wrote about Sadie Mae and Miss Ida's friendship. I think the first thing that attracted Dee to Reese was his care for Miss Ida. I will confess, I think there's something to be said about measuring a man in how he treats his elders. Reese definitely passed that test for Sadie and for me.

As I was finishing the book, I read Lin-Manuel Miranda and Jeremy McCarter's *Hamilton the Revolution*. In it LMM says, "That's the whole show...Ron tells you a story and he's the star of the story. I tell you a story and I'm the star of the story. **History is entirely created by the person that tells the story**." It was one of those **yes** moments I love having when I'm reading. For me, what LMM is saying is, perspective is everything.

I love that Miss Ida spent a lifetime choosing a happy perspective. She told her story from the perspective of her best moments every day and passed that gift on to the others in her life. It's something I work to do as well. Writing this book has encouraged me to redouble my finding "glee" efforts.

I hope it inspires you to find some of your own.

Holly

ABOUT THE AUTHOR

Award-winning author Holly Jacobs has over three million books in print worldwide. The first novel in her Everything But... series, Everything But a Groom, was named one of 2008's Best Romances by Booklist, and her books have been honored with many other accolades. She lives in Erie, Pennsylvania, with her husband and four children. You can visit her at *www.HollyJacobs.com*